Turning Tables

TURNING TABLES

Alice Takawira

TURNING TABLES

ISBN eb: 978-8-9858937-0-0

ISBN pb: 978-8-9858937-1-7

Editors: Caroline Tolley, Mike Robinson, and Graeme Hague
Proofreader: Stephanie Parent
Formatter: Erik Gevers
Cover Design: Mark Thomas

Dedicated to my beloved mother

Pauline Zemura

My pillar of strength,
my biggest cheerleader,
and now my guardian angel.
I will always love you.

Rest in eternal peace.

Part I

Chapter 1

Maita

Missing my flight was not an option. My mental health was at stake, and the crippling urgency to reclaim a lost love was driving me insane. I had to get on that plane, and nothing would get in my way—not the never-on-time bus to the MARTA train station, or the slow train ride to the airport, and certainly not the brunette British Airways agent in her perfectly pressed uniform. Panting and drenched in sweat, I finally made it to the British Airways gate A7. After racing in a panic through the terminal and unapologetically pushing my way past flustered travelers, my shoulder aching from the weight of my carry-on bag, I arrived seconds after the gate closed. Would she let me through?

With a trembling hand, I gave the agent my boarding pass. She examined it, her expression giving away nothing. My heart was pounding in my chest, and the rhythmic throbbing echoed through my ears like a drumbeat. I crossed my fingers, held my breath, and prepared for the worst.

"Ma'am, we don't allow anyone onto the flight once the gate has closed," she said, scanning my boarding pass. "You're late, but I'll let you in. Thank your lucky stars that I'm at the gate and not my colleague."

"Thank you so much, I have to make this trip, and it can't wait," I replied, exhaling with relief and gratitude.

"Well, hurry and get seated. We can't delay much longer. You're in seat 18A."

I fumbled through the narrow aisle looking for my seat and

could sense the accusing glares from passengers who were strapped in and waiting impatiently for takeoff.

I was pleasantly surprised when I reached seat 18A and noticed that it was my preferred window seat. Still pumped with adrenaline from my run from security to the departure gate, feeling hot and clammy, I struggled to open the overhead cabin while carrying my oversized bag. I was the only standing passenger when the flight attendant announced that everyone must take their seats and get ready for takeoff.

"I'll get that for you," the gentleman in seat 18B said, pointing at my bag as he got up to assist me.

"Thanks," I replied, noting, even in my unsettled state, his piercing brown eyes and handsome features. Before handing him my leather bag that faithfully served as both a handbag and carry-on luggage, I quickly dug in and pulled out my most treasured possession, my iPod. Although the screen had an irregular hairline crack, and most of the ivory coating had worn off, exposing a silver-gray metal, it worked perfectly. I stepped aside as he opened the overhead bin, and with one swift move exposing toned arms that complimented his firm physique, he stuffed my bag into a narrow space between a black laptop bag and a red backpack.

"Go on, then," he said, motioning for me to get into my window seat so he could take his aisle seat next to me.

"Thank you," I whispered again, not sure if I had bothered him. I heaved a sigh of relief and thought how a glass of red wine would be most welcome at this moment.

My hair was a mess, and I was sure that I reeked of sweat and fatigue from all that running through the airport. I felt sorry for the kind man sitting beside me. How unpleasant for him to be cramped next to me on this long flight. I made a note to freshen up as soon as the pilot gave the all-clear to get up. I buckled my seat belt and closed my eyes to calm down and relax.

My thoughts drifted to the excruciatingly slow MARTA train ride, the reason I was late to board my flight. It was continuously interrupted by multiple stops, making me frustrated, restless, and disappointed by the speed or lack thereof. My anxiety slowly brewing. This experience had me looking forward to being in London, where I would enjoy the efficiency of the London trains and buses that were always on time, to the second.

I felt the plane transition from taxiing to takeoff as it gained speed, and I was on my way. Two and a half months in London would be a welcome break from my studies at Emory University, and I was excited about spending time with family and friends. I planned to unwind at my mother's house in Chatham. As always, she would pamper me with delicious home-cooked meals, especially *sadza* and beef stew. I was so ready for summer barbeques, club-hopping, and partying with my sister and girlfriends. It felt like going home.

As much as I was looking forward to chilling out and having fun on this vacation, I had to stay focused on my two missions. The first: to work and save money to pay for my tuition in my final semester at Emory—which had a hefty price tag. I dreaded my second mission—to make right what I had messed up. Thinking about it stirred a sinking feeling of regret, and it cast a dark cloud over everything, including my plans to have a good time in London.

As always, music was the best distraction for me, and it often saved me from sinking further into depressing thoughts, especially when that dreadful feeling best described as a heartache threatened to overwhelm me. Ironically, sad love songs were the ones that lifted my spirits. I knew which song would fit my mood. I opened my eyes, took my iPod from the seat pocket, scrolled through my playlist and selected the *Secrets* album by Toni Braxton. With the volume cranked up, my head resting on the seat, and eyes shut, I began to fantasize about the day I would come face-to-face with the man who was the reason for my pain.

As Toni Braxton's deep, almost masculine voice washed over me, it carried me to a time when someone adored me so much that he became consumed with the fear of losing me. The painful truth was that I misinterpreted his affection as possessiveness and control, and I left him. Now, I would do anything for a second chance, but did he still feel the same? Did he long for me as I did him? As the music played, and the plane floated in the sky, I felt at ease, and slowly drifted off into dreamland.

*****

The airplane had been rattling and shaking for some time. Initially distant, the motion grew louder and more vigorous, finally piercing my dreams and waking me with a jolt. I gripped my armrests, fear bursting through me. Was the plane losing control? Turbulence had always terrified me.

"Lord, please get us to London safely," I prayed under my breath. "Oh God, please make this stop." With my eyes tightly shut, I held my breath as the plane suddenly descended, then ascended, shaking all the while and taking my intestines with it, making me nauseous.

I opened my eyes briefly and realized with surprise that most passengers were calm—reading books, typing on their laptops, watching movies, or sleeping in peace. A lady across from us, in the middle row, was just as panic-stricken as I was; she too, was close to tears. The gentleman next to me was staring at something straight ahead, undisturbed. The plane made a sudden dive, and this time many passengers yelled in fear. I joined them, which got the attention of my neighbor.

"Bloody turbulence," he muttered. "Relax, it will be over soon." He smiled at me reassuringly.

Just as I was about to reply—*bang*! The plane jolted, and this time seemed to tilt. Even more passengers cried out with fright.

I had experienced frightening turbulence, but this was the worst yet. I whispered, "Oh *Nkosi Yami,* I don't want to die, not like this, Lord." I must have said it out loud, because the gentleman next to me burst into laughter, and I knew he was laughing at me. How could he find humor in the middle of this terrible situation? And how insensitive of him to laugh at me.

The captain's voice came on the speakers. "Folks, we're encountering severe turbulence. I expect it to last another fifteen minutes. Please be calm, and remain in your seats with your seat belts fastened."

That didn't ease my nerves, because fifteen minutes was a long time to be on this roller-coaster ride. I clutched the armrests again. Then I felt a tap on my shoulder. The gentleman next to me smiled and said, "Sorry, I didn't mean to laugh at you. It's just so funny the way everyone is panicking. It'll be over soon. Just a little bump on the road, I guess."

I relaxed my hands and sat up. "No need to apologize. I can never get used to turbulence and always freak out."

He leaned toward me. "Well, think about it, as long as the overhead oxygen masks don't spring out, and no one is throwing up like in the movies, we're fine. Cabin pressure is good, no problem."

"You're probably right, but that doesn't mean we won't nosedive into the ocean."

"And we won't live to feel the impact. It would be so fast you wouldn't get the chance to complete your Hail Marys, but that quick prayer you made earlier might work." He chuckled. "Sorry, I couldn't resist laughing."

"Did you hear me pray? I thought I was whispering."

"Ha, it wasn't much of a whisper. Amazing how religious we get when faced with danger." Then he placed his soft hand on mine, and patting it gently, said, "Don't worry, we're going to make it to London okay."

His actions and words were comforting, even as the plane continued its violent shaking. "Thanks. I hope it will end soon."

He reached for a bag under the seat in front of him, and with a steady hand pulled out a little zipped purse. He brought out a bottle of pills, took one out, and turned to me. "Here, try one of these. This pill is an all-natural herbal sleeping aide that will help you relax. It always works for me." He must have noticed the suspicion and confusion on my face, because he quickly added, "Okay, fine, I'll take one first."

He popped a little brown pill into his mouth, swallowed, and smiled. I hesitated. Taking any medication from a stranger was dangerous, of course.

Just then, the plane lurched again, tilting to the right. Someone behind us screamed. The pill fell out of the gentleman's hand and landed onto my lap. Without thinking twice, I put it into my mouth and swallowed.

He patted my hand again. "Trust me, you will be fine."

I took a deep breath. "I hope so." I wasn't sure what I'd just done. Closing my eyes again, I decided to ignore the vibrating airplane and wait for the sleeping pill to take effect.

"When I wake up," I said, eyes closed, "this crazy ride had better be over."

"It will, and everything will be all right," he replied.

I don't know for how long I was asleep. I woke up a little disoriented, then quickly remembered I was on a flight to London.

"Hi, did you sleep well?" asked my friendly neighbor.

I smiled back, and remembered he had given me a sleeping pill.

"Hey, you're the creepy man who drugged me," I said.

He laughed. "Saved you is more like it. You were freaking out, praying, and chanting Hail Marys because of a little turbulence." He made a funny face and began imitating me in a cartoonish voice. "I don't want to die, Lord, not like this, Lord!"

We both laughed, even as I replied, "That's not funny; I was afraid."

"Okay, I won't laugh anymore, I promise." Though he continued to. Then he turned to me and extended a hand. "My name is Chris. Christopher Medley."

I shook his hand. "And I'm Maita, Maita Shumba."

Chapter 2

Chris

My legs had started to cramp from sitting at the British Airways gate A7 for the past two hours. I had paced up and down the terminal to break the monotony of sitting and waiting for the flight to start boarding. I also had coffee from the café across from the gate, which tasted terrible. I longed for a good cup of English tea. I was glad to be going back home, where at last I would enjoy a cup of Yorkshire tea with a splash of milk and a heaped teaspoon of sugar, one of the few things I missed since I moved to Atlanta.

Finally, after a long and tedious boarding process that included a British Airways security check and reviewing passports and visas for non-British passengers, I settled into my aisle seat. I had begun to think that the window seat next to me would be vacant—hard to imagine British Airways not filling up all seats in the summer—as it was almost time for takeoff, and the seat was empty. Someone must have missed their flight. If that were the case, great: just more room for me to stretch out.

However, when I saw a woman pushing her way through the aisle, appearing a little confused as she looked up at the seat numbers, I knew she was heading for the vacant one next to me. I almost raised my hand to direct her and save her the trouble.

When she found her seat, she tried to open the overhead compartment and could barely lift her carry-on bag. I wondered how that huge bag could be considered hand luggage. It was all too much to watch her struggling, so I offered to help as any gentleman would. The passengers sitting opposite us, already buckled into their seats, couldn't be bothered to assist this petite woman with a big bag.

One thing I disliked about flying economy was the cramped

spaces. The first time I moved to Atlanta, Digi-Mechanix, Inc., my new employer, had already paid for my business-class ticket; this time, it was on me, and I intended to save every penny I had for a down payment on a house. Thus, I would survive the long hours sitting in this tight space. My neighbor in seat 18A, who just made the dramatic, big-bagged entrance, had already shut her eyes. She had iPod earphones on, and looked like she was in no mood to talk. Fine with me.

Turbulence eventually woke her, and I couldn't hold back the laughter when she began praying in both English and another language I couldn't understand. As a frequent flyer, I was accustomed to the rough and tumble of turbulence, and I remained calm. On the other hand, my neighbor could barely open her eyes, and she was holding on to her armrest with a tight grip as if this would magically steady the plane.

Feeling a little guilty for laughing at what was probably one of the scariest moments in her life, I offered some comforting words, which thankfully eased her. I was glad when her expression changed from fear to a smile; although weak, it was a smile all the same. Her eyes, now open and relaxed, gave away signs of fatigue, so I offered her a relaxant, one of the many remedies that I carried with me when traveling. It worked. When she woke up, there was no doubt she seemed better rested, and in a better mood.

Something about her had grabbed my attention. Perhaps her unusual accent, or her amiable demeanor, which made it easy to talk to her.

"Where are you headed?" I asked.

"London, for my summer break," she replied, shifting uncomfortably in her seat.

"Hmm, family? Friends?"

"Both," she said.

Short and to the point. Maybe my neighbor didn't want to talk, and I had become that irritating passenger who wouldn't stop. "Your accent is different, not quite American. African, maybe, but I can't say for sure because you also have a slight

English tone. Where are you from, if you don't mind my asking?"

She started to laugh. "Are you Professor Higgins now?"

"You know *My Fair Lady?*"

"Why is that surprising?" She sounded defensive.

"It happens to be one of my favorite musicals," I lied. In fact, I couldn't stand musicals because I didn't have the patience for all that singing.

She lit up. "Mine, too. I love it. I've watched it so many times. I love singing along to it."

Now, that did surprise me; not your average girl, I guess. "I'm hardly a Professor Higgins, but I am curious about where you're from." I tried to change the conversation away from *My Fair Lady;* otherwise, she would soon find me out.

"I'm from Zimbabwe," she said. I must have looked clueless, because she quickly added, "It's in Africa. I'm African." There was pride in her tone.

"Oh, I know that, just can't recall if it's in East or Southern Africa."

"It's in Southern Africa."

"Interesting. Do you live in Atlanta?"

"I'm a graduate student at Emory."

"Emory University, that's an outstanding institution. I've heard good things about it. So, who is in London?"

I probably came across as being nosy at this point, but I was intrigued and didn't know why.

"I have family and friends in England," she replied. And with that, she switched the subject. "I'm hungry; I must have missed dinner, thanks to you and that sleeping pill." She smiled, and I was relieved that I hadn't upset her. Why was I so ready to be in her good graces anyway? I just met her, for goodness's sake.

I pushed the button to call a flight attendant. "No problem. I'll have them bring your dinner." Soon after calling for the flight attendant, I realized I was doing something that she could have done herself. I must've appeared eager to impress her.

"Thanks," she replied. "Was the food any good?"

"The best you can expect on a flight," I said. "I had to wash it down with some wine." I was tempted to continue my line of questioning, but felt a little intimidated. What did I know about Zimbabwe? I had read something about war or political troubles there. But that was like most of Africa—war, hunger, and diseases. Of course, I knew Africa wasn't all the doom and gloom the media portrays it as. I had once made a connecting flight through Johannesburg in South Africa, and the airport was as modern as anything in the West. Plus, I'd read about beautiful tourist attractions and once considered going on a safari. Would I sound ignorant if I asked where *exactly* Zimbabwe was on the African continent, next to South Africa or closer to the center? Was it landlocked? I bet the average person probably had no idea, so why did I feel pressure to be knowledgeable? No one had ever called me ignorant, but... I guess I was hard on myself.

My train of thought was interrupted by her asking, "You must be English. Were you visiting Atlanta and returning home now?"

"Indeed. Quite obviously, my accent gives that away. I now live in Atlanta. I relocated from England two months ago, and I'm going home to Oxford to complete my packing." I was glad this time she had initiated the conversation.

Before I could ask another question, the flight attendant approached us, turned the call light off, and asked, "How can I help you, sir?"

"This young lady missed dinner. Could you bring out some food for her?"

"Sure, no problem. Chicken or beef, ma'am?"

"I'll have chicken, thanks."

"And some red wine for me," I said and turned to her. "Anything to drink? Wine perhaps?" First, I offer her a pill, and now alcohol. Odd sequence. And why was I acting like I was on a date, ordering food for her and all?

She said, "Red wine would be great, thanks."

I cleared my throat.

"Getting back to our little chat," I said. "How did you end up in Atlanta?" I figured an open-ended question would get more out of her. Then it occurred to me that I had forgotten her name already. Mita? Moyta? Should I ask her?

"Okay, here's a quick summary," she said. "Born and raised in Zimbabwe, I graduated from the University of Zimbabwe, relocated to England, worked there for two years, and then moved to Atlanta for graduate school. This summer, I'm going to London to work and to visit my family and friends."

My first thought: how old could she be, old enough to have done all that? She didn't look a day past the age of maybe twenty-two. Instead I asked, "Wow, you have an interesting life. Have you worked in England? What did or do you do?"

My mind raced with questions. Was it that easy to come from Africa and work in a foreign country? How did she do it? And was it legal work? I had heard of asylum seekers and all types of immigrants working and living illegally in England. It occurred to me that this was the first time I had ever had such a conversation with an *African immigrant.*

"I'm a physical therapist," she said, "and I worked at the North Middlesex hospital in North London. Now I'm studying for a master's in public health. Is there anything else you would like to know? My national insurance or social security number, perhaps?"

I wasn't offended by the sarcasm; I was actually impressed. She was proud to be African, educated, and well-traveled. "You have done well," I said, not sure if that was an appropriate response. I continued to ask questions. "How easy is it to come from Africa and work in England or study in America?"

She smirked. "How easy was it for you to get a job in Atlanta and move from Oxford?" Had I upset her with all the questions, or was this her way of talking? She added, "I bet you had to get that H-1B visa to work in Atlanta. I had to get the equivalent to work in the UK, the work permit, and a student visa to study at Emory. Life of an immigrant, right?"

She got me. I had categorized her as an immigrant, yet I was one, too; I just happened to be white and British. I was a typical ignorant white boy. I started to laugh out loud at myself.

She looked at me, puzzled. "Did I say something funny?"

"No, no, not at all. I just had a funny thought."

When the flight attendant brought her food on a tray, she opened the tray table and prepared to eat.

The flight attendant placed a bottle of wine and a plastic cup on my open tray table and offered her some wine, too. I felt edgy and a little excited and wanted to open the wine bottle and chug it down. Why was I getting so worked up from a simple conversation? She had some effect on me.

She poured wine into the little plastic cup, raised it to me, and with a big smile on her face said, "Cheers."

I raised my cup. "Cheers," and took a huge gulp. I sat straight-faced as she ate, and I drank. I wanted to get back to talking, but had to let her eat.

She broke the silence: "I'll need more wine, I just know it. It's not the best, but it's going down fast."

"I feel the same, and I have drunk most of mine. I'll call for more." She liked red wine too.

When she finished eating, the flight attendant cleared the tray and brought us more wine. I can't recall the details of what we talked about afterward. I remember we discussed everything from music to movies and politics, and we laughed numerous times, all the while drinking more red wine. We never discussed our backgrounds or immigration history again. She had an opinion about everything—except sports—and when she referred to football as soccer, I teased, "I can't believe you've become that Americanized already. You can't call it that once we get on English soil."

"Just watch. Soon you'll be using American lingo too, and watching Monday Night Football." We laughed when we discovered that neither one of us had any clue about American football.

We both got tipsy from the wine, and I noticed fatigue in her big brown eyes.

"I think I'll take a nap," she said.

"I might too." I checked the travel details on the screen in front of me. "Hopefully, when we wake up, we'll have arrived in London."

"That would be great. I can't wait to get out of here already. Good night, Chris."

I was surprised she remembered my name, and although it's not a difficult name, I had only mentioned it once ages ago, many wine bottles ago. I still couldn't remember her name.

"It's Maita," she said softly.

She must be a witch. Had she read my mind? "Of course, I remember your name," I lied.

"No, you don't." She chuckled.

I sat up in my seat. "Well, how do you know?" I asked, still trying to keep up with the lie.

"You'd be the first non-Zimbabwean I ever met to remember it the first time around. I usually have to spell it too."

"All right, you got me. I didn't remember it. If you don't mind, could you please spell it for me?" Hopefully the letters might imprint it in my memory.

"M-a-i-t-a, and it means 'thank you' in Shona."

"It's a beautiful name, Maita. And, I must add—you have a beautiful accent. Whatever mixture it is, it's beautiful."

"Thanks, my friends call me Bubbles," she replied. "I'll try to sleep now." She smiled, pulled the small British Airways blanket up to her chest, placed a sleep cap over her eyes, and laid back. I stayed up for a few minutes, staring at Maita as she slept. She was undeniably beautiful, fun and stimulating. I wanted to know more about her.

Chapter 3

Ade

A wasted day off, spent waiting for my new washer and dryer delivery. It was now three p.m., well past the three-hour window between eight and eleven. It was a bad idea to take the whole day off from work; that was precious time that I could have utilized better. Three months into the year, I had already used up two weeks of my annual leave when I'd traveled to Nigeria for my cousin's wedding. In hindsight, I should have arranged for an afternoon shift at the hospital.

I called the delivery man again. This time, his phone didn't go straight to voice mail, he answered.

"Sorry, sir," he said, "but we're stuck in the worst traffic jam. Looks like we'll have to book you for another time. You can call our office to reschedule."

"I wish you had called me earlier to let me know about this traffic jam," I shouted. "I could have made better use of my time." If my cell phone were a landline, I would have slammed it hard.

I had to make the best of what was left of the afternoon, and at the top of my to-do list was grocery shopping and collecting my shirts from the dry-cleaner. I did neither; instead, I settled for lounging on the couch, drinking hot chocolate, and surfing the internet on my laptop. I really wanted to check my email, but I was hesitant and continued to browse aimlessly.

I was anxious every time I opened my Gmail account. Checking my email evoked the same reactions I had when expecting test or exam results: sweaty palms and teeth-grinding. Her emails had become more frequent, and they made me uncomfortable, but I couldn't figure out why.

"Come on, this is ridiculous," I said aloud. "Be a man, and get over it."

Reading her emails brought back memories, good and bad. Most of the time, truthfully, they filled me with resentment. I had just recovered from the worst kind of heartbreak a grown man like me could experience. Now I was in a good place, and my career and personal life were on an upward trajectory. I didn't need her, or thoughts of her, to drag me down again.

*****

It all began earlier this year, on Valentine's Day. It was just another day at the hospital when my pager rang as I was performing ward rounds. I picked up the phone at the nurses' station.

"Dr. Ola, a call for you on line four. It's an international call."

I thought it was a call from Nigeria, but my family and friends always called me directly on my mobile phone, and never via the hospital switchboard.

"Okay, thanks," I replied. "Hello."

"Hi. Is this Ade?"

I held my breath for a few seconds. I knew that voice. How had she gotten my work phone number?

"Bubbles?"

"Yes, it's me, long time. How are you?"

I paused to think. "Err, I'm fine," I said slowly, still confused by this unexpected call. "How did you get my number?"

"I did a little research; you can find anyone on the internet these days," she replied with that Miss Know-It-All confidence.

Before she could say any more, I asked, "Why are you calling me now? What do you want?"

This time she paused, and stammered back, "I-I wanted to talk to you. I know it's been months, but I need to—"

"I'm at work right now. You called my work number."

"I'm sorry if I disturbed you. I had no other number to call." Her tone was now soft and warm.

There she goes again, I thought, remembering how difficult it was to resist her voice. Aware that mine sounded harsh and combative in comparison to hers, I paused and said, "Listen, I'm busy now. Let me give you my mobile number, and you can call me in about three hours when I get off work."

She took the number and said, "Okay, thanks, I'll talk to you later," then hung up.

"Dr. Ola, is everything all right?" Nurse Gemma asked, with a worried look.

"I'm fine, just a little family issue, nothing major."

And I walked off.

At exactly six p.m. that evening, my mobile phone rang. As much as I was dreading the call, Bubbles had aroused my curiosity, and her motive was suspicious. I'd prepared myself by rehearsing hypothetical conversations in my head. I was ready to *handle* her smart mouth.

She had a sharp tongue and never ran out of things to say. She could dish out a sarcastic or hilarious response to any situation. She never lost an argument and always had the last word. Bubbles could justify anything; whatever it was, she had a logical answer for it. I often told her she had chosen the wrong profession. She should have been a defense lawyer—one that I would hire.

I let my mobile phone ring for a while, not wanting to appear over eager to talk to her. Finally, in a calm and controlled voice, I answered, "Hello."

"Hi, Ade, it's me again."

"I know, Bubbles. How are you?"

"Good, I guess, just a little stressed out by school assignments. How are you doing?"

How did I answer that? "I'm doing well, can't complain." I figured, since she called me, I'd let her do most of the talking. She would have to lead this conversation.

There was an uncomfortable silence until she said, "I'm glad you're fine. How is work?"

She was attempting to engage in small talk, like this was a normal conversation. It wasn't, though. Unlike her cheerful voice earlier, she sounded timid and downtrodden, not the Bubbles I used to know. The Bubbles I knew would have gone straight to the point with tremendous confidence. What had happened to her?

"How did you know I worked at this hospital? I just started here in January. Have you been spying on me?"

I'd attempted to lighten the mood and put her at ease. I could sense she was smiling as she replied, "I have not been spying on you, but I have been thinking about you. I never stopped caring for you."

That was an unexpected statement, for which I had no response.

She continued, "I lost my phone with all my contacts, including your cell number, so I had to find other ways to get to you. I knew you had moved to a new hospital because you started applying before I left. I struggled to remember which ones you applied to, so I looked up all North London hospitals and narrowed it down to two."

"You did all that? Why? Why didn't you just email me?"

"You must have changed your email address, because your Hotmail account isn't active. Trust me, I tried."

"You're right. I use Gmail now, like most people. Well, what do you want, Maita? Do you know what it has taken me to get over you? You up and left without even saying goodbye. Then you conveniently lost my number. I haven't heard from you in seven months. What am I supposed to think? I guess I didn't mean anything to you. After everything we had been through, you just walked away." This outburst was part of my previously prepared speech.

"I'm so sorry I left you like that. I don't know what I was thinking at that time—"

I didn't let her complete the sentence, because I was now so wound up and had to get this off my chest. "I went through a rough patch. I was clinically depressed, and I'm not joking. I was so broken I couldn't even concentrate at work and lost fifteen pounds. You have no idea how much you hurt me. I went through the stages of grief, and I mean it. I was angry for a long time and then in denial, thinking you were coming back. I've been through it all. Finally, I accepted that you were gone for good, and then today you call me. Why? To hurt me again?" I was almost shouting, aware of the tremor and anger in my voice.

I didn't intend to disclose that much detail, especially about my weight loss and clinical depression, but the emotions that had been brewing inside me for months erupted, and I divulged too much. Contrary to what I had planned, my impromptu rant portrayed a weak and bitter man.

"I'm so sorry, Ade," she said. "I truly am. It was selfish of me to leave the way I did. I didn't mean to disappear. When I arrived here, I was overwhelmed with this place, I had so much adjusting to do, and it was all too much. I've been under immense pressure with classwork, and finding my way here has been a struggle. I had no idea how difficult it would be. I neglected to call you, but I never forgot about you."

I heard a sniffle; was she crying? Yes, she was sobbing.

"I have come to my senses," she added. "Things are better now, and I miss our friendship. I just wanted to talk to you."

Such vulnerability from the typically feisty Bubbles was surprising. I had expected a defensive response explaining her way out, never accepting blame. And yet, I admired this new ability to be honest about her feelings, and to admit she was wrong.

I softened my response. "You could have given me a chance to say goodbye. I tried to call you and later found out from your sister that you had gone already. I realize we had been going through stuff, but it was nothing we couldn't have talked about before you left."

"I'm so sorry," she repeated. "Believe me, I am."

Never one to stay angry for too long, I decided to change the conversation. "So, have you made it in the land of milk and honey? Is it as good as they make it look on telly?"

"No milk and honey for me, just a lot of studying. I don't even have a car, and you can't get anywhere without driving. So I'm usually stuck on campus. Student life sucks."

"Well, at least you followed your dream to study in America. Hopefully you'll get a good opportunity when you graduate. You should be proud of yourself."

I had been a supportive boyfriend. She had so much drive; it was fun to watch her plan and scheme, and she always accomplished the things she set out to do.

Her go-getter attitude had rubbed off on me as well, inspiring me to apply for a fellowship in cardiology after she encouraged me to move on to the next level. I even upgraded to a flat in a better neighborhood shortly after we started dating. While I'd been content with my one-bedroom flat, she would say, "You work so hard only to come home to this little place? Come on, live a little." Never mind that, at that time, she stayed in shared nurses' accommodation at the hospital where she worked. That was because she was saving money to pay tuition for the master's program in America. It was admirable, her ability to be focused, disciplined, hardworking, and yet still enjoy life.

"Do you like Atlanta better than London?" I asked. "Or do you miss the cold weather, constant drizzle, and gray clouds?"

"I miss my family and friends, but I like it here. By the way, when will you sit for the USMLEs, the American medical boards, so you can come and practice here? I remember that you had started to prepare for the exam."

"I won't be moving anymore. I've been promoted to a consultant position, and plan to enroll for a fellowship here. I bought a new house, and I'm in a relatively new relationship with a lovely girl. So, I will stay put and see how that works."

I couldn't tell her that the only reason I had planned to move to America and practice medicine there was because I wanted to be part of *her* American dream. We could have gone to Atlanta together. She would have graduated and gotten a job, and I would have pursued my medical career in cardiology. We could have had the cliché happily-ever-after. But she left me, and the dream and ambition had left with her.

"Congratulations on the new house," she said, in a more solemn tone. "And I'm happy that you have settled into your new home and things are working out for you." The mention of my new relationship was deliberate, of course. "So, who is the lucky lady?"

"Lucky lady? I think I'm the lucky one. I met her when I was going through a difficult and depressing time, and she helped me get back to being a happy chap." She was silent. "She's also from your country, believe it or not."

"How nice, which part of Zimbabwe? How long have you been together?"

"Just a couple of months. It's still new. Noma is from Bulawayo, just like you. Enough about me, though: who is the lucky guy that you are dating? Have you found yourself an American man?"

"No such luck. I'm so busy with school and haven't had time to socialize." Her voice now reduced to a whisper.

"What? You, Bubbles, no time to socialize? I find that hard to believe. You were the life of the party. I'm sure the guys in your class, at the very least, would be after you. Come on, it can't be that bad."

She forced a laugh, I could tell, and replied, "I haven't met anyone of interest. I guess I'm not looking anyway. Maybe I'm holding on to the past."

What did she mean by that, and why did her words make me uneasy? "Well, Bubbles, it was good to catch up with you. I really must go now." It was time to end this conversation. I had already said too much.

"I enjoyed talking to you, Ade. I'm glad we got back in touch."

Another uncomfortable silence followed. Before I hung up, she added, "I would like to *keep* in touch, if that's okay."

"Yeah, sure, you have my number now."

23

"You can have mine, if you like."

After a short pause, I decided to accept it. "Sure, what is it?"

She gave it to me and then asked, "Can I have your new email address?"

*****

That was how her email communications began. At first, I didn't know what to make of her messages. She sent short, one-line sentences such as *How was your day? I hope you are well. I am checking in on you.* Then, she slowly progressed to sharing details of her daily activities, like the time she overslept and missed an Epidemiology test. I tried to keep my replies simple and to never really engage. I didn't want her to get any ideas.

After all, I was with someone else, and I considered it inappropriate to be chatting with an ex-girlfriend. My current girlfriend and I were in the early stages of our relationship, the so-called honeymoon phase, and I didn't want to jeopardize it over someone who could easily walk out on me again.

And yet, each time I turned on my laptop, I could neither ignore nor explain the trepidation that resulted. When there was no new email from Bubbles, I was disappointed and worried that she had disappeared again. I wanted to stay angry at her, to avoid falling for her, but holding a grudge against Bubbles made me feel worse. She had come back into my orbit, and in typical Bubbles fashion left me feeling confused.

Chapter 4

London, UK
May 2005

Maita

On my third day in London, a longtime friend named Rosie—short for Rosemary, and pronounced *Rhozee* by most Zimbabweans—came to spend the afternoon with me. She lived in Newham, East London, and had driven over an hour through traffic to Tolworth in the South. I enjoyed and appreciated her company, considering that she would rather be working a shift for extra cash. Rosie was a nurse, and she hated it, but it was her only chance at getting citizenship and a respectable career. Like most African immigrants in the United Kingdom, she'd taken up nursing because it guaranteed a work permit and a path to permanent residency. It was relatively easy to get into a nursing program, and the demand for healthcare workers was so high that most of them worked overtime and earned a good living.

Rosie accepted every shift that was thrown at her and hardly ever turned down an opportunity to make extra money. She worked days, nights, weekends, including bank holidays, and would drop everything without hesitation to rush to whatever hospital or nursing home needed her.

Working so much was necessary to maintain her expensive lifestyle. Rosie indulged in luxury brands and wore only the finest clothes and shoes, boasting a collection of designer handbags. She carefully coordinated a pair of Chanel sunglasses with a Chanel handbag. Her choice for a car was no different: Rosie was the proud owner of a black 2004 BMW X3. It was a costly habit to shop on King Street and Covent Garden, and unlike me, she couldn't stoop to bargain-hunting in high street stores like Next or Oasis.

When I lived and worked in London, I had to be thrifty, saving every penny for university tuition. At that time, Rosie and I each lived in shared employee accommodation at the hospitals where we worked. A year later, I lived in graduate student housing on the Emory University campus, but Rosie still shared a flat with two other girls and, of course, all her expensive possessions.

We'd come a long way from sharing a dorm room in boarding school, late-night chats about boys after lights out, being study partners, and dreaming of going to university. I was heartbroken when she didn't make enough A-level grades to advance to university. I moved on to Harare, and she stayed behind in Bulawayo, got married then divorced, and struggled as a single mother whose estranged ex-husband wanted nothing to do with her or their son. We rekindled our friendship in London after a chance meeting in a Tescos supermarket, and we picked up from where we left and carried on like we were in high school. Although we lived different lifestyles, we had a bond that blurred the lines between sisterhood and friendship.

"Okay," Rosie said, "so this guy you met on the plane is a white dude, *angithi*?"

"Yes, he is handsome—dark hair, brown eyes—average height, probably five-foot-ten, and he has a nice olive tan, most likely from the Atlanta heat. He must be about thirty years old. He sort of resembles a young Sean Penn." We were sitting on my sister's living-room floor on a mattress that we'd positioned against the wall, where a couch should have been.

My older sister Mercy lived in a two-bedroom flat with Wendy, her classmate from nursing school. They had just moved into the newly built modern flat and were in the process of putting it together. Mercy and Wendy lived in their separate bedrooms and shared the living room, bathroom, and kitchen. Each bedroom was fully furnished with a bed, TV, and a couch, leaving no incentive to complete the lounge with even the most basic sofa.

"What's his name?" Rosie asked.

"Chris," I said. "So we land at Heathrow Airport, and I'm waiting for my turn to get into the aisle and walk out of the plane. That's when Chris asked for my UK number. I was quite chuffed, but acted nonchalantly and told him I didn't have one. Then he said, 'Well, give me your sister's number. I can call you on her mobile.'"

"So, he was serious, or else he wouldn't have bothered to ask, *angithi*?" Rosie said, using a favorite Ndebele word to urge me on.

I continued, "I guess we had a terrific conversation on the flight, and we talked for hours. Chris made me laugh a lot, and certainly kept me entertained. But I don't think I'm his type. He didn't seem like he could be into Black girls."

Rosie shrugged. "You never know, don't be fooled by looks. I almost dated an Indian guy once, a medical student, after everyone had assumed that Indians never date outside their race, let alone an African. He was on my case for a long time, but I didn't find him attractive or fun. He was more your type—nerdy."

"Hmm, that's what you say now, but let's be honest, back then you declared that you wanted to date Zimbabwean dudes *only*. And I told you how unrealistic that was when the pool of Zimbabwean men in London was so small." And with a chuckle, I added, "Now that the clock is ticking and options are running low, you've opened up to dating *anyone,* including that Polish plumber that couldn't speak a word of English."

"Okay, so you gave that Chris guy Mercy's number?" Rosie said, deliberately ignoring my last comment.

"Yes, and guess what? As soon as I got here, Mercy told me he had called three times to check if I had arrived safely."

Rosie's eyes widened, and she gasped with excitement.

"Hmm, how interesting, but sounds like a stalker. This dude doesn't even know Mercy, and he is already blasting her phone."

Considering that we had only just met, it did seem a little too soon to be calling so much.

Just then, the doorbell rang. I glanced at my watch, wondering who it could be. Mercy and Wendy were working long shifts at a nursing home nearby. They would be done later in the evening around 7:00 p.m., and it was just 3:00 p.m.

"Can't be the girls. Besides, they wouldn't ring the bell since they have keys, right?" Rosie said, as if she read my mind.

"Yep, but Mercy gave me her key this morning. She may have left work early," I replied, slowly getting up from my comfortable position.

A quick look through the door spy hole confirmed no one was at the door, but a box had been delivered. I opened the door and was surprised to see that the white box was addressed to *Maita*.

Puzzled, I reread the mailing label. Who could have sent this package to me, and what was in it?

"Rosie, hurry, come and see!" I shouted, and she rushed to the door.

"What is it? Whose package is that?"

"Someone addressed it to me, but who sent it? Who knows I am staying here? What if it's a bomb?"

Rosie laughed. "You haven't changed a bit, have you? Ever so dramatic. What bomb? I'll get it, if you don't." She stepped outside and attempted to pick up the box, but it was too heavy. "Goodness, what's in here, bricks?" She bent down to read the mailing label. "It was sent by…"

She paused, then stared up at me with a questioning look. "A Christopher Medley. Do you know anyone by that name?" Before I could answer, she gasped. "O-M-G! It's the guy you met on the plane. *Angithi,* you said his name was Chris, right?"

"You have got to be kidding me. How can that be? I didn't give him my address." I crouched down to examine the box and mailing label.

Rosie couldn't contain her excitement. "Come on, let's get this box inside and see what's in it. It says here, *fragile, handle with care.*"

I was trying to wrap my head around what was happening. Why would Chris have sent me a package within days of meeting him? I was flattered, and also a little concerned by how quickly it had happened. Rosie motioned for me to help lift the box; it had to weigh more than fifty pounds. She took the lead, heaved the box up, and I assisted in carrying it into the lounge. Then she grabbed a knife from the kitchen and cut it open.

"He sent you wine, lots of wine!" There were three by four rows and columns of bottles separated in square compartments. She pulled out a bottle, and then another, and exclaimed, "An assortment of French wines. And wait, there's a note."

I was speechless, still trying to comprehend how this box wound up at Mercy's flat. Rosie read the handwritten note out loud:

Dear Bubbles,

I thoroughly enjoyed your company on the BA flight. I thought I would surprise you with a selection of wine. We both love red wine and enjoyed a good drink together. I hope we can have dinner —and more wine— soon.

Sincerely,
Chris

Jumping with joy like a toddler who'd unwrapped a gift from Santa, Rosie said, "Not only is he romantic and thoughtful, he wants to see you again!"

My enthusiasm however was delayed, my mind processing the not-so-obvious details, how eerie it felt for him to address me as Bubbles. It was too soon to be that familiar, especially after I introduced myself as Maita. I'd only mentioned my nickname briefly. He must have made a mental note of that; he was paying attention.

"How did he get this address?" I asked again.

"Simple, Mercy must have given it to him. He went out of his way to impress you. He even called you Bubbles, so that means *you* must have gotten very comfortable with him." Then she turned to me with a worried look and asked, "What happens to your plan to get back with Ade?"

"Nothing has changed. Certainly not because of a box of wine from a good-looking guy I just met."

The wine was an unexpected and romantic treat from Chris. We'd clicked on the flight from Atlanta, and there were moments when I thought I felt a reciprocal attraction, but I wasn't sure if it was imagined, especially after drinking lots of wine. Yet I didn't think our interaction would last beyond that flight.

Perhaps I was biased to assume that a seemingly successful young white English male would not be interested in a young Black African student. I had never dated outside my race—not by choice; that was just the way it was. Apart from previous work colleagues, my social circle was predominantly Black, and that provided little chance of mingling with potential boyfriends of another race.

Rosie didn't waste time trying to figure out how that carton of wine found its way to Mercy's doorstep. She uncorked a bottle of Pinot Noir and we indulged. I drained my glass in three gulps.

"You have to call him and thank him," Rosie said, handing me her cell phone. We had returned to our perch on the mattress. "Look, he even wrote his number on the note."

"You're right, I should thank him. I also need to find a way to let him know that I am not going to have dinner, or anything, with him. I don't want to lead him on." I signaled for Rosie to refill my wineglass. Chris was a nice guy, but I was preoccupied with reuniting with Ade and had no desire to be with anyone else.

"You don't have to tell him all that now. He hasn't formally asked you out on a date. Don't be too quick to blow him off."

I was sure that Ade and I would be back together by the end of the summer, so why entertain anyone else? Instead of reaching out to Chris, I had to figure out when I would contact Ade to let him know I was in London. Hopefully, he would ask to see me. I had to stay focused on my mission to win Ade back—my desire to do so was stronger than my more superficial attraction to Chris.

Keeping such thoughts to myself, I sipped more wine as Rosie went on about how she needed romance in her life—she wanted a guy like Chris. About three glasses later, as the wine worked its way through me, relaxing every muscle and elevating my mood, I decided it was time to call Chris.

Chapter 5

Chris

On my first day back in Oxford, and after a few hours of sleep, I stopped at The Iron Horse, a local pub around the corner from my mum's house. It was empty for a Wednesday night, with barely ten people drinking there—surprising for the legendary quiz night that brought the regulars.

I took a seat at the bar and felt at home. The bartender was nowhere in sight, probably on a bathroom break. With a warm feeling of appreciation I scanned the dimly lit interior, inhaling the familiar thick, musty smell of stale beer and cigarette smoke ingrained in the walls, furniture, and floor.

I'd been drinking here since I was fourteen. My mate Jimmy and I would offer to do dishwashing and cleaning for the owner, old Georgie. In exchange, he would sneak a can of Guinness for us to share. The place quickly became my refuge.

"I don't see anything wrong with drinking early," Georgie would say. After all, he started at twelve, and his love for the pub inspired him to run his own. "Just don't drink yourselves silly. Drink enough to have a good laugh; no need to get drunk like them hooligans."

Well, that was a bit difficult to do in those early years, because we never knew when to stop. The more booze we guzzled, the less we could distinguish tipsy from drunk. Everything blurred, the girls prettier with each pint, or shot. Of course, we also got a lot braver.

So there began my career in drinking. Nowadays, fed up with

the watered-down American beers, I had switched to wine and didn't drink beer much anymore. My friends Jimmy and Donnie would indeed have a go at me for turning soft. I had developed a taste for more sophisticated beverages and now enjoyed wine tasting and exploring wine bars, something my old pals would never understand. They had already called me names for being too "upper class."

Me, upper class? What a joke. Since I had traveled the world—worked in France, Sweden, Japan, China, Australia, and now Atlanta—they thought I had changed on them. My clothes were too conservative, my food and drink choices too expensive, and in their eyes I'd become a bore. Why couldn't I just enjoy a night out at the same old hole where we pulled girls? One-night stands and all, get legless on booze and stumble out of the bars sometime in the early morning hours, with a local lass to take home for a shag?

Well, if you've never traveled more than fifty miles from the council estates where we grew up—then yes, maybe you would find me a little sophisticated.

"Good to see you, Chris," said a familiar voice, breaking up my thoughts. "Been a while. How's it there in America?"

It was Timothy. He was the long-serving bartender we'd nicknamed Grumpy because, well, he always seemed to be in a bad mood. Timothy used to growl at us to quit being loud and rowdy, especially during a good football game. We soon learned that he was a kind-hearted, easygoing man who, despite working in the town's social hub, just wasn't good at socializing.

He said, "I hear you're doing well out there. You liking it?"

"It's great. I like it a lot, and I'm excited about starting my new job. I'm pleasantly surprised by how much I like it there."

I placed an order for a pint of Guinness.

"You still like Guinness, ha? So, which city did ya move to? I hear the place is so big, they've different time zones in one country."

"I live in Stockbridge, a city south of Atlanta, in Georgia." As I said this, I could tell by his expression that he didn't have a clue about any of the places I mentioned. Relocating to America—and to Georgia of all places—wasn't something I ever imagined. Everyone often talked of moving to New York, California, and certain areas of Florida. Not the South, often characterized as backward and ignorant. And yet here I was, back home in Oxford to wrap up my packing, load all my belongings into a container, and ship everything to my new home in Stockbridge, courtesy of Digi-Mechanix, Inc., my new employer.

"What's it like then? I bet it's so different from Oxford you might need a translator," Grumpy said, laughing with a smoker's wheeze, giving away his years of smoking, inhaling secondary smoke, and drinking—all unavoidable occupational hazards.

I had a lot to say in response, but didn't know how to sum it up and package it in a way that could help him imagine the place, to understand the differences in cultures, demographics, food, music, and so much more. Thankfully, before I could come up with a good answer, Grumpy's attention shifted to new customers, a party of three that sat two barstools away from me.

The city of Atlanta had surprised me. Contrary to expectations, it was more diverse than I imagined. Predominantly Black, with a sweltering mix of Blacks, whites, Hispanics, Asians, gays, and straights. I mingled with African Americans at a professional level and just about everywhere. With no prior experience living and working in a multicultural environment, I thought this was wonderful.

Earlier in January, after I accepted the job offer, I was invited to Atlanta to meet the company executives and my future workmates. As part of the orientation process I was invited to an office meeting with my new team. Walking into the boardroom, I noticed that the group of people sitting around the large oak conference table differed from those I'd worked with in previous jobs. There were three women and five men: Asian, Black, and white, all young-looking. A burly African American man got up to welcome me.

"I'm Jamal," he said, "head of logistics. Welcome to the ATL.

You will love this city." And with a broad smile, he directed me to an empty chair beside him. "We're glad to have you come on board."

"Glad to be here," I said. I made my way to the chair, reassured that I had made the right decision when I accepted the job.

Had I been born and raised in London, I would have been more exposed to people of various multicultural backgrounds through interactions at school and work, as the streets of London are indeed a melting pot. On the other hand, Oxford, where I'm from, is majority white. Growing up, the only person of color I saw regularly was the Pakistani man at the off-license in my neighborhood, and maybe an occasional waiter or waitress.

I was reminded of a night years ago, after partying and binge drinking, when Donnie and Jimmy got into a fistfight that ended badly, and we had to go to the local hospital.

"Why do we have to wait this long to be seen by the doctor?" Donnie complained, bracing his chest to minimize the pain from what we suspected were broken ribs.

"Can't you see that this place is crawling with Black and Asian doctors and nurses?" Jimmy said with a scowl. "These damn immigrants are clueless. They're messing up the system."

"Where are the white doctors and nurses then?" I said, disgusted by Jimmy's comments. "Go and find them and stop whining." It wasn't the first time they'd expressed their dislike for people of color, which made me uncomfortable. At that time, our local hospital was the only place I knew that had significant numbers of various races and nationalities.

Two pints and a shot of tequila later, I was chattier and in good spirits. The three strangers that I saw previously at the bar invited me to their table. Feeling unusually generous, I ordered a round of drinks for them all. I began entertaining them with stories about my new life in America, and the beautiful girl I'd met on my flight back to London.

"Sounds like the beginning of a romantic movie, meeting on a flight and all," said the red-haired lady, who I assumed was one of the guy's girlfriend. "I hope you got her number, and asked her out."

"It seems a bit too early, don't you think? I reckon I'll wait for her to get settled. I have her sister's number. Did I mention that she doesn't live here? She lives in Atlanta."

"Oh, you've gone international. Two Brits find love in Atlanta, what are the odds?" said one of the guys, who had a thick brown beard. With his shoulder-length hair and massive body, he could play a Viking role in a movie; he just needed a horned helmet. I figured he was the redhead's boyfriend by how his hand permanently rested on her thigh, and their proximity.

"She isn't British, actually." I was suddenly aware that I would have to clarify Maita every time I told this story, because most people would probably assume she was white and British like me.

"Is she an American?" asked the red-haired lady.

"No, she's African, from Zimbabwe."

"Oh, African, huh?" she replied with a raised eyebrow. "That's an interesting twist."

What did she mean by that?

"I worked with a guy from Cameroon once," the Viking lookalike said, wiping beer froth from his beard. "Nice fella. They are hard workers, those Africans. His English was poor, could hardly understand a word he said. Does she speak good English?"

"Yes, she does. Cameroon and Zimbabwe are two very different countries," I said, feeling a little irate.

"Yah, but they are all Africans, same thing."

"No, they're not, silly." The redhead rolled her eyes. "It's like saying all countries in Europe are the same. Take the English and the Polish for instance, we're different, we speak different languages—"

"Yah, yah, I get it." He brushed her off.

"I think I'll go now," I said, getting up. The conversation had taken an annoying turn.

"Already?" said Mr. Boyfriend. "Thanks for the beers. Good talking to you."

"Good luck with the beautiful lady from Atlanta," his girlfriend added.

"You're welcome," I said to Mr. Boyfriend. With a nod to his red-haired girlfriend, I added, "I think I'll take your advice and call her first thing tomorrow. I'd better hurry before she forgets about me."

As I walked out, I had an even better idea—a surprise that would ensure that she'd never forget about me.

* * * * *

Three days since returning to Oxford, I was preoccupied with packing my belongings into boxes, arranging to ship furniture, and finalizing the details of a leasing contract with Sarah, my property manager. She had called to let me know that my three-bedroom, semi-detached house was now available to prospective tenants.

"You have to clean it up, and make it presentable as soon as possible."

"Easier said than done," I said, scanning the mess and clutter of boxes in my living room. "I'll need more time. Hold off on advertising and give me a few more days."

"I'll give you a week. Don't forget to send a payment for the plumbing work done at the flat last week, and you still need to go there to check out the damage to the floors before I send out the contractors."

And she hung up. I was overwhelmed with the many tasks I had. "The joys of being a landlord," I muttered, and slumped onto my leather couch.

When I was twenty-one years old and starting an engineering apprenticeship program, I purchased a one-bedroom flat. For ten years it was my home until I bought my current house a year ago. Sarah placed tenants in the flat and had managed it since. At thirty-two years old, I was the proud owner of two properties.

Now, I had plans for a third. Houses in Atlanta were spacious and affordable, and they made English homes look like dollhouses. They came decked with en suite bedrooms, walk-in closets, sizable and functional basements, and huge backyards. I wanted to buy one before the year was over. My tri-level semi-detached house, which I was very proud of, now seemed so dull and tiny.

Despite the exhaustion and stress from packing and sorting out issues concerning my flat, I was happy overall—that rare moment in one's life when everything appears to be going well. The highlights: a new position as a senior engineer for Digi-Mechanix, Inc., a promotion and significant pay raise, climbing the property ladder in Oxford, and the prospect of buying my dream home in Atlanta.

Then there was Maita—or Bubbles.

She'd been on my mind since the day I met her. I remembered her beautiful smile and hypnotizing brown eyes. As we sat side by side, drinking wine, laughing, and talking, it felt like the best ten hours I had spent with any girl. The conversation was effortless, the laughter was genuine, and we realized that, while from very different worlds, we had so much in common. That girl who'd scrambled late onto the plane—who I even, at one point, hoped wouldn't show up—turned out to be more than I could ever have imagined.

Did she feel the same about me? Did I ever cross her mind? With all the talking we did, we never discussed our respective love lives. She mentioned being single, but never asked me about my situation. I didn't get into it because there was nothing to tell. I broke up with Mabel almost a year ago, after three years together. My parents liked her, and there was immense pressure from my mum for me to *settle down*. She always said that Mabel was the one.

"Mabel is a lovely girl and has a good job at the Council. You two would do great together," my mother would say.

Dad felt the same and would grumble, "I guess I'll be that old man who never had grandchildren. No one to call me Grandpa.

Can't you see that time is running out?"

Unfortunately for them, my relationship with Mabel was unfulfilling, and I eventually got bored of her. She also had a volatile temper, perhaps no different from mine, and I cringed in thinking about some of the fights we had. Especially the time when she accused me of flirting with her friend, Sheila, whom we called Shilz. After a night of drinking with friends at a karaoke bar, we returned to Mabel's flat, both of us drunk and wobbly. When I tried to kiss her, she pushed me away.

"Oh, *now* you wanna get some, after ignoring me all night? Why don't you go to Shilz? Get your filthy hands off me…"

"What are you on about?" I asked, irritated and confused.

"Don't pretend like you don't know. We all saw how you were all over Shilz. It was pathetic." She kicked her shoes off and stomped off to the bedroom.

I followed her. "Oh, come on with the false accusations. There you go again, why are you so jealous of her? You're the one that insists on inviting her each time we go out—"

"Oh, so it's my fault now, huh?" she shouted, with both hands on her hip. "You just can't resist her platinum-blonde hair, is that it? Or her big tits? What is it, huh?"

I knew by the way she was already hyperventilating that I'd aggravated yet another fight. The alcohol-fueled argument spiraled out of control, going beyond my flirting with Sheila to further ridiculous accusations of sleeping with her other girlfriends.

When I shouted, "You're a jealous, insecure bitch!" she came at me with a table lamp. I grabbed her by the wrist, and we wrestled for the lamp. Finally, I pushed her hard against the wall and she fell. The lamp-turned-weapon tumbled from her grasp. It was clear right then that we were not suitable for each other, and I feared that our fights would one day escalate to something fatal. We agreed to go our separate ways, and I was relieved.

Last Christmas at my parents' dinner table, Dad began to nag me about getting married and starting a family. My sister, Nicki, tried to escape the discussion and got up from her chair, but she immediately sat down when Mum gave her a disapproving look.

"You're not getting any younger," he said, with a mouth full of mashed potatoes. "Most of your mates, including that no-good lad Jimmy, are married, and they have kids. Meanwhile, you're globetrotting with that job of yours."

"I can have kids at any time, even when I'm sixty," I said, annoyed. "I'm not the one with a biological clock that's ticking."

Dad was speechless. Mum and Nicki gasped in unison.

"Leave me out of this," exclaimed Nicki. "Don't drag me into your issues. That's not fair."

I felt terrible for referencing my sister that way, but I was fed up. The focus should be on her, not me. Nicki was thirty years old and still running around with the village goth crew. She was tattooed from her neck to her toes, wore excessive black makeup, and smoked incessantly, cigarettes and weed. We all knew she was on drugs too, but no one said anything to her. I guess the family had written her off.

What would Nicki and my parents say if I told them that I was attracted to a Black African girl? Even though Dad was begging me for a daughter-in-law and grandchildren, I knew he wouldn't accept Maita because he'd once expressed his old-fashioned views on biracial couples. I decided not to tell them about her. I wasn't ready for any negativity, and merely thinking about my family dynamics began to dampen my mood.

I made a conscious decision to shift my focus from the past to the present, something more positive. Maita was all I could think about really, giving me a warm feeling. According to the postal tracking record, she had received my wine gift, and I was waiting impatiently for her call. I desperately wanted to call her sister's number, but didn't want to bother her.

Communication would be better if Maita had a mobile phone of her own, and a local number to use during her time in England. If I had to, I would buy her a phone, if that's what it would take to get in touch whenever I wanted to.

After hauling more boxes from the house's upper level, I was hot and tired and went upstairs to my bedroom to take a break. I lay on my bed, stared at the ceiling, and wished I had air-conditioning or a ceiling fan to cool me down. I was seriously considering taking a cold shower when my phone vibrated in my pocket. I sat up.

The caller ID was an unknown number, I hoped it was Maita. No one had my mobile phone number except my family and property manager. My friends didn't know that I was back in Oxford—I hadn't told them I was coming home. I wanted time to sort out my move before any distractions.

I thought about ignoring the call and taking a shower or nap, but my thumb involuntarily clicked the *answer* button.

"Hello," I said.

"Hi, may I speak to Chris?" The voice was immediately familiar; it was her, Maita. What a pleasant surprise! My heart began beating so fast and loud, I thought she would hear it.

"This is Chris. Is this Maita?"

"Yes, it's me. I'm calling from a friend's cell phone. How are you doing?"

"I'm good. How have you been?" It was insane how nervous and boyish I'd become. I cleared my throat and took a deep breath.

"I'm great and well-rested. I just received the box of wine you sent to me. Thank you so much. What a lovely surprise. You got me on that one; I wasn't expecting that at all."

"You're welcome, from one wino to another. I'm sure you will enjoy it."

An awkward silence followed. I had to keep the conversation going.

"How is your sister?" I asked. "She was my partner in the surprise. I asked for her address, and she agreed to keep it between us." I was desperate to get Maita talking like she did on the flight, but she wasn't as cheerful as I expected and was relatively subdued.

"Trust Mercy to keep a secret. I'm having some of that wine with a friend. She says, 'Hi' and 'thanks.' We're already drinking our second bottle." Someone giggled in the background.

"My pleasure," I said. "I enjoyed your company, you know, and—"

Before I could complete my sentence, she said, "Chris, I have to get off the phone. My friend has an incoming call from work, and she has to take it. Thanks again for the wine. Can we chat later?"

I felt like someone had splashed a bucket of ice-cold water onto my face. Was Maita bluffing, just trying to get me off the phone?

"No problem, when can I call you?" I hoped she would give me the green light to call on her sister's phone again.

"You can call whenever, at this number. I have to go now. When I get a phone, hopefully soon, I will get in touch."

"Okay, talk to you later, then."

That didn't go as well as I'd hoped. Did Maita's friend really have an incoming call, or was that a way to get me off the phone? Maita said she would call me when she got her phone, so did that mean I couldn't reach her on Mercy's number? I lay down on the bed like before, staring at the ceiling again, trying to understand what just happened. Did I have to wait for her to make the next move?

Perhaps Maita wasn't that into me. Maybe I was moving too fast. It had only been three days since we met. "Forget about her," I told myself, but I just couldn't.

Unfortunately, now it seemed like the feeling wasn't mutual. Just when I had become optimistic about the future, a single phone call had crashed me down from cloud nine.

Disappointed, I turned onto my side, curled up, and decided it was time for a well-deserved nap.

Chapter 6

London, UK
June 2005

Maita

Mercy called me into the kitchen to help unpack the bags of groceries piled on the kitchen counter. By the looks of it, she had spent a lot of money, which left me feeling bad for not helping with food and living expenses. Nothing was free, after all, guest or not, friend or family—you couldn't live in anyone's home, or crash on the couch, without at some point contributing financially.

"How much do I owe you for this?" I asked, placing a carton of milk into the refrigerator.

"Don't worry about that now," Mercy said. "You can start to chip in after your first paycheck. For now, you can make dinner and wash the dishes, which would be nice."

"Sounds fair. Hopefully, I'll start work next week." I was glad to delay paying bills.

It was June, over a week since my arrival, and I was eager to begin work. Motivated by an ambitious agenda and limited time, I felt like each passing day was a missed opportunity to earn money and rekindle my relationship with Ade.

Mercy and Rosie were aware of my hopes to make amends with Ade, who I'd left behind a year ago after a series of heated arguments. I hadn't even said goodbye. Honestly, it was all my own pride and arrogance.

Now the tables had turned. I had come back for him, but he had moved on. Mercy told me to forget about Ade, to focus on Chris. Although she had never met Chris, she liked him from the details I had given, her brief phone conversation with him and the whole surprise with the wine.

Rosie, on the other hand, had always been fond of Ade, and was rooting for him. However, she had her own relationship woes: her boyfriend had left her for someone else. So even though she was sympathetic to my cause, Rosie couldn't help but revert to the case of her heartbreak.

Getting back with Ade occupied my mind all day, every day. The blend of regret and sadness was a constant feeling in the background, and although I would laugh and chat with the girls, I never felt true joy. Being in London worsened my agony, because I was so close to him and yet so far away. We were in the same city and time zone, living under the same summer skies. He was just one or two trains away, a bus ride away, a phone call away— yet I couldn't gather the courage to contact him.

"I don't understand why you won't call him," Mercy said, after expressing that she'd had enough of my whining. We were sitting on the mattress in the living room, relaxing.

"He doesn't know that I'm in London," I said. "I haven't talked to him in over a month since he told me to quit calling him. I stopped calling, but I just can't stop thinking that I can change his mind if we meet face-to-face."

"Ouch, that must have hurt," said Mercy. "I'd leave him alone. I have too much pride."

"Not if you feel the way I do. I know that when he sees me, he will remember the connection we had. Besides, I look twice as good as I did back then."

Mercy rolled her eyes at me and shook her head as she got up to go to the kitchen for more wine, and to fix a snack. She couldn't believe the effort I had made to impress Ade—the expensive Brazilian wet and wavy weave in my hair, an immaculate manicure and pedicure, and expertly threaded and shaped eyebrows that complemented my smooth and flawless skin. My battle with acne was behind me, and my confidence was at its highest.

Arranging a meeting with Ade, either lunch or dinner, would be my greatest challenge. I had to find the guts to make that dreaded call and ask him out.

The following day, I decided to do it. Pacing back and forth in the bedroom, I flipped open the cell phone that Mercy gave me. I slowly punched Ade's number on the worn keypad, then sat on the bed, my heart pounding hard. With a trembling finger, I pressed the call button.

His phone rang until voice mail kicked in. I felt some relief when he didn't pick up, because I wasn't sure that I was ready to talk to him, but I didn't want to leave a message either.

Feeling lonely and demoralized, and with no enthusiasm for anything, I got into bed, aware it was eleven thirty in the morning. I rested my head on the pillow, and without warning a flood of tears flowed uncontrollably, soaking my pillow. I had reached the bottom of the pit and hated the way I felt; regret and desperation combined—the worst kind of feeling. My mood had swung like a pendulum from one extreme to another: from moments of confidence that I could waltz back into Ade's life and we would fall in love all over again, to times like this when I felt like I had already lost the battle, and had no chance of redeeming myself. It felt like torture.

*****

I ended my relationship with Ade, mainly because I'd been afraid of commitment. A year ago, in 2004, as the day of my departure to Atlanta drew closer, Ade became more clingy and overbearing. He counted down the days on a calendar, lamenting about how miserable he would be without me. He didn't want me to spend a day or weekend away from him. When I'd visit my mother, sister, or girlfriends, he would call me on my cell phone repeatedly, demanding that I return "home" to his flat, where I lived six out of seven days of the week. If I told him that I planned to sleep over at Mercy's or Rosie's place after a night of partying, he would plead with me to get a taxi to be with him instead.

This uncharacteristic behavior by the usually easygoing Ade soon became irritating—and a turnoff. In his defense, he said that he was trying to make the best of the little time we had before we embarked on a long-distance relationship. His biggest fear, he confessed, was that I would meet someone and leave him. I reassured him that I would do no such thing; besides, we could travel back and forth between London and Atlanta, and eventually, he could join me.

Ade surprised me when he suggested that perhaps the best way to secure our relationship was if we got married before I left. It was an unexpected proposal—and, at the time, unwelcome.

Feeling stifled, pressured, and a little upset by his attempt to trap me into marriage, I rejected him. He accused me of not being invested in our relationship.

"This confirms what I've been saying," Ade said, "that you're going to move on without me."

"You're right, and I need to keep my options open. I don't want restrictions." It was only a heat-of-the-moment reply to hurt him, but unfortunately, he believed it.

"Don't blame me for your paranoia and insecurities," I continued. "You're trying to tie me down with emotional blackmail, and it's not working. In fact, I need a break from all this drama."

The exchange erupted into a big argument. Ade was furious, and I was upset. We became intentionally cold to each other, our interaction marked by tension and the occasional silent treatment. This unpleasantness had a physical presence; it was so repulsive that even when we rode on the bus to work, we sat on separate seats.

I wanted an apology for his accusations, but Ade didn't believe he owed me one. He blamed me for the rift between us and stated that I was insensitive to his feelings. Neither one of us backed down. For days, we went on ignoring each other until I packed my bags and moved out of his flat. I returned to my shared accommodation where I had already given my thirty-day notice.

I expected Ade to come begging me to return to his flat that we had shared for over a year, but he didn't. This infuriated me. We were both too proud to give in, and I began to believe that, indeed, I needed my space and freedom to start a new life in America without a nagging boyfriend.

Due to my pending move to Atlanta, I brushed off the standoff with Ade as a minor issue compared with what lay ahead. I was looking toward a new and exciting experience in America. I reconnected with my childhood friend, Lindiwe, who lived in Phoenix, Arizona, and she was already making plans to meet me in Atlanta for a long overdue reunion. My last days in London were a series of farewell dinners and parties, and I didn't invite Ade. Leaving for Atlanta without seeing or talking to him was the best way to punish him for being unreasonable. Both our egos prevailed, and the rift between us widened.

He eventually tried to reach me by phone, but I didn't answer. I couldn't explain why I was still so upset. At that point, I just wanted to punish him unnecessarily. After a few missed calls, he gave up, and I never returned them; instead, I left London without saying goodbye.

Adjusting to student life was overwhelming, and in trying to navigate my new world, I didn't prioritize mending fences with Ade. Seven months went by before I reached out to him, ironically on Valentine's Day. I should have done it earlier, but back then, my pride wouldn't let me.

What had been a childish and foolish game to me was a big deal for Ade. He indeed feared losing me, and maybe sincerely wanted to marry me out of love. Although we each had a hand in our relationship's demise, he'd made an effort to call, but I stubbornly left the country without a proper farewell.

*****

Sleep eventually took over my mental postmortem of past

events—until I was awakened by the cell phone on the nightstand. It was after three in the afternoon. I couldn't believe I had slept that long. Confident that it was Ade calling back after seeing a missed call, although it would be an unfamiliar number, I was still hopeful. I sat up, noting the damp patch on my pillow. Finally, I thought, I would talk to him. After one look at the caller ID, though, I answered with a disappointed sigh.

"Hi, Chris."

"Bubbles, I didn't hear from you today and decided to check up on you. You okay?"

"Yeah, I'm fine." Why did he assume such familiarity as to use my nickname? "I'm just getting up from a short nap."

"The weather is lovely today. You can't stay in all day. Get out and enjoy the outdoors. Maybe I should come get you and bring you here, to Oxford."

It wasn't the first time he had suggested that I should go to visit him. "I'll consider your offer after I start work."

"Are you ready to get back to your old job? You must have left a good impression on your boss for him to let you come work for the summer."

I forced a smile. "I'm a little nervous about getting back to physiotherapy and working in the community after a year away. My brain can remember health economics principles, bio stats, and public health policies, but my physio is a bit rusty. I'll have to read up to refresh."

"That's impressive."

"Well, I have no choice but to dive into the deep end and get on with it. I need this job, and the money."

"Bubbles, I have to say, you amaze me. Graduating from Zimbabwe, working as a physiotherapist in London, going to America for graduate school paying out of pocket, then coming to work in London for the summer, just like that. I can't even navigate the various visa requirements for my job. And here you are, switching them around like crazy."

"You flatter me, Chris. I guess it's the hunger in me. Getting a working holiday visa for the summer wasn't easy, but I tried anyway. I had a gruesome telephone interview with an agent from the British consulate. Fortunately I passed, and got the visa. My old boss, David, was more than happy to have me fill in for a colleague who is on maternity leave. Good thing I maintained my physiotherapy registration with the UK Health Professions Council. It's all God's work, trust me."

Chris replied, "Hmm, I'm inspired. So, when do I get to see you?"

I wasn't ready to meet him, not before I had an opportunity to talk to Ade.

"Can I call you after I get my work schedule and settle into my new work environment? When do you go back to Atlanta?"

"I'm supposed to go back in a week, but I've extended my stay. I have to sort out my house, and there are some delays with the shipping company."

"I see, so there's still time. I'll be in touch."

In a deflated tone, he replied, "All right, I'll wait for your call."

The subtle pressure in his response told me he *expected* a call from me, sooner rather than later. I was flattered by his eagerness, and I was interested enough to reciprocate, but it had to be at my pace.

Just as I placed the phone down, it rang again, startling me. I answered immediately, without checking the caller ID. "Hello?"

"Hi. Someone called me from this number."

It was Ade.

Once again, my heart rate shot up. The moment had finally come.

"Hi, Ade, it's Bubbles."

"Bubbles? Your caller ID is a local number."

"I'm in London. I arrived last week."

He was silent for a few seconds. "Oh, well, welcome back. What brings you here?"

I wasn't going to make it obvious I was here for him, not yet anyway. "Well, for starters, my mother lives in Kent, and my sister is here in London, so there is that. Then work. I'm here to work."

He must have been walking and talking simultaneously; I could hear his footsteps, which seemed at a quick pace, accompanied by loud, rhythmic breathing as if he were mildly out of breath. "I see. How are your mum and sister doing?"

"They're well. Mercy was asking about you." That was a lie, and I don't know why I even said it. I guess it was an attempt to remind Ade that he was once a part of my life, and my family knew and liked him.

He ignored that. "So, where will you be working? Same hospital as before?"

"I will work for the same trust but not inpatient. I'll be in the community in North London."

"I see," he said. He had stopped walking; I heard a car door open. "I'm sure you'll do well. That was your old home, your territory." There was a pause. "I have to get off the phone, my phone battery is low and I don't have my car charger."

I was silent for a moment, wishing I could engage him longer. "Oh, okay, so you have to go already?" I hoped that my voice didn't give away my disappointment.

"Yes," he replied. His car engine started.

"No problem," I said, making an effort to steady my voice. "We can catch up later."

With fingers crossed, I pressed the phone to my ear, hoping to hear him say he would call me back. "Okay, I have to go, goodbye."

And he cut the call.

I was crushed. I threw the phone on the bed, slowly got back under the covers, and cried again. It was apparent Ade didn't want to talk to me beyond pleasantries. Perhaps he was rushing home to his girlfriend. The thought of him being with another woman deepened my sorrow. How was I going to initiate another conversation without exposing my desperation? Was I even going to see him after coming this far?

I forced myself out of bed and got out my iPod. I needed to drown this feeling in music, and hopefully it would muffle my crying and the pain. Another Toni Braxton song, "I Don't Want To," was my choice, a song about a broken heart. I buried my head under the covers, still crying, and let the music play.

Chapter 7

London UK
June 2005

Ade

The last time I talked to Bubbles on the phone must have been about two months ago, in April. I had wrestled with how to break it down to her, to make it clear that I wanted nothing to do with her. It was evident from her email messages and random phone calls that Bubbles wanted us to get back together. I never initiated any contact; I just replied to hers. Even when she shared details of her personal life and made it very clear that she was single, I offered no information in return.

I don't go out to clubs or socialize much, she would write from America. *On any given Saturday night, you can find me in my bedroom watching reruns of* Friends. Yeah, right, not the Bubbles I knew. Bubbles got that nickname because of her love for *bubbling,* a phrase she and her friends used to describe partying and having a good time. A childhood friend had named her Bubbles as a joke because of her easygoing nature, tendency to be a social butterfly, and being the life of the party. And the name stuck.

I find it hard to believe that you could be in a city like Atlanta and resist going out to have a good time, I wrote back. *People change, but not that much.*

Although she liked to *bubble,* she never did anything stupid—as far as I could tell. Bubbles kept a level head and always stayed focused; just one of many things that made her attractive.

It felt good to have her call me, especially after the pain of the break-up, how she'd left without saying goodbye before we could resolve our misunderstandings. She'd left me and never looked back.

Now look who was crying.

It was karma.

However, as the frequency of email messages and phone calls started to increase, I knew that I had to stop feeding my ego and tell her to stop. I was getting mixed feelings. At times I was angered by memories of how I'd broken down after she left, and yet a part of me felt drawn to Bubbles again, which scared me.

The decision to cut her off was inevitable when Noma, my girlfriend, stumbled on an open email on my computer. She was upset that I was still chatting with an ex-girlfriend. I realized then that maintaining a relationship with Bubbles wasn't worth destroying the one I had.

Noma and Bubbles were opposites. Maybe that was why I liked Noma—to get as far away from my past as possible. They were the same height, but Noma was curvier with wide hips and a sizable derriere, giving structure to her thicker body. Her breasts were at least two cup sizes bigger. I preferred slim and slender women, like Bubbles, and initially I hadn't been attracted to Noma. Unlike Bubbles, Noma was an introvert and a homebody. She hardly missed church on Sundays, and had me attending Bible study classes with her. As a Catholic who hadn't been to church in over a year, I welcomed the idea of attending church regularly, but I couldn't relate to the Pentecostal way of preaching. I later stopped going to church. Still, Noma brought calm into my life when I was distraught, and she helped me get back on my feet, refocus, and recalibrate. She nursed me back to a healthy social and mental state.

Shortly after I bought my house, Noma moved in. Unlike Bubbles, she was a natural homemaker who loved to clean, cook hearty meals, and to decorate the home. It was refreshing to have someone take care of me. We got along well, and I was happy, comfortable, and content. My sister, Bola—short for Bolanle—liked her, and they hung out sometimes, but not in the same way that Bola and Bubbles used to get along. They had similar personalities, and Bola was devastated when Bubbles left me. It broke my heart to watch my sister mourning the loss of my relationship.

After Noma found the email from Bubbles on my computer, I decided to end all communication with Bubbles. I waited for her next phone call.

"I don't think it's a good idea for us to keep talking," I said to her. "I told you I have a girlfriend, and it's not fair to her."

"Well, it's not like we're hooking up," Bubbles said. "Tell your girlfriend to stop being petty. We're just old friends. You're allowed to have friends, right?"

I wasn't a naive third grader, and I knew what she really wanted. I replied, "We may be friends, but we can't constantly be talking and emailing anymore. Can you respect that?"

She said she understood, wished me well, and that was that. Since then, I hadn't heard from her.

Now she'd called, told me she's in London. I decided not to call Bubbles back, and if she called me again, I would have to tell her off once and for all. Who would have thought I would ever be the one doing that when, just a year ago, I was in pieces because of this girl? I sometimes wished I'd never met her, but she had some kind of hold on me, and I was desperately trying to fight it.

As I drove into my driveway, I saw Noma getting out of her car and walking to the front door. She must have just gotten back from work too. My commute home usually took forty-five minutes, but today it seemed like fifteen. Driving in silence was atypical of me, no music playing, no background noise from talk-radio hosts—just the smooth hum of the BMW engine, backgrounding the constant thoughts of Bubbles.

Part II

Chapter 8

London, UK
March 2003 – 2 years prior

Maita

Midday, and the physiotherapy team on the geriatrics medical floor was having lunch in the office. Food from the hospital canteen was greasy and not appetizing, so I preferred to bring in lunch, or order local takeout. Three months into my job as a junior physiotherapist, I was gradually getting acquainted with everyone. It was my second job, after six months at a government hospital in Harare.

My work colleagues were generous in showing me the ropes, helping me adapt to a different culture and foreign work environment. I was the primary physiotherapist to a geriatric ward. Natalie Clark, a senior physiotherapist, was my supervisor. She provided oversight and guidance, a godsend who held my hand and trained me on managing a medical ward.

Natalie, who'd emigrated from New Zealand, reminded me of Carrie Bradshaw, Sarah Jessica Parker's character from the series *Sex and the City*. She was short, petite, and curvy, and had long dirty-blonde hair. When she was out of her work uniform—the blue pants and white tunic that we all wore—Natalie displayed an eccentric, Carrie-like dress code and love for designer shoes. She was twenty-eight, five years my senior, and we got along like age-mates, professionally and socially.

A single woman without children, Natalie enjoyed traveling and exploring Europe, indulging in fine cuisine, designer clothes and shoes, and hitting popular London nightclubs and bars. I was new to the UK and its healthcare system, living alone in

North London, far from my family and friends who were spread across South London, East London, and Kent. She expressed genuine concern over my well-being and sometimes called after work to check up on me. Her generosity, including the rehabilitation team, enabled me to settle comfortably at the North Middlesex hospital.

On that Monday afternoon, when we all had lunch in the office, Natalie announced with a twinkle in her eyes, "Maita, I forgot to mention, someone on your ward has been asking about you. I think he likes you, and he's not one of your patients."

Everyone turned to me.

"You mean, she has a secret admirer?" asked Josh, a fellow junior physiotherapist who was nerdish and goofy, and a lover of gossip.

"I bet it's that nurse, the Caribbean guy; he's always checking you out," chimed a senior physiotherapist named Jennifer.

With a mischievous look, Natalie continued. "Keep guessing. There aren't that many men on the ward. This person has been asking about you quite a bit, and I know you've seen him because he frequents your ward."

I tried to conceal my intrigue. "Can't be anyone of interest to me. If the mysterious person you speak of were any good, I'd have spotted him already, so I'll pass. If I see anyone I'm attracted to, I'd be the one asking about him."

Everyone laughed. Becky, an occupational therapist, asked, "Are you sure you don't like the red-haired fella from housekeeping services, the janitor? He works on the ward." Again, everyone laughed out loud.

I shook my head. "No way, I'd rather stay single, thank you very much." The red-haired janitor wasn't attractive at all. Short and overweight, with an acne-ridden face, his smile exposed yellow and brownish teeth desperately in need of a dentist. It dawned on me that I was hypocritical to dismiss the janitor so harshly, because I too had a terrible case of adult acne, which made me wonder why anyone would fancy me.

Natalie said, "Well, I'll tell you who it is later. Promise you will at least talk to him."

"Natalie, why are you so invested?" Josh asked. "What deal have you made with this mystery man?" He'd taken the words right out of my mouth.

Getting up and gathering her notepad and stethoscope, Natalie said, "I just think he's really nice, that's all. Guys, I have to dash to a family conference that starts in three minutes. If I sit around here talking, I'll be late. Maita, I'll fill you in on all the details later." She tossed leftovers in the trash and rushed out the door.

With lunch break over, everyone hurried off to their various duties. I made my way to the cascade ward to get started with my afternoon treatments. Staying alert and energetic during the second half of the day was difficult, especially after a satisfying lunch. This particular Monday was more challenging as I struggled to recover from my weekend hangover, and I'd already begun counting down the days to the end of the week. My birthday was on Sunday.

As usual, my birthday weekend would be one big party of drinking and club-hopping with Mercy and my girlfriends. We'd go to Moonlight, a trendy Afro-Caribbean nightclub in central London, where we were guaranteed a good time.

In prepping for my next physiotherapy session, I stood at the nurses' station, reviewing the patient's medical chart. My attention soon diverted from the paperwork to Saturday night plans, how to do my hair, and what I would wear.

"You must be having a good day, smiling to yourself."

Like a child caught cheating, I stiffened and glanced over my shoulder.

"At least one of us is enjoying work today," he said. "Or something in that medical record must be the reason you seem so happy."

Standing in front of me, fiddling with the stethoscope on his thick neck, was one of the doctors who frequented the geriatric medical floor. He was easily recognizable as a minority Black physician with a striking, dark-chocolate complexion, square jawline, and medium frame. He extended a hand, and in what sounded like a West African accent said, "I'm Dr. Ola."

We shook hands. It seemed odd to do so, too formal for the ward setting.

"Hi. Maita," I said. I indicated my name tag, and noticed he didn't have one.

"I know, Natalie told me you're the physio managing this ward."

I wondered, could he be the person she was talking about?

My questioning expression must have given him the need to clarify. "I'll be the senior house officer on this ward for the next few months. I like to know the therapists and nurses on my team."

"I see. Well, it's nice to meet you, Dr. Ola," I said.

He replied, "I hope I didn't disturb you. I'll let you get back to work, then."

With a smile and quick nod, I said, "Sure, my work awaits."

How friendly, I thought, as he walked away. Unlike most of the doctors around here.

Later that afternoon, I was in the office clocking out on the computer when Natalie walked in. I turned to face her.

"I think I met the so-called secret admirer. Is it Dr. Ola?" I asked.

She giggled. "Yep, that's him. You have no idea how long he's been asking about you. I think since the first time he saw you on the ward. He approached me after a care plan meeting, and in his words, he asked if *the Black physio* was the primary therapist on the cascade ward. When I said yes, I could tell from his reaction that he was into you. He asked me your name, and every time I see him in meetings, he asks about you."

She was enjoying this, I could tell.

"So," Natalie said. "What do you think?"

"Let's not jump to conclusions. He just introduced himself as the doctor in charge, and he wanted to meet his team members."

"Yah, but what do you *think* of him?"

"Think of who?" interrupted Josh, who had quietly entered

the office.

"Oh, nothing," I replied, signaling to Natalie that I didn't want to discuss it further. I continued to type.

"We are talking about a difficult patient," Natalie replied. "Maita, let's continue this tomorrow. I have to head out."

We didn't get another opportunity to talk about Dr. Ola, because Natalie was busy with meetings all week. On Friday, the rehab team surprised me with a birthday cake and card. Everyone had chipped in and ordered Chinese takeout for lunch.

"Thank you so much, you guys are the best!" I said, before digging into my sweet and sour chicken. Unfortunately I had to rush the cake-cutting in order to complete my afternoon patient rounds and leave work earlier than usual. I planned to spend the weekend in Lewisham at my sister's place, and it would take ages to get from North to South London on a Friday evening.

Once again, at the nurses' station, I was signing a daily note when a familiar voice said, "Happy birthday. How come I didn't receive an invite to the party?"

I turned. "Dr. Ola, hi. How did you know about my birthday?"

"Word travels fast. I have my sources. So, the cake was just for the rehab team?"

"My birthday is on Sunday, and my workmates decided to celebrate today. There is some leftover cake if you're interested."

"I already had too many carbs for lunch. Maybe I'll get invited to the real party this weekend?"

I closed the medical chart and placed it on a pile of medical records that needed filing. Opening another patient's medical chart, I said, "Unfortunately for you, there is no other party."

His mouth drooped, seemingly intentionally. In an animated voice, he said, "Oh, well, I guess I missed out."

It was cute, and I laughed.

Switching back to a serious voice, he asked, "Can I take you to dinner to celebrate your birthday?"

We were at the nurses' station, discussing birthday parties and dinner dates in the middle of a workday. Instead of standing around, I should have been working to leave at least thirty minutes earlier than usual. "I'm not sure about that," I said, trying to think of an excuse to get out of this conversation without being rude.

"Okay, let me have your number. We can talk later." He wasn't about to give in. Looking around to see if anyone was watching or listening, and pretending to be looking down at the open medical chart, I whispered my number. He scribbled it on his notepad.

"Thanks, I have to run. I'll call you later." After cheerfully tucking the notepad into his lab coat pocket, he was gone.

When my work was finally complete, I quickly made my way to the main hospital entrance. Natalie came running after me.

"Hey, did you get a chance to talk to Dr. Ola?" She caught up with me, and we walked out together.

"Yes, I did. I felt a little awkward now that I know he *is* the secret admirer. Did you tell him about my birthday?"

We had stopped at the shuttle stop; this was where I got onto the mini-bus that ran between the North Middlesex hospital and St. Anne's hospital, where I lived at the employee housing on the hospital campus. I shared a three-bedroom flat with a nurse and a physiotherapist.

"This morning Dr. Ola saw me bring in the cake, and I told him it was for your birthday."

"He wants to take me to dinner."

She jumped in excitement. "You will go, right? He is such a nice guy, come on. I think you two would be great together."

I lowered my voice as more people joined us at the shuttle stop. "Natalie, he's not my type."

She gasped. "What do you mean?"

I looked around and whispered, "Not here, in case someone hears us." I pulled her to the side, away from bystanders and fellow employees. "I'm not attracted to him like that. He isn't my sort of guy."

"I don't understand. Dr. Ola is good-looking and smart.

What else do you need?"

I searched for the right words. "I agree, he isn't bad-looking, but... he's a little bit on the chubby side of things."

With disappointment in her eyes, she said, "I think you have it wrong. Okay, just go on one date, just one, and if he bores you to death, then fine." She seemed sincere and determined. "Let's make a deal. If you go on one date with him, I'll give you two tickets to see *Chicago* on the West End. You can have them if you go with him." We both enjoyed West End plays, and often talked about going together on a girls' night out.

"Let me think about it, and not because I want the tickets to *Chicago*." Natalie's sincerity moved me—she cared about me on a personal level. "He has my number, so if he calls, I will hear him out, and maybe I will go to dinner."

"Yes!" she shouted, as if her favorite football team had just scored a goal. "Great, keep me posted. I've got to go, and here comes your shuttle. Enjoy your birthday, and have a good weekend."

She 'd done it. Natalie had convinced me to go on a date with Dr. Ola. Now I just had to wait for him to call.

*****

That night, I settled down to a bowl of rice and curry beef stew, whipped up in thirty minutes—a new target for all my meals. Frustrated with eating late after lengthy meal prep and fed up with take-away, I was determined to perfect my skills in making fresh, tasty, quick, and easy dishes. I shared a kitchen with Deepa, a fellow physiotherapist from India, and Ivy, a nurse from Trinidad. Ivy and Deepa prepared elaborate meals using a multitude of ingredients and fragrant spices. Rich aromas of cumin seeds, turmeric, cinnamon, and coriander would waft from the kitchen.

Wrapped in a warm fleece blanket and supported by fluffy pillows, I sat on my twin bed, eating and watching a *Law and Order* rerun on the television. Just as a series of commercials ended and the episode resumed, my cell phone rang.

Though tempted to ignore the unknown number, I answered. "Hello?"

"Hi, is this Maita?"

"Yes?"

"It's Ade. You gave me your number at work today."

"Oh, Dr. Ola?" I asked, thinking that maybe I heard his name wrong.

"Yes, my full name is Adeboyega. My last name is Olamide, so at the hospital, I am Dr. Ola. But please call me Ade."

Wishing I had opted to pay the subscription for my cable package so I could pause the *Law and Order* episode, I grunted, "Huh."

"Did I get you at a bad time?" he asked.

"No, no, you're fine."

"You seem distracted. I can always call another time."

I put my bowl of rice on the nightstand and sat up. "I'm good; we can talk. How are you?"

"I'm fine. I just got in from work, and I'm knackered."

"Long day at work?"

"Long days is more like it, and I've been on call back-to-back," he said. Then he quickly changed the subject. "So, how's the birthday girl doing?"

"Chilling, watching *Law and Order*, having some curry beef stew."

He must have expected to hear something more fun, or I came across as being lonely. "Come on, that sounds too miserable. It's your birthday week, or rather, month. You should be pampering yourself. I like to go all-out for my birthday, and I celebrate throughout the month."

"You must be high maintenance then," I said.

He laughed. "Me, high maintenance? Hardly, but every November, I try to enjoy myself, that's all."

"In that case, I've been shortchanging myself for the last twenty-three years. Oops, did I just give away my age?"

He chuckled. "I can keep a secret. I promise I won't tell your age. If you allow me, I would love to treat you to dinner and even better, for what's left of your birthday month."

This unexpected offer, especially on the first phone call, made me pause for a while to process it. What a generous guy, I thought. No one had ever made such an offer to me.

He broke the silence. "Hmm, I realize I may have overstepped here a little. Maybe you already have someone treating you for your birthday."

"No, no, it's fine," I said. "There's no one treating me for my birthday. That is a rare offer."

He sounded relieved. "Okay. Can I take you to dinner sometime next week?"

My acne made me reluctant to go on dates. How could he be interested in me with the unattractive blemishes and pimples that populated my face, which layers of foundation couldn't even hide? Then I remembered how Natalie had literally begged me to go on a date with Dr. Ola, and so for her sake, I said, "I'm tied up next Friday and the weekend."

"Does Thursday evening work for you? I know getting out on weekdays can be a challenge. I had already planned to get off work early on Thursday, so if you have time, we can meet then."

"Sure, Thursday will work," I said.

"Great," he said with audible excitement. "Do you have a preference for food types or restaurants, or can I take you to one of my favorite spots?"

"You choose," I said.

"No problem, I will make a reservation at my favorite Thai restaurant. It's in central London. Hope that's okay."

"A little far, but it should work. I will have to leave the hospital early too." Already I was dreading the trip into central London on a Thursday evening, with all the rush-hour crowds on the trains.

"I will call you tomorrow with details," he said.

"All right then, talk tomorrow."

"Okay, good night," he said.

As soon as I got off the phone, I called Rosie. She was my

go-to friend for everything girls like to talk about—boys, fashion, gossip, and more. We were both single and struggling to navigate the complicated dating scene in London. We often went out to parties and clubs in the hope of meeting someone.

"Hey, what's up?" she asked, sounding half-asleep.

"Were you sleeping? Did I wake you up?" I asked, checking the time. It was barely eight o'clock.

"Yes, I just completed two night shifts and a long day, and I'm exhausted."

"Well, it can wait. It's nothing important, just that someone asked me out on a date. I can fill you in tomorrow."

"No, wait, what? A date?" Suddenly she sounded alive. "With who? I will sit up for that."

"Okay, so there's this African doctor at work. I think he's Nigerian—"

She said, "A doctor from work? Wow. Do you know how many times I've desperately tried to catch the eye of a doctor on my ward?"

I knew she would react that way. "Well, he isn't exactly my type, and to be honest, I should be glad that someone like him is interested in me. My acne is on a roll."

The sleepy, groggy voice was gone. "Here we go again, Miss Picky. What's wrong with him?"

"There's nothing wrong with him. I'm just not attracted to him."

"You said he's not your type. What do you mean, he doesn't look like Denzel Washington?"

I laughed. "Well, yes, Ade certainly isn't Denzel, but that's not it. I can't explain. You know I like guys that are slim, not too skinny, and not too big either. He's good-looking but could do with shedding a few pounds. He just isn't getting me excited, that's all."

"Bubbs, he's an African doctor who clearly sees past your skin. He is a rare commodity compared to the trash we meet. *Angithi,* you like the smart and nerdy type dudes anyways. If he's young and single, he's a catch. Period."

If I hadn't been more interested in telling her details of my phone exchange with Ade, I would have argued that relationships involve more than someone fitting a hypothetical profile. There was more to a connection than one's social status or profession. Being a doctor wasn't all it took.

"Just go on a date with him, and if you still feel the same, then you can at least say you tried." She had a point there.

"How about I hook you up with the good doctor, if I still don't fancy him after our date?" I asked, as a joke.

To my surprise, Rosie replied, "Honey, give him my number if you don't want him. It's hard to find an educated, professional man these days." She was sincere, causing me to consider this seriously. Rosie would make a good girlfriend.

"He's taking me to dinner next Thursday. I'll tell you all about it."

"I know I should be more excited for you, but I'm in a shitty mood because my sister keeps calling and demanding more money for one thing or the other. I'm working overtime to keep up with my bills here, *and* bills in Zimbabwe. It's exhausting"

Rosie's older sister in Zimbabwe was raising Rosie's three-year-old son. When she enrolled in nursing school at London City University, Rosie had no choice but to leave him behind. Now she was working hard to bring him to London, but her ex-husband was giving her a hard time. He wouldn't sign documents for their child's passport application.

"I'm sorry you have to go through all that. People back home don't know how expensive life can get here in London. Get some rest, we can catch up tomorrow."

"Cool, let's talk later. I took a sleeping pill, and it's starting to take effect. Good night."

"Later," I said, and cut the phone.

*****

The following Thursday, I arrived at work an hour early, determined to complete my afternoon rounds in time to beat the rush-hour traffic into central London. I told Natalie about the date, and she couldn't contain her excitement. She even offered to take over some of my patient treatments, so I could leave work early. Unfortunately, I forgot to tell her to keep it between us, and at lunchtime, she announced the pending dinner date to the entire rehabilitation team. Everyone was in favor of this potential relationship.

"Dr. Ola is one of the kindest doctors," Josh said, and everyone agreed. "It's such a good match since you're both African, and there won't be any cultural or language barriers." Clearly he was unaware of how far from the truth that statement was, and I struggled to conceal the shock on my face. He seemed to sense it though and added, "You do get what I mean, right?"

It wasn't the first time my work colleagues had talked about Africa as if it were one big country, or assumed all Africans spoke the same language, ate the same food, and had one universal *African* culture. I once was called to the ward to be a translator for an elderly Ghanaian patient who couldn't speak a word of English. The nurse manager was surprised to learn that I couldn't be of assistance because I came from a different part of Africa and spoke an entirely different language.

Typically, I would have responded to Josh's remarks with a sarcastic comment, highlighting his ignorance. I knew though that most of my colleagues had limited knowledge of Africa, and as the group was sincerely excited for me to be going on this date, I just smiled and let it go.

To avoid getting caught up in traffic, I brought a change of clothes to work, a pair of white pants, and a black strapless top that I knew complemented my slender neck and shoulders. I untied my hair extensions and let them cascade onto my shoulders and back. Next, I had the task of applying makeup, something I dreaded.

The biggest challenge was covering up the blemishes from past acne breakouts and current inflamed pimples. After exhausting the possibilities of over-the-counter products, I'd consulted a beauty therapist. Her treatments were expensive and ... ineffective. I was waiting on an order for an American product called Proactiv, hoping the commercials were honest. As a last resort, I had gone to see my GP, who prescribed a topical antibiotic cream that seemed to be the best solution yet.

That Dr. Ola was actually attracted to me *did* boost my confidence.

After washing my face in a bathroom used for patient rehab, I applied a thick layer of concealer and makeup and stared with dissatisfaction at my reflection. I thought of canceling the date at the last minute, but when Natalie knocked on the door and shouted, "If you don't leave now, you'll get stuck in traffic," I had to proceed.

"I'll be right out," I shouted back, and quickly wrapped up my beautifying process.

I arrived at the restaurant fifteen minutes early on a chilly evening in March and waited outside, braving the cold. Sitting inside the restaurant was an option, but Dr. Ola had called to say he was on the way and would arrive in less than five minutes. But the five turned into ten, and now at fifteen minutes, I was ready to get inside when I spotted him walking in quick strides toward the restaurant, a laptop bag hanging from his shoulder. He wore the same shirt and pants he'd worn at the hospital. His shirtsleeves were still rolled up to his elbows, as if he'd just walked out of a patient's room, and the only items missing were his lab coat and stethoscope.

No sweater or jacket in this cold?

Looking scruffy, with the top button on his shirt undone and beads of sweat covering his forehead, he said, panting, "Sorry, I'm late. You shouldn't be waiting in the cold."

"No worries, I was here early, so you're not late," I said, continuing to study his shabby appearance that was turning me off.

"Shall we?" He gestured to the door, then opened it for me.

This would be a long night. Natalie would have to give me credit for trying.

ALICE TAKAWIRA

Chapter 9

Ade

When one of the house officers called in sick, the workload piled up, forcing me to scurry through my day with hardly a moment for small talk or rest. There would be no time to go home and prepare for my date with Maita. I contemplated calling to postpone to a day the following week, but couldn't bring myself to let her down on our first date. After much anticipation, I couldn't afford to mess this up.

Forfeiting tea and lunch breaks paid off. I made it to the restaurant just on time, though not in the most presentable fashion. The train station was a fifteen-minute bus ride away from the hospital, and I had to run to catch the bus seconds before the automatic doors shut. Arriving at the train station, I had less than sixty seconds to get to my platform before the train departed. After all the running, my unfit body was aching, and my chest felt like it would burst open. The small bottle of cologne that I kept in my bag came in handy for a moment such as this. I sprayed a generous amount onto my neck, wrists, and behind my ears.

Maita was waiting outside in the cold, staring at me as I approached, looking prettier than ever. She always had her hair or braids tied into a bun or ponytail at work, but today she'd let them down, which made her look more mature. She wore more makeup than usual, she didn't have to—she was beautiful either way. Her pink lipstick magnified a gorgeous smile, making her irresistible. When she took off a black coat, she revealed a slender figure in form-fitting white pants and a black lace strapless top that showed off toned arms. I had never seen her out of the physiotherapy uniform, which I realized now didn't do her justice. I already liked how her uniform fit so well, and now I was blown away. I couldn't stop staring at her. As we took our seats at the table, the words slipped out: "You look beautiful."

She seemed surprised. "Thank you."

"I'm so sorry I look a bit disheveled. I had no time to change and clean up because work got super-hectic."

Maita replied, "Don't worry about that. We both made it, and that's all that matters. Thanks to Natalie, I was able to leave early. She covered for me."

Nodding, I said, "Natalie's your girl, isn't she?"

"She is, and my boss too."

I smiled. "Well, we thank God for Natalie." I meant that in more ways than one, because I knew Natalie must have put in a good word for me. Maita broke out into laughter.

"Yes, trust me, we're here because of her," said Maita.

I didn't understand what she meant by that, or why she found that so amusing. Before I could ask, the waiter came to take our orders. She asked for a Malibu and pineapple cocktail, and I ordered a gin and tonic.

"So, tell me about Maita," I said, taking a long sip of ice-cold water. The running and sweating had left me dehydrated.

"You go first. I get the feeling your story will be more interesting than mine. Besides, the birthday girl calls the shots."

"Okay, fair enough. Ask me anything."

She delved right in, asking endless questions about my background. She had me describing my Yoruba family, growing up in Nigeria, and how I left Lagos with a scholarship to study medicine at the Birmingham Medical School.

"Do you think you'll ever return to Nigeria?"

"No way, not any time soon. There's too much chaos there. I like the predictable lifestyle in England." I continued to quietly admire her beautiful smile that showed off those perfect white teeth.

She lit up. "You and I both. Every African I ask tells me they have a five-year plan to work here, then return to their country with cash loads. Always with a plan to start a business, build a mansion, and live like a king. You're the first person who admits that you're here for the long haul."

"You know back home, only the corrupt politicians and their cronies get to live the good life," I said. "I'd rather be here making an honest living."

She nodded. "Tell me about it. In Zimbabwe, for the majority of people, you can be the hardest working and most honest citizen, but if you have no connection to someone important, or if you're not willing to get your hands dirty with bribes, you may never get a job, own a house or a car."

"Is that why you left Zimbabwe? Getting away from the corrupt system?"

"Sort of. Because in a way, it all boiled down to a corrupt and mismanaged government that couldn't pay civil servants, including doctors, nurses, and other healthcare professionals. As a newly employed graduate, I was fed up and frustrated by the never-ending strikes and protests for better pay. The hyperinflation made our salaries worthless, and the future seemed bleak."

She took a sip of her cocktail and continued.

"On one hand, the government doesn't seem to value your service, and on the other, you have recruiters from the UK, Australia, America, and even the Middle East begging you to come work for them. It was a no-brainer, a win-win for the recruiters and me. And in my opinion, a loss for my country because it's not just me. So many doctors and nurses have left, and more are still leaving. My mother left Zimbabwe and continued her nursing career here."

I said, "Well, in the end, you do what you have to do. We have a similar situation in Nigeria. Government doctors get paid very little. I couldn't afford to rent my place because in my country a tenant has to pay two years rent in advance—"

"Wait, did you say two years rent in advance?" She laughed. "That's crazy."

I said with a chuckle, "I tell you, when I first came to Birmingham, and the rental agent told me I only had to pay first and last month's rent, I was so shocked at how trusting the system is compared to back home. It was refreshing to work and be paid my full salary, on time, every time. For me, there is no doubt that practicing medicine here is a better option, and as you said, everyone benefits because I'm providing an essential service to this country, and I get to enjoy living here. I like it here."

The waitress came and placed more drinks on the table.

"You mentioned that your parents have properties and businesses in Nigeria," Maita said. "Couldn't you have stayed and joined the family business?"

"I've always wanted to be a physician, and I don't think I have what it takes to be a successful businessman in a cutthroat environment like Nigeria. I'll leave that to my dad. I'm quite happy to be out here saving lives."

She raised her cocktail glass. "Cheers to that." Then she chirped, "You're living an honest life now, but I bet that you weren't so honest on your scholarship and visa application. Like most immigrants, myself included, you probably wrote a sob story about how you would return to Nigeria full of ideas and advanced skills, to practice medicine in your home country and to help the poor."

"Hah, of course. I needed a good sad story explaining why a scholarship was so important. And what better to say than that I would give back to my countrymen?"

I raised my glass for another toast and echoed, "Cheers to that," and we laughed.

Great conversation and good company, coupled with a delicious meal and cocktails, were the things I needed after a hard day at work. Frankly, I hadn't had such a fun time or date in a very long time.

"Call me Bubbles," she said at one point.

"Bubbles?"

"Yes, that's my nickname. Maita is too formal. Save that for work."

"Bubbles? Like Michael Jackson's pet, Bubbles?" I asked,

puzzled.

"No, I have superpowers, like Bubbles from *The Powerpuff Girls.*" She said this with a straight face.

"You're joking, right?"

"I do have superpowers, passed on from my grandmother," she insisted, leaving me speechless and confused. Then she burst into laughter. "Of course, I don't have superpowers."

"Phew, for a moment there, I thought you were going mental. I thought I had a psych case on my hands."

"A little humor can't hurt. You should have seen your expression."

Her friends called her Bubbles or Bubbs, so she'd at least added me to her list of friends. Although six years my junior, Maita was mature, and I could immediately sense an independent nature. The more we talked and laughed, the more I was drawn in. We touched on every topic—work gossip, politics, music, tabloid rumors, books we liked—everything but details of our love lives.

Then she said, "On a more personal note, I assume you don't have a girlfriend. Otherwise you wouldn't have asked me out to dinner."

"Correct," I immediately replied.

"How come? A guy like you can get any girl."

I was flattered. "I'm glad you have a high opinion of me. I've been single for a while. And you?" Part of me didn't want Maita to reply, fearing that the answer may ruin what was turning out to be a perfect date, and I wanted to savor the moment.

To my relief, she replied, "No boyfriend, and I've been single for a while too. Hard to make friends in this country."

"Well, here's to new friends," I said, raising my glass for yet another toast. Maita did the same with vigor, spilling the cocktail onto the table and her lap.

"Oh, great," she exclaimed. "The day I decide to wear white pants is the day I spill on my clothes." She frantically tried to wipe off what she could with a napkin. "How embarrassing."

"Hey," I said calmly. I leaned across the table and placed my hand on hers. "It's no big deal. Don't worry about messing up your clothes. It's just me here. Never mind everyone else. Let's have another round."

My words seemed to put her at ease. "Thanks, it's getting late. We'll soon be the last ones here. We should probably start packing up." Maita had suddenly become self-conscious.

"Bubbles," I said, aware that it was the first time I used that name. It felt so natural, like I had known her for ages. "Please let me have one more drink with you. I will get a cab and take you home. I know it's late, and it's a weeknight, but I don't want this night to end. One more drink, please. I'm having too much fun."

She glanced at her watch. "Of course, one more drink."

I knew right then that I wanted to spend more days and nights like this, take care of her, keep her happy. The name Bubbles suited her well. It made me think of luxurious bubbly champagne, combined with a festive ambiance and easygoing atmosphere, and that was how I felt in that moment. I was intoxicated.

And I wanted this feeling to last forever.

Chapter 10

Maita

Getting up for work the next morning was torture after one too many cocktails and staying out way past midnight. Ade and I had to get a taxi from Central to North London. He walked me to my door, gave me a warm hug and light kiss on my cheek. When I was safely indoors, he left.

That morning, I called Rosie as I sat in the back seat of the shuttle that took employees from St. Anne's Hospital to the North Middlesex hospital.

"This better be good for you to call so early," she snapped.

"Girl, you have no idea how much fun I had last night," I said. "He was such a gentleman, and we had the best conversation I've had with anyone in a long time." I lowered my voice after one of the passengers looked at me with a disapproving eye. "All this time, he was right there in front of me. How could I have been so blind?"

"What a surprise, considering you didn't want to go on a date with him in the first place. So, I take it he's not so bad after all?" She didn't sound as excited as I expected. Perhaps it was too early in the morning to be having this conversation, or she was disappointed there would be no hooking *her* up with the good doctor.

"Yes, a pleasant surprise. I think we connected well, and we seem to have so much in common. I'm suddenly interested in him. I just hope he still likes me. I may have gone overboard with the cocktails. Who knows how sloppy I was in the end."

"I'm happy for you, Bubbs. I'm sure he'll ask you out again."

"Well, things will be a bit weird at work today. I hope I can keep a straight face—"

"Bubbs," she interrupted, "I have to go. I'm already late and

81

running on empty. I'm so hungry and need a strong coffee to keep me awake. Can we talk later?"

"Sure, no problem. Call me when you get a chance."

That first date with Ade was the beginning of many dinners, movie nights, and nights out in London. We quickly grew attached and became inseparable. We maintained a professional relationship at the hospital, occasionally engaging in casual and flirtatious conversations, which left us yearning for the end of the workday. Later, we would meet up at his flat. My shared accommodation wasn't ideal for an intimate rendezvous, so the one-bedroom flat he was renting became our default love nest. Ade turned out to be more than I had expected: a very caring and kindhearted man who was smart and witty, with a great sense of humor.

About two months into our relationship, he introduced me to his siblings. His sister, Bola, had just graduated from dental school. The youngest, his brother, Olugbenga, also known as Gbenga, with a silent *G,* pronounced *benga,* was in medical school in Birmingham. Bola and I immediately hit it off. After all, we were age-mates, and she often came to visit her brother and spend weekends with us. The three of us would go out to eat and watch movies. Occasionally we'd stay in and have lengthy conversations that ranged from intellectual discussions and arguments, to shallow celebrity gossip, indulging in snacks and cocktails till the early morning hours.

It wasn't long after I met Bola that I introduced Ade to Mercy, and my friends, Rosie, Josephine, and Grace. He enjoyed being around them and found us to be a fun-loving and easygoing group of girls, often referring to us as the *crazy gang.* Everything was happening so fast that, six months into dating, he asked me to move in with him. I was already at his flat six out of seven days, and together we rode the bus to work, often walking to the bus stop hand in hand.

Being a live-in girlfriend took our relationship to the next level. Unsure if I was ready for this big step, I left some of my belongings at my shared flat and continued to pay rent. At whirlwind speed, we went from work colleagues to living together like a married couple—a happily married couple.

We shared everything, discussed budgets and finances, argued, made up, traveled, and shopped together. Ade, an avid history buff, enjoyed traveling to various historical sites across Europe. He encouraged me to get a Schengen visa, which enabled me to travel freely within the Schengen zone. Since I was saving money for university, he paid all expenses on these sometimes spontaneous trips around Europe. We visited the Archeological Museums of Firà and the Museum of Folkloric Art in Santorini, Greece, and explored the Colosseum and Vatican City in Rome. In Germany, we joined a walking tour that included the iconic Brandenburg Gate, the Berlin Wall, and Holocaust Memorial. Being with Ade was fun and intellectually stimulating.

"Your birthday is coming up soon. It will be exactly a year since we met," Ade said as we lay in bed in the dark, snuggling tightly on a cold December night. "I have the best birthday present and anniversary gift. I planned to surprise you, but because it involves getting an American visa, there can be no surprises."

I sat up. "What have you got up your sleeve?"

"Two things. We both want to go to Las Vegas, and one of your favorite musicians has a residency at the Colosseum—"

"Elton John's *The Million Dollar Piano* residency!" I cried, and leaped onto him, hugging and kissing him. Unfortunately, the American embassy denied me a visa, stating that I had to apply from my country of origin. It didn't make sense to travel to Zimbabwe then, because I'd have to go back a second time to apply for a student visa. So we celebrated my twenty-fourth birthday and our first anniversary of dating in Paris—an excellent romantic alternative.

I met his parents when they visited from Nigeria. They split their time between Nigeria and the UK and had two homes, one in Lagos, and another in Surrey. I was aware that this was a big deal for Ade, who had never introduced any girlfriend to his parents— and it made me nervous. We were invited to their house in Surrey for dinner, and within minutes I knew I had nothing to worry about because his mother gave me the warmest and most welcoming embrace.

On my second visit to their home, she began addressing me as "my daughter," and I noticed Ade's face light up every time she did this.

Ade's mother was a short, stout, and quiet woman, who spoke in a soft voice, preferring to let others talk while she listened, and only chiming in when prompted. Her opinion of me mattered to Ade, and he wanted to be sure she approved of our relationship. So, when she called me on my cell phone and said, "My daughter, before I return to Nigeria, you must come, and I will teach you how to prepare some of Ade's favorite food like *jollof* rice," Ade was pleased, and I was happy.

Ade knew that I had plans to go to America—and that Emory University in Atlanta had accepted me for a master's program.

"Don't worry about paying bills here. Focus on saving your money. I'll take care of everything." He was my biggest cheerleader.

"Let me pay for groceries," I said. "That's the least I can do."

"No, you need to have a chunk of your paycheck directly deposited into your savings account. We're in this together."

"I already set that up with my bank," I said. I think I impressed Ade with my determination and discipline.

Ade told me, "My uncle in Miami told me I should relocate to America for better opportunities as a physician. I'm looking into it now so that I can join you." Until now, he hadn't considered moving to America. He began to research the process of getting his American credentials so that we could be together. He added, "I doubt that you'll want to return to England after completing your master's program. Most people who move to America never look back."

"Don't be so sure. I might have a terrible experience there and come right back."

He shook his head. "I'd better get my act together and start preparing for the American medical boards."

A year and a half later, it would be over, his American dream lost, and my romantic fairy tale a sad story told in the past tense.

Chapter 11

London, UK
July 2004

Ade

"What's so bad about having a baby now anyway?" I fumed, my nose flaring in anger. "Will you quit being selfish and for once think about us? It's not the end of the world. You can always continue with your grand plans after."

Hyperventilating, and my blood boiling in a fury, I turned the steering wheel and swerved to the left, slamming on the brakes, stopping the car at the side of the road just two blocks from my flat.

Maita sat in the passenger seat, defiant and straight-faced, which infuriated me more; any reaction was better than none.

I said, "These things happen, okay? We are two grown folks, working and able-bodied. There is no reason why we can't have a baby. But oh no, not if it interrupts Bubbles' plans."

"Ade, you're overreacting. We don't even know if I'm pregnant or not. My period is ten days late, and of course, it's a possibility. But let's not make conclusions until I take the test."

"That's not what makes me mad," I said. "You just told me that you can't afford to be pregnant now, not a month before you leave for Atlanta. What's that supposed to mean? I'm upset because you never considered what I would want. It's my baby too."

We were driving from Boots pharmacy, where we'd purchased a pregnancy test. Recently, I had noticed how Maita was downcast and distant. Attempts to cheer her up were futile. I figured she was miserable because she would soon be leaving her circle of friends—and me—to go to Atlanta alone. Even after surprising her with a brand-new cell phone, dinner at a favorite restaurant, and a spa treatment that she had been asking for, Maita continued to be in a low mood, even losing her appetite.

Then she finally told me the reason, on a Saturday morning at our dining table, exactly four weeks before she would depart to America.

"My period is about ten days overdue, and I've been feeling weird, no appetite, and nauseous. I think I'm pregnant." Maita looked down at the table, deliberately avoiding eye contact as she pushed a bowl of cornflakes aside.

I froze, holding my cup of coffee midway between the table and my mouth. "What? Are you sure?"

"How can I be sure?" She scowled, still looking away from me.

"When was your period due? Are you *sure*?" I placed my coffee down, rose from my chair and wrapped an arm around her shoulder. It was evident that she was uncomfortable, and she recoiled when I said, "It's not bad news, right? Even though we didn't plan it, it's a good thing?" Although I seemed calm, inside I was bursting with excitement. "Let's go to the pharmacy and get a test."

She shrugged my arm off and shook her head. "Not now, we can wait a few more days. I-I don't want to get all worked up. Maybe I have miscalculated my days."

"No, let's go now, I'll drive. Besides, it will be our first ride in my new car." I had just purchased a silver 2003 BMW 5 series. When I'd brought it home a day ago, Maita's reaction was less than enthusiastic. And yet, she had been harping on me to get a car, so we wouldn't have to ride the bus to work. I thought the car would lift her spirits, but it didn't.

"I'll go alone if you won't come," I said, collecting my wallet and car keys from the kitchen counter.

Reluctantly, she stood up and sighed. "If you insist," she said, and followed me out the door.

Maita remained silent on the drive to the pharmacy and didn't comment or show interest after I proudly showed off my new car's DVD player and navigation system. At the pharmacy, she didn't attempt to select a pregnancy test, and silently stood beside me as I struggled to decide which test to buy, as if it was my task alone. Then, as we drove home in silence, she said, "I don't want to have a baby. I can't afford to be pregnant a month before I start university."

That was the moment I veered to the side of the road and stopped the car. Engine off, the unforgiving summer heat started seeping fast into the car, and my T-shirt and khaki cargo shorts trapped heat like an unwelcome blanket.

"So, what will you do if the test is positive?" I asked, turning to look at her. Maita didn't answer, but I knew what she was thinking. Sadness washed over Maita as she covered teary eyes with one hand and turned to look out the window while fanning her face with the other.

"You're enjoying this, aren't you?" she said, still turned away from me. "I shouldn't have trusted you in the first place. You said you'd be careful and would always use a condom, but you must have been reckless and didn't put it on properly, or it burst and—"

"Are you going to blame this on me?" I shouted. "You're the one that complained about the pill making you gain weight. Plus you hated the idea of the IUD. How is this my fault?" I started the engine to get the air-conditioning running. I was sweating, hot with rage.

"Can we just go home and do this test already?" she said.

Too angry to argue, I got back on the road. I didn't look at her, nor did I say another word.

When we arrived home, she went straight to the bathroom and shut the door. I knew I wasn't welcome, and waited impatiently, pacing back and forth. I couldn't stop grinding my teeth, and I rubbed my sweaty palms together to calm my nerves, which didn't work. Each passing second my anxiety level increased, and I had a strong urge to storm into the bathroom and witness the result on the pregnancy test for myself. I wanted her to be pregnant. I wanted her to be the mother of my child. I wanted her to stay with me forever.

I desperately wanted the test to be positive.

After what seemed like an eternity, she flung the door open and with a broad smile shouted, "It's negative." She had two pregnancy tests in hand, each with an evident and clear negative sign on the test window. "I had to be sure, so I took two tests." Her expression was bright, almost radiant. "Oh, *Nkosi Yami*, what a relief."

I turned away without a word.

Maita's period started that evening, and she was overjoyed. "I'm not taking any more chances," she announced as we prepared for bed, an obvious hint to the fact that we would no longer be having sex, at least not for a while.

Our relationship had started to fray at the edges by then, but it began to come entirely undone after the pregnancy scare. I was afraid that Maita would go to America and forget about me. I wanted to be with her all the time, to be reassured that she wouldn't leave me. Maita complained that I was too clingy, that she needed space.

As the departure day drew closer, I noticed a degree of arrogance in her actions, as if she knew that I was breaking down inside and enjoyed seeing me beg for attention.

"How long will you be gone?" I asked, dismayed that she'd decided to spend her last day off work with Rosie, shopping for "college clothes" instead of spending the time with me— especially since I'd taken the day off just to be with her. "I wanted us to go have lunch at Bola's place," I said, pleading. "It will be your last time to see her before you leave."

"I already promised Rosie that we'd meet up, and she took a day off work too. You know that's a big deal for Rosie to take a day off."

"Yeah, but it's also a big deal for my sister to prepare lunch for us, don't you think?"

"Tell Bola that we can have dinner sometime next week."

She was slipping away and I couldn't help but think that the distance between us would doom our relationship. "Maita, what's really going on? Is there something you need to tell me? You can talk to me. I feel like you don't want to spend time with me, and we have less than two weeks left before you leave."

"Nothing's going on. You're overreacting. It's not like I'm going and never coming back. We talked about this already. Maybe I'm just excited to be starting something new and you're feeling left out."

I had made up my mind about Maita; I loved her and wanted to spend the rest of my life with her. I was saving for a ring, and to afford the right time and place to propose—a romantic trip to the Maldives. Next summer, in 2005, when she would return to London for a summer break, I would have saved for the perfect proposal.

As events unfolded, I felt a need to act fast, so I changed my plans and decided to propose before she left for Atlanta. Next summer we could have our wedding, the wedding of her dreams. I smiled just thinking about a destination wedding, with our families and close friends.

I purchased a 14-carat princess-cut ring, more affordable than what I had initially planned to buy, but very much her taste. I wanted to surprise Maita, and with guidance from Gbenga, my all-knowing brother, I hired a private chef who came to my flat, and she prepared a dinner for two. The chef set our little dining table as if it was a table in a fancy restaurant with appropriate tablecloths, plates, and silverware, and I decorated the flat with roses and scented candles.

When Maita finished work, I sent her on a wild goose chase for dried fish at the local African grocery store. I knew that the store didn't have dried fish in stock, and they would redirect her to another store that was at least forty-five minutes away. I needed time to prepare for my big surprise. After some persuasion, she agreed to buy the fish because she knew that I liked to cook on the weekend.

That evening, the setting was complete. I played Maita's

favorite playlist from her iPod, a mix of 90's R&B love jams, shuffling from Keith Sweat to Boys II Men. After a quick shower, I dressed casually in a white short-sleeved cotton shirt and black jeans, and eagerly awaited her arrival.

Maita gasped when she opened the door to the dimly lit, red fluorescent light, and the sweet jasmine scent from the strategically placed candles.

"Wow, what's all this?" she said, looking around in amazement. I was glad that she was finally happy about something. My plan seemed to be working.

"Welcome to The Lovers' restaurant," I said with a dramatic flair, pointing at the dining table. "Dinner for two." I took the grocery bag and headed for the kitchen.

"You put all this together? I didn't know you had it in you. I'm impressed, and hungry too."

Maita had no idea what lay in store.

She walked to the dining table and gasped. "I *know* you didn't set this table. Wow, is today Valentine's Day?"

"Darling, why don't you go and freshen up, then come down for dinner?" I said, approaching her from behind. I placed my arms around her waist, kissing the back of her neck.

For the first time in weeks, Maita didn't push me away. She turned around and kissed me lovingly. It felt like the first kiss that usually followed days of courtship and flirting. After days of no intimacy, I wanted to forgo dinner, rip off her work clothes and devour her right there, but staying focused on my plan was more important, so I held back and said, "Bubbs, let's save this for after dinner. Go get ready."

When she came back to the dining room, I was stunned. She wore an above-the-knee, body-hugging black dress, accentuating her petite, curvy figure, toned arms, and thighs. She even made an effort to wear bright red high heels. She had tied her braids into a bun, which made her look more slender, especially with her defined cheekbones and long neck.

"You look gorgeous," I said, almost at a whisper.

"I thought I should dress the part." She smiled.

Still dazzled by her beauty, I pulled out a chair for her and became the default waiter. I poured wine, and served our food which had been expertly prepared and garnished.

For the first time in close to a month, we were that happy couple again. I was doing the right thing, I knew.

I had to marry her.

After a three-course meal that included slow-roasted porterhouse steak and a side of sautéed collard greens with caramelized butter, I was ready to make my move. I had a bottle of champagne waiting for the post-proposal celebration.

I got up to refill her glass, then went to turn off the music. I wanted one hundred percent attention. Before Maita could protest shutting down the music, I rushed over and was on one knee.

"Maita," I began, almost choking on my words. "You have brought nothing but joy into my life, and I want to spend the rest of my life with you." I opened the small jewelry box that I held, revealing a shiny white gold ring. She was staring at me wide-eyed and shocked. Was it not obvious by now?

"Maita, will you marry me?"

I expected her to jump out of her chair screaming and crying, "Yes! Yes!" as they did in the movies, maybe a big hug that would topple us to the floor, or even for her to snatch the ring and immediately try it on as she shouted, "Of *course* I will!"

But Maita sat there, speechless, a distant look in her eyes. I waited, still on one knee, thinking that maybe she didn't hear me—that perhaps I had to repeat my proposal.

Now my hand was shaking as I waited.

She slowly got up from the chair, ignoring that I was still kneeling with an extended arm and a ring in my hand. And then I saw it: the look of disapproval, and I instantly knew that Maita would reject my proposal.

"Ade, I thought this was a romantic farewell dinner. I didn't expect you to propose…"

"That's the point of a surprise," I said, getting up, feeling dejected and upset by her insensitivity. "Surprise party or not, I just proposed to you, and you can't even give me an answer."

"I need to think, I'm not ready—"

"Not ready for what? It's yes or no, and I'll take it as a no."

"Not ready for marriage—you know I'm not ready, I have all these plans…"

"Again, with your plans. What's so special about going to university in America? You act like it's a life and death issue, and nothing can get in the way of the Great American Dream."

"Just because you're ready to be tied down doesn't mean that I have to," she yelled back. She reached for the glass of wine and took a gulp.

"Tied down? Is that how you view this relationship? So, you want to go to America and meet other people? Is that it? Is that why a baby or a husband would be a disruption to your plan?"

I stuffed the jewelry box into my pocket, feeling hurt. Again: no regard for my feelings, or the future of our relationship.

"Ade, you have a nerve. First, you try to get me pregnant, and when that didn't work, you decide getting engaged would do. So, you don't trust me. You think that maybe I'll cheat on you or something, and you have to mark your territory. Is that what this charade is all about?"

She took off her heels and let the braids down. No need to continue the sexy look; it was time for war. "You have become the whining and nagging boyfriend, breathing down my neck. I can't even go to the loo without you asking when I'll be back."

"That's not fair. I have been nothing but good to you. Is there anything wrong with wanting to spend as much time as possible with you? Soon we'll be in a long-distance relationship, and I know I'll miss you."

"I don't *want* restrictions! A baby or a ring are ways to control me, maybe even stop me from leaving. So no, I can't marry you, not now."

Her reply dumbfounded me. I felt my shoulders drop, my spirit crushed. Even some of that undying love for Maita seemed to wither. She didn't care for me as I did her. She could leave me if she met someone else. She wasn't ready to be committed to us.

"You don't love me," I said. "You want to keep your options open in America."

"I said I don't want restrictions or to be tied down, that doesn't mean—"

"You're selfish, and I don't know why I didn't see this before. You don't care about us. You're only concerned about your dreams, your goals, and not me or us. I thought we were in this together, and planning a future for us."

"Ade, I'm tired of your whining. I do care about you, and us, but that doesn't mean I want to be engaged or married now. You need to stop being paranoid and insecure. If you can't trust me, then we can't be together."

She stormed upstairs to the bedroom. I was left standing at the dining table, staring at the unopened champagne bottle in the ice bucket, the ring tucked deep in my pocket, my heart bleeding.

Part III

Chapter 12

London, UK
June 2005

Maita

"I can't believe it's been three weeks since we arrived in London," I said, "and I've made it through my first week back at work."

I was stuck in a traffic jam on my way home, talking to Chris on my phone, which was cradled in a car phone mount. I had to shout for him to hear me clearly, because the air-conditioning unit in the 1998 Nissan Maxima—a gift from my mother—made a loud cranking sound as it blew lukewarm air. What should have been a one-hour commute from the Wood Green office in North London to Tolworth would eventually take close to two hours because of the slow-moving traffic.

"Was it any different from the last time you worked there?" Chris asked.

"In-home physio differs from in-patient physio in many ways. I'm out in the community alone, driving from one patient to the next, as opposed to being in a building working alongside other therapists.

"It does feel good to be back," I continued. "I missed the one-on-one interaction with patients, and I enjoy working with the elderly. So far, so good." I took a sip of Red Bull, which helped keep me alert during long drives in the summer heat. "Plus, my schedule is very flexible. I can take coffee breaks or window shop between visits. What's not to love?"

"And I get to talk to you all day," he replied.

Chris called me multiple times a day—in the morning on my

way to work, between patient visits, during my drive home, and into the night. He'd extended his stay in the UK by an additional two weeks due to logistical problems with the shipping company, and to resolve issues with the tenants at his flat. When he repeatedly stated that he wanted to see me before returning to Atlanta, I began to suspect that he had manufactured the delays to buy time.

Through our lengthy daily phone conversations, we discovered that we clicked in more ways than one. Chris wanted to know every detail about my everyday life.

"What music are you listening to now?" he asked.

"I can't get enough of James Blunt's 'You're Beautiful,' and I love the new song 'Speed of Light' by Coldplay."

"No way! I just bought Coldplay's CD today," he said.

"I fell in love with Coldplay after their first album *Parachutes*," I said. "You want some Chris Martin trivia?"

"Sure, I think I know quite a bit about him," he replied confidently.

"In what country was Chris Martin's mother born?"

"England, of course," he said, matter-of-factly.

"Nope, she is from Zimbabwe. Back then it was called Rhodesia."

"Oh really, I never knew that. Ha, so Chris Martin has some Zimbabwean roots. Very interesting."

"Yep, he has African roots."

"Interesting. I didn't think you listened to that sort of music. I thought maybe African music, or R&B—"

"What's that supposed to mean?" I interrupted, irritated. "Let me guess. You thought I'd be into hip-hop and soul?" It wasn't the first time he had expressed surprise at my choices, and I didn't seem to follow whatever stereotype he had ingrained in his mind.

"I didn't mean anything by it... just that... well, I thought maybe you'd like—" he stammered, and I had to terminate the call before I said anything I'd regret.

"I need to get off the phone and concentrate on my driving.

I'll talk to you later. Bye."

Chris called that evening to apologize for making assumptions. In the weeks that followed, I learned that he disliked R&B, and found hip-hop, jazz, and rap completely distasteful.

Unlike me, Chris wasn't into reading books—fiction or nonfiction—and he wasn't interested in anything associated with academia.

"University degrees are overrated," he said. "After all, I began my career as an apprentice in mechanical engineering and rose in the ranks to management level without a degree." He wasn't impressed by my ambition to obtain a master's degree, and he couldn't understand why I would pay so much money for it.

We learned so much about each other during this discovery stage: he was an atheist, and I was Christian. Our views on religion became another source for heated arguments and discussions that had us talking endlessly. Although I preferred a man who had the same values as mine with regards to religion and education, Chris was an exception. I liked that he was ambitious with plans to keep rising up the career ladder. He wasn't a Christian, but he believed in being a good and honest citizen of the world, and we both had our sights on achieving the American dream.

The possibility of getting into a relationship with him crossed my mind, but I still had unfinished business with Ade. In fact, Chris became my phone companion, and a welcome distraction from the unbearable pain of waiting for Ade to call me back. It had been two weeks since I'd let Ade know I was in London, but he hadn't returned my call—an obvious sign that he didn't care.

With each passing day spent waiting for Ade's call, my anxiety grew into a constant gnawing pain. The message was clear: he was over me and in love with someone else. Despite all this, I remained hopeful and believed that he would change his mind if we met face-to-face. Many times I was tempted to call or text him, but my pride wouldn't let me. Mercy and my friends encouraged me to focus on Chris, who was interested in me and wanted to be more than friends, but I couldn't get my mind off Ade.

The dilemma with Chris and Ade forced me to make a decision. During my lunch break at a Nando's restaurant, with two more in-home patient visits left for the day, Chris made his usual afternoon call.

"Hey, Bubbles," he said. "I don't have much time left, and my boss wants me in Atlanta. I need to see you before I leave. Can we meet up soon?"

"What do you propose?" I asked with a mouth full of fries and peri-peri chicken.

"I'm coming to London next Friday. Let's do something that weekend. Can you take any days off?"

I almost choked on my food and took a sip of my Sprite. "Days off? I just started the job, like yesterday."

"I want to take you out on Friday and would love for you to drive to Oxford with me. We could spend the weekend here. A road trip would be fun, don't you think?"

The idea of a road trip was tempting. After all, he'd been good company through the British Airways flight. Sitting next to him for hours in a car would be no different, except we would be alone for the first time, and on our first date—cause for caution. Perhaps a simple dinner date was safer. But I desperately wanted to suppress the pain I was feeling, and going away for the weekend seemed like a good idea. Although I was still carrying a torch for Ade, I liked Chris and had warmed to his charm.

"All right," I said, "I'll talk to my supervisor and ask for next Friday off. I've never been to Oxford. This will be a good time to visit the famous university."

"I knew you would mention the university, no surprise there. I don't know what the big deal is with Oxford University. But if Bubbles wants to go there, then we're going."

Smiling, I replied, "Well, what else is the city of Oxford famous for except the university? I think it'll be fun. Let's do it."

I could hear the excitement in his voice when he said, "Great, let me know about Friday so I can start planning."

After that call, I knew I had to make up my mind about Chris and if we would—should—take our friendship to the next level. That, of course, depended on Ade. I couldn't handle the anxiety any longer, and I couldn't keep Chris in limbo while waiting on Ade.

I had to face my fear and call Ade—again.

Without planning or thinking things through, I immediately dialed Ade's number. It was the middle of the workday. He was probably busy at the hospital and would ignore my call, but I took a chance.

"Hello?" he answered, after the second ring.

I gathered myself and sat upright. "Hi, Ade, it's Maita again." This time I spoke with authority and had a take-it-or-leave-it attitude. If he turned me down, it would be the last call.

"Hi. Is everything okay?"

"Everything is fine. Well, kind of fine. I need to talk to you in person. I would like us to meet up, maybe for lunch or dinner?"

There was no turning back now... unless he declined my offer.

After a long pause, he replied, "Can't we discuss whatever it is over the phone?"

I wanted to snap back and say that if I could say it over the phone, I would have said it already. Instead, with a calm and controlled voice, I said, "I prefer to say this face-to-face. It doesn't have to be over lunch. We can meet at a bus stop or the train station if you like." I couldn't resist the sarcasm that slipped out.

"When do you want to meet?"

"Saturday, if you're free."

Again he paused. Playing hard to get, I thought. I braced myself for the worst and was pleasantly surprised when he said, "I have a few things to do in the morning, but I should be done by noon, so yeah, maybe I can make it. Where do you want to meet?"

I had no idea of a venue. I hadn't thought that far before making this spontaneous phone call. "There's a restaurant in Covent Garden that's good. We could meet there for lunch, if that's okay. I can text you the details."

"That's fine. I can make it to that part of town after one."

I was so relieved he'd agreed to meet. Realizing that I was holding my breath, I exhaled, relaxed and said, "Okay, I'll be in touch. Bye."

Saturday seemed like a long way away. I wanted it to come sooner, so that I could move on with my life. Sadly, I didn't have the same feelings about meeting Chris and was confident that, after my date with Ade, I would have to tell Chris to go on to Atlanta and forget about me.

Chapter 13

Maita

During my entire commute from work, I spoke to Rosie on the phone, unpacking a detailed word-for-word account of my conversation with Ade. She shared in my excitement, listening attentively and urging me on.

With joy in my voice, I made a reservation for two at The Arbor restaurant in Covent Garden. Certain that my enthusiasm would be detectable, Chris's phone calls went unanswered for the rest of the day. That evening, I rummaged through my closet to select the perfect outfit to wear on this crucial date.

Saturday's weather forecast was gloomy. I woke up to gray clouds and a cold drizzle, the sort of weather one expected in the winter. I had to switch the flirty summer dress I'd set aside for warmer clothes. Mercy had planned for us to go to Kent and spend the weekend with my mother, but the long-awaited day had finally come, and I would have to join her later that evening.

Mercy came into the bedroom, where I was sitting on the bed surrounded by a pile of clothes, deciding between a pair of jeans and leggings.

"Why don't you call him and postpone the lunch date?" Mercy asked. "Do you really want to go all the way to Covent Garden in this horrible weather?"

I set aside the pair of jeans that I had settled on. Without making eye contact, I replied, "You have no idea how much guts it took for me to ask him out on a lunch date. Come rain, come sunshine, I'm going to go."

"Yeah, unless he calls to cancel," she said. "Remember, he may not be as invested in this as you are. Just don't get your hopes too high. And you would appear desperate if he canceled, but you insist on meeting up."

The truth was brutal to take, so I lashed out. "You don't want this to work, do you? You're so fixated on Chris, yet you barely know him."

"You're overreacting. I hate to see you this way. The Bubbles I know is stronger than this. Don't give him power over you."

"What are you *on* about? Being honest about my feelings does not make me weak—"

"But it can make you vulnerable," Mercy cut in, "and before you know it, you'll become that desperate ex-girlfriend that can't move on."

Offended by the reference to weakness and desperation, I said, "Thanks for the vote of confidence. Now please leave me alone to deal with my weak self."

"That's not what I said or meant," she said, before walking out and closing the door.

I tossed clothes from the bed in frustration, crumbled to the floor and cried. How did I get to the point of almost begging a man to take me back? I wished I'd never left him. How could I have been so stupid to not realize his proposal had been sincere? He wasn't trying to trap or tie me down. Why was I so afraid of commitment back then?

It was almost ten in the morning, and I had to get ready to reach the train station on time. Consoled by the idea that the day would have a better ending than this horrible start, I gathered the strength to get up.

I arrived at the Covent Garden underground station and quickly made my way out of the station onto the square. The rain had stopped, the dark clouds had started to clear, and the sun was peeking shyly from behind a cloud, providing a glimmer of hope for a warm and bright afternoon. As usual, Covent Garden was bustling with life. Tourists and local shoppers filled the streets, street artists played music, others sang, some made cartoon portraits for paying customers, and others dressed up as characters and posed like live statues or mannequins. The sidewalk cafés and restaurants were buzzing and inviting, and the designer shops were tempting to those who dared to enter. The vibrant ambiance captured my attention, and for a moment I forgot how nervous I was about my lunch date.

I occasionally stopped to check my reflection in shop windows. I was both attractive and classy in skinny blue jeans, a pink satin Ralph Lauren shirt, a black leather biker jacket, and black leather boots that added an extra three inches to my height. I remembered our first date almost two years ago, how I'd lacked confidence because of my acne problem. Now, my smooth acne-free face, brightened by pink lipstick that matched my shirt, gave me a spring in my step.

I arrived at the restaurant just in time, and there he was, waiting outside. Suddenly I was nervous again, and as I walked toward him my legs felt like jelly, my underarms perspiring. I plastered a smile on my face.

He had changed—for the better. Ade stood tall and strong with a fresh haircut and a handsome, clean-shaven face. He'd replaced the excess weight with sculpted muscles. His gray shirt and black jeans enhanced his slender appearance, and he looked more attractive than he did two years ago when we met.

"Hi," he said. "Good to see you after so long."

"Same here," I replied, a little disappointed that he didn't offer a hug but instead a gentle nod.

"You look great," he said. "America seems to be working for you."

"Thanks, you look good too."

"Shall we?" he asked, and extended a hand in the direction of the door to the restaurant.

In uncomfortable silence we walked down a flight of narrow stairs to the basement. When we arrived in the dimly lit restaurant with its luxurious 1920s decor and classical music humming gently in the background, he broke the silence.

"Trust Bubbles to find a spot like this. This restaurant is beautiful. How did you even know about this place?"

I was glad he was impressed by my choice—my first score for the day. Before I could respond, the hostess asked if we had a reservation, then showed us to a table tucked away in a back corner. There was a candle, creating an intimate atmosphere suggestive of a romantic date. I noticed Ade raise an eyebrow at the setup, and I was a little embarrassed.

"I'm not surprised," he said. "You always liked the finer things."

"I'm glad you like it," I answered.

"The setup and the decor are very classy. I hope the food is good too. Do you recommend anything?"

I shook my head. "I've only been here once, and all I can tell you is that I enjoyed the food, but I can't remember what it was."

He seemed satisfied with that. Just as I thought we could move onto menu choices, he said, "I assume you came here on a date. Looks like the sort of place for romantic dinners."

Why did he care? Was he trying to find out if I was dating someone?

"No, I was here with my sister and some friends. This place looks different at night. The lighting was different, the music was dance and pop, and the bar was jam-packed with people. I guess they switch it up to a less formal place after dinner."

He nodded as he looked around. "I probably need to get out more and explore the London scene a little. I'm missing out on all this cool stuff."

The waitress came to take orders for drinks. I knew I needed something substantial to get through this date without being a nervous wreck, but I didn't know what to order.

Ade said, "Let me guess. Malibu and pineapple, or a martini."

I shook my head. "I'm into red wine now." I regarded the waiter. "I'll have a glass of merlot, please."

Ade said, "Okay, well, what else has changed besides your favorite cocktail? I can already see you look amazing. You always did, but you're glowing more than before, and you look happy."

"Happy" was the last thing on my mind; evidently, I was doing an excellent job of pretending. I had rehearsed this day several times over in my head. I wanted to show him the old, fun, and bubbly Maita. Hopefully, he would fall in love again with the Maita he remembered.

Unfortunately, my imaginary conversations never happened, because he seemed to be in control of the narrative. He asked about my graduate classes at Emory. "How is it there? Do you enjoy being a student?"

"It's stressful," I said. "I have volumes of assignments and projects with never-ending deadlines. I sometimes second-guess myself about why I'm getting my master's."

"Bubbles, you're a smart girl, and I have no doubt you will do well," he said.

"Thank you for that." Ade always was supportive and encouraging, but I was a little perplexed by all the compliments he was dishing out.

He said, "You don't plan on coming back to England for good, do you?"

I knew he would ask me about returning to England, and I had prepared a response. I had to be careful with my answer, because this was where I would begin to lay the groundwork for the conversation about us.

"Well, it depends," I said scanning the menu.

"Depends on what?"

I took a sip of my wine and looked him in the eyes. "Depends on if I have anything to move back for."

He looked down at his menu and paused. "Unless you're coming back for your family. Your mum is still here, right? Well, apart from that, I believe America has more opportunities than England, and with your drive and personality, you'll do well there. There is nothing for you here."

My eyes stung with tears, and I stared blankly at the menu to conceal my disappointment. Did I have to be more direct, to let him know that I would return to London if he asked me?

"I agree, America may have more opportunities, even for doctors like you. Why don't you move to the States, like you wanted to when we were together?"

I took another sip of my wine, ready to go in on this matter once and for all, then the waitress came to take our food orders.

He handed his menu to the waitress and in a low, gentle voice replied, "Bubbs, my life is here. My family is here, and I have no intention of moving anymore. I will soon begin a fellowship in cardiology, and I don't want to do a residency in America. I decided to stick it out here."

"I would move back to the UK if I had to. It's not like I never lived here before, so I can easily adjust to the British life again." This statement was my way of letting him know that I would come back to be with *him*. I hoped he got the message so I wouldn't have to spell it out. It was torture sitting across from him, struggling to say the right words.

"You were never truly happy here," said Ade. "From the day I met you, you talked about relocating to America. I look at you now, and you're glowing. It looks like life is treating you well. You should work on getting your papers there—"

Fed up with holding back, I said, "Would you come if I asked you? I would come back here, if you asked me."

I held my breath, and time froze for a brief moment. The guests disappeared, the music stopped. It was just us and the loud throbbing of my heart pounding in my chest— I braced myself.

"I can't leave my girlfriend," he said. "We're building a life here, so I don't think I'll be coming to America."

Slowly nodding, I forced a smile, fighting back the tears.

"I'm happy for you, that's really nice," I managed to say, unable to disguise my deflated and hollow voice.

"Bubbs, you're a beautiful and smart girl. You will find someone. It took a lot for me to come here today. I wasn't sure if it was a good idea, especially since I'm with someone else. I'm sure you understand how this could be a problem for my girlfriend."

I was speechless. Ade immediately changed the topic, probably feeling bad for being so brutally honest about his new relationship, and at the same time telling me to back off.

"So, how are your girlfriends—Rosie, Grace, and Joe?"

I was still digesting what he had said, but I played along.

"They're all good. Rosie is still working her crazy hours." My voice was low and hoarse, and it became harder to mask the pain I was feeling.

"We had some good times with your girlfriends," he said.

I wanted to say, *we could go back to those good times if you gave me a chance.* Instead, I said, "Those days are gone. Life goes on." My phone rang before he could reply. It was Mercy.

"Are you still coming to Kent?" she said. "How's the date going?"

"Yes, I'm coming. Okay, goodbye." I placed the phone on the table. "That was Mercy. We're supposed to be meeting in Kent." Immediately I regretted saying this, because it gave him an excuse to end both the uncomfortable conversation and lunch.

"Well, don't let me delay you. Are you going to your mum's in Kent?"

"Yes, but there's no rush. I might go tomorrow instead." As disastrous as this lunch date was, I didn't want it to end, but wanted to prolong this day, sit with Ade, and engage him. I wasn't ready to leave, especially when I hadn't convinced him to give me a second chance. This meeting could be the last time I saw him, my last chance to win him back.

We sat in awkward silence, then the waitress appeared with our food. The food looked delicious and well garnished, but I had lost my appetite. Ade broke the silence and as we ate, he talked about how he enjoyed his job and looked forward to the cardiology fellowship. He had plans to travel to the Middle East with a group of friends, and next they would go on a safari trip in South Africa and Zimbabwe. He was training for a triathlon and was considering becoming a vegetarian. Life was great.

"How is Bola?" I asked.

"She's doing good. Got engaged last month. Now all she talks about is her big wedding."

"Congratulations to her. Pass my regards."

It seemed like their lives had moved on, and I was stuck in the past. He wiped his plate clean, and with my appetite still gone, I struggled to finish my food. The wine kept me going.

"Well, I need to get back home," he said. "I have a few things I need to do around the house. Let me get the bill."

He motioned to the waitress. He was eager to leave. There wasn't much more to say, really. It was almost four, but it felt like we had only just sat down and talked for a minute. I couldn't bring myself to make small talk, and I was waiting for him to resume the conversation.

"You were right: the food here is great, as is the service. I think I'll come back here and even try it out after-hours."

I wanted to respond sarcastically to the fact that he would bring his girlfriend to a restaurant that I had introduced him to, but instead I said, "I'm glad you liked it. It's always good to try out new places."

"You always liked exploring new restaurants and all. Do you do much of that in Atlanta?"

"No, I'm too broke to eat at a restaurant. I eat from Subway, or I buy groceries and cook my food at home."

He laughed. "Oh, come on, Bubbs, it can't be that bad. I'm sure there's at least one guy who can take you out to fancy restaurants. And let me guess, you're still cooking your favorite chicken and pasta dish."

He paid the bill, and we got up to leave.

"Yes, I still cook that dish," I said. "Do you remember how you used to like it?"

"Yes, I do," he said. He led the way up the stairs and out into the street and daylight. The sun had gone back into hiding, and dark clouds were forming again.

"Thank you for lunch," I said.

"My pleasure, it was good to see you again," he said.

My phone began to ring again, and I knew it was Mercy. I ignored it.

"Let me walk you to the station," he offered.

"Sure," I said, realizing that my long-awaited date had come to an end, and that it would probably be the last.

I walked beside him and wished he would hold my hand, like

old times. We used to walk hand-in-hand to the bus stop every morning. Those were some of the small acts of love I took for granted, and now I yearned for the slightest sign of affection. As we approached the Tube station, the reality of the situation hit me—that this was the true end for us, that there was no chance of salvaging anything from our past relationship. I had spent close to two intimate hours with him, yet I was empty inside. He chose her over me, and that hurt more than anything else. I couldn't let him walk away from me, not without a fight, and certainly not after I had come this far.

We stood at the Tube station entrance as people walked past us, rushing in and out, oblivious to the unhappy ending that was unfolding. My heart was heavy and broken, and I couldn't hide it anymore. Raindrops began to fall, followed by a drizzle. I turned to him.

"Ade," I said. "I-I am sorry for hurting you. I am so very sorry that I left you, and now I understand the pain you must have experienced. I guess I wasn't ready to take the next step. I know you're with someone else, but I-I can't move on. I miss you so much, and I want you back. That's why I came to England. I thought that if we had a chance to talk face-to-face, you would forgive me, and we could start over. I shouldn't have left you the way I did. I shouldn't have left you at all. I was young, stupid, and naive. You have no idea how I have been hurting. Please give me a second chance." Tears streamed down my face.

He was genuinely shocked. "Maita, please don't cry. You know I loved you, and I will always love you, but we can't be together anymore. My girlfriend is a good person, and I can't just leave her. I couldn't do that to her. Please don't cry."

"Do you love her?" I sobbed, and before he could answer, I said, "Ade, I also met someone who is really into me. I just met him, and he wants us to date, but I can't bring myself to be with anyone else because I still love you and want to give us a chance. Please tell me you'll give us a try. I will move back here—"

He pulled me close. "Maita, I love you. I still do. Please don't cry. I can't bear to see you cry. I do love you, and you know it."

"Then why can't we be together?"

He didn't have an answer. Instead, he pulled me closer and kissed me on the lips, a long, passionate and unexpected kiss. We kissed in the rain, like lovers. I became overwhelmed with mixed emotions, heartbroken that he had turned me down, and now comforted by his tight embrace. We were both wet from the rain, and neither one of us seemed to care.

"I love you, Maita," he whispered in my ear.

"I love you too," I replied, hoping that he had finally come through, and he was going to give me a second chance.

"Maita, listen to me," he said with a firm tone. Looking me straight in the eyes, as if he had just snapped out of a hypnotic trance, he said, "I cannot be with you anymore. You must give this other guy a chance. We had it good back then, but it's over now, and I want my new relationship to work. You should also move on with *your* life."

Once again, I was confused and speechless. What we had just experienced when we kissed was real, and it was a solid and deep yearning for each other. So why was Ade refusing to be with me?

Unable to say anything, I cried uncontrollably.

"Please, don't cry," he begged.

Just then, my phone rang for the third or fourth time.

"Listen, Maita," said Ade. "You need to get going. Don't keep your sister waiting; she keeps calling. I need to go too. I hate to leave you like this, but sometimes we have to make tough decisions. It's over between us. Please do take care of yourself."

He hugged me tightly and kissed me on the cheek, then walked away and left me standing alone in the rain. It was only moments later I realized he'd called me Maita, not Bubbles.

Chapter 14

Chris

The day I'd been waiting for finally arrived—my first date with Maita. It came on a bright and sunny Friday after a cold and rainy week, and I was glad the weather had changed in our favor.

Since last Saturday, she had been unavailable, not answering my calls for the entire weekend as if she had disappeared off the face of the earth. This silence was unusual and worrying, but I told myself not to panic, and planned to call Mercy if she didn't resurface on Monday. I was relieved when Maita called me early Monday morning and said she had been feeling unwell and had slept through the weekend.

"Will you be fully recovered by Friday?" I asked with fingers crossed.

"I should be good to go. I had a bit of a fever Saturday night, and my temperature is back to normal now. Besides, I won't get another day off any time soon."

Her supervisor had approved the day off at the last minute; this date almost didn't happen. "I changed the plans a little," I told her. "Not only will we drive to Oxford, but we'll go to the seaside in Bristol." I had a full day planned, including visits to some tourist sites in London and lunch.

She replied cheerfully, "That sounds like fun. I can't wait for Friday already."

I waited for her outside the Waterloo Tube station. Although we had been speaking on the phone daily, I was a little nervous about our first date, and needed to impress Maita and show her a good time.

My phone rang. It was Maita.

"Hey, I'm here. Where are you?" she asked.

"I'm outside the Waterloo station on the Westminster exit.

And in case you forgot what I look like, I'm the good-looking guy in a pair of blue jeans and a black T-shirt."

"Okay, I'm making my way out of the station. I was heading that way anyway, and should be out in a few seconds."

As she walked toward me, I gazed at Maita with admiration, reminded of why I had become so infatuated with her. She was striking with her glowing brown skin, eyes that seemed to sparkle in the sunshine, and a beautiful, warm smile filled with perfect white teeth. Her skinny black jeans complemented her slender, petite frame, paired with a sky-blue lace top revealing just enough skin and black bra beneath. Comfortable-looking ballet-flat shoes completed her outfit. She was carrying the same brown leather bag she had on the BA flight.

I embraced her with a warm hug. "Finally, we get to talk in person," I said. "And you look and smell good." I took in the feel of her soft body against mine, and the floral and spicy scent of her fragrance.

"Yes, finally, and you look good too," she replied.

"What perfume are you wearing? I love it."

"It's Chanel Chance, eau de parfum; I like to smell richer than I am," she said, and we laughed.

"Let's walk over to my car so you can put away your bag. I'll carry it for you."

"Thanks." She handed me the leather bag. "So, what have you planned for us?"

I smiled. "Our day is jam-packed with activities. I know you've done all the tourist stuff in London. You just haven't done it with me. Let's start with the London Eye, a walk over London Bridge, lunch, then Buckingham Palace and whatever else you want to do. We can head out to Oxford later this evening, then Bristol tomorrow."

She smiled and nodded. "Sounds like you have it all worked out. I'm here for it."

From the moment we met outside the Tube station, we talked like people who had known each other forever. It felt natural, and the conversation flowed. She had a great sense of humor, and we seemed to get each other's jokes. It was just like it had been on the flight. We delved into a dynamic conversation that kept us both engaged. We agreed on most issues, and disagreed on some, including pretty big subjects like religion. Unlike me, she was passionate about politics and social issues, and seemed to be informed about tabloid gossip and current affairs in Zimbabwe, the United States, and England.

"Geez, how do you keep up with it all?" I marveled. "Do you watch the news for fun?"

"I do actually. In Atlanta I listen to a news channel called NPR, and here I always check into BBC World News. But I love Entertainment News just as much, so there you have it: a healthy balance."

"Well, I'm all about football and cricket," I said. "I watch ESPN and Sky Sports, and that's about it. I listen to the morning news to learn about what happened in the world while I was sleeping, and evening news to catch up on the day's events, and that's all the news I need. I don't need a play-by-play commentary of the war in Iraq. It upsets me, and that's all they go on about."

Because I knew the lines would be long, I had purchased advance tickets for the London Eye, so we had ample time before our ride. We walked along the Thames, enjoying the street performers' entertainment, then sat on a bench facing the river and watched the boats on the water. I couldn't stop myself from stealing admiring glances at her beauty. I'd enjoyed every minute with Maita thus far, and was so glad we would be together for the entire weekend. We took several pictures together with her digital camera. The first time I held her close, with the confidence a man has with his girlfriend, was when we had a picture taken during our ride on the London Eye. We wrapped an arm around each other's waist, drew close, our cheeks touching, and a kind stranger snapped the photograph. Right then, I knew that she felt the same for me. Neither one of us had to say it out loud. The feeling was mutual—we were attracted to each other.

We walked across the majestic London Bridge and took more pictures together, before hopping onto a double-decker bus and heading to Soho, where I had made a reservation at a French restaurant. I was never a fan of the London buses, but that day, as we sat upstairs on the bus, chatting and giggling like teenagers, I didn't want the bus ride to end.

She liked the Moulin Rouge-themed French restaurant, located between a Thai and an Italian restaurant. We had a corner table at the back of the dimly lit room, and the small candle centerpiece, coupled with the dim red florescent light and red velvet wallpaper, created a romantic ambiance. I ordered a bottle of pinot noir.

"This is a beautiful restaurant," she said. "I bet it turns into a full-on cabaret at night. Have you been here before?"

"No, I did a Google search, and it had excellent reviews," I said. "Are you okay? You seem to be deep in thought all of a sudden. Why the sad look?"

I was genuinely concerned, as her mood had shifted rather suddenly from energetic to subdued.

She shook her head. "It's nothing, this place has a familiar vibe... never mind. I'm good. I'm marveling at what a beautiful day this has been, and I'm taking it all in."

I was glad to hear that. "I can't tell you how happy I am. Who knew that a girl from Africa would capture my poor British heart?"

She lit up again and took a sip of wine. "Never underestimate an African queen like me, and consider yourself lucky."

We raised our glasses and made a toast.

"To new friendships, happiness, and more days like this," I said, and I meant it. Because I was falling in love with Maita.

After our late lunch, we walked around Soho, then hailed a black cab that took us to Buckingham Palace. We posed for several pictures, walked the streets with throngs of tourists, sat for cocktails at a sidewalk bar, then got onto the Tube and headed back to Waterloo station where I had parked my rental car. We were tired, but also pumped and excited.

"Are you okay to drive?" she asked when we settled into the Peugeot.

"Yes, I'm good, after all the walking we did. And I've been drinking lots of water. It should take us about an hour-thirty with traffic. We should get to Oxford around eight thirty."

"Please tell me you have some good music in this car," she said, as we drove off.

"I knew you would ask about the music. I have some CDs you can choose from, including Maroon 5, Coldplay, and a few others, in that case in the back seat."

She reached back for the case and said, "I get to be the DJ while you drive."

She flipped through the CD case. "DJ Bubbles needs more than soft and alternative rock—"

"I believe I have a Michael Jackson CD in there, his greatest hits," I replied quickly, wishing I had more to offer.

She shook her head and smiled. "I love Coldplay and Maroon 5 too, but we need variety. You're going to have to step up your music game."

Chapter 15

Maita

We arrived in Oxford at about nine o'clock at night. Because it was a Friday evening, the traffic was heavy, and the drive had taken a little longer than expected. Exhausted from the day's activities, I longed to take a shower and dive into bed.

Music and great conversation served as a good distraction from the traffic jams. I connected my iPod to the car radio and played a mix of songs from "Gold Digger" by Kanye and Jamie Foxx, "Hollaback Girl" by Gwen Stefani, "One, Two Step" by Ciara, to "Boulevard of Broken Dreams" by Green Day. We never ran out of things to talk about, just as it was the day we met on the British Airways flight. He was a godsend, because being with him made me realize that I could be thoroughly engaged and enjoy the company of another man. Why did I think that Ade was all there was, and that he was *the one* for me? If he was, why was I enjoying my time with Chris, and why was I now attracted to him?

Reviving my relationship with Ade wasn't the ultimate key to my happiness. By merely stepping into uncharted waters with Chris, in so little time, I already felt rejuvenated.

While Chris concentrated on the road ahead, bopping his head to the music, I replayed the conversations I had with Ade on our lunch date, reliving the agonizing rejection.

After a week of complete misery following that meeting, this beautiful day out with Chris was a breath of fresh air and reminded me that I was still an attractive young woman. I thought about the possibility of dating Chris. Perhaps that would unshackle me from the past, help me get over Ade. Or at least dull the pain.

We arrived at Chris's split-level three-bedroom house—a

beautiful, modern semi-detached home in an affluent suburb of Oxford. There were boxes everywhere, because he was in the process of moving, but his couch was still in place, so I sat down and relaxed. "I like your place. It's more modern than the typical England houses."

"Thank you," he said, settling onto the couch next to me. "It's a new build, definitely modern, and I got to add my finishes, including a fountain outside. I will show you tomorrow. I lived here for just a year before I was headhunted and moved to Atlanta. I haven't had the opportunity to enjoy my house."

"That's too bad," I said. "At least you get to keep the house. Just pray for good tenants." I got up and walked over to gaze at the rectangular fish tank mounted on the wall, where several exotic-looking fish swam about. "This fish tank is lovely. Was this your idea, too?"

He nodded. "Yep, I did all the decor myself. I feel bittersweet about leaving this to some stranger. Let me give you a tour, then we can call it a day. I'm exhausted."

After taking me up the spiral stairs to the third level—his bedroom with an en suite bathroom and an office—he offered to order some pizza for dinner. I was still digesting the big lunch we had, so I declined and said I wanted to take a shower and go to bed. He took me to one of the guest bedrooms on the second floor. "This is your room. It's a mess with all the boxes, but the bed has clean linen, so you're good to go."

We stood in the doorway, and he motioned for me to enter. "Thanks," I said. "Is the bathroom the door on my right?"

"Yes, I have clean towels in there too," he said. Without warning, he wrapped his strong arms around my waist and pulled me close. "Before you go to bed, I just wanted to say that this has been one of the best days I've had in a very long time. Bubbles, you are an amazing girl, and I'm so glad you're here."

His actions and words were unexpected, and I couldn't think of a response.

He continued, "I hope I'm not coming on too strong—"

"Chris, you have no idea what this day has meant to me. I feel the same way. You just have no idea."

He pulled me closer and kissed me on my lips, and I kissed him back. Locked in a tight embrace, we stumbled into the bedroom, almost tripping over some boxes, as we continued to kiss passionately. He threw me onto the bed, and I knew what was going to happen next. We were enjoying the moment, and we let our emotions get the better of us. Neither one of us wanted to stop. He began undressing me, struggled to strip off my jeans as I yanked my top off.

There we were, making love on our first date. Like every experience with Chris, the first time we made love seemed natural, as if we had been together for years. He was alternately gentle and aggressive when he needed to be. All the pain and agony I had bottled inside after Ade left just melted away.

My body responded and allowed Chris to enter. With each thrust, I screamed in joy and pleasure, joy in knowing that I could feel this way again, and I was free from my past—free from Ade.

Part IV

Chapter 16

Atlanta, GA
January 2007 – 1 year, 6 months later

Chris

At the start of the New Year, I was in reflection mode. Typically, I would adjust previous and yet-to-be-achieved goals and dress them up as brand-new resolutions. This time, my goals for 2007 were genuinely unique and relationship-orientated: to be a better boyfriend, more caring, less quarrelsome, and to control my temper. Hardly objective goals and hard to measure success, but the results would be evident in a happier Bubbles.

At the moment, a year and a half since we started dating, our relationship was on shaky ground.

Unlike my past relationships, this one had a unique set of challenges. The first time we had a negative experience as a biracial couple was during our extended first date, when we drove from Oxford to Weston-super-Mare in Bristol. Tourists flocked to this seaside resort during summer, so it wasn't surprising that all the bed and breakfast places I called were fully booked.

I decided to try my luck at a small lodge I spotted as we drove into the town. It was a three-minute walk to the beach and half a mile from the Grand Pier. When we arrived, Bubbles was on the phone with her mother, and I went ahead to check in.

A woman, who was probably in her late fifties or early sixties, was at the front desk confirming a reservation over the phone.

"Yes, we do have rooms available. A party of six just canceled their booking. You're in luck." She paused to listen to the potential guest on the other end of the phone. Smiling at me as she adjusted her thick-framed glasses, she said into the phone, "Certainly, you can have a separate room for the kids." She completed the phone call and turned to me with a wide smile. "Good afternoon, sir, and welcome to The Seaman's Lodge."

"Thank you, I need a room for one night," I said.

"Brilliant, one guest?" she asked in a cheerful singsong voice, looking at a computer screen.

"No, two guests, I'm with my girlfriend," I replied, happy to call Bubbles *my girlfriend* for the first time.

Just then, Bubbles appeared next to me, and I took her hand in mine and squeezed it. The woman looked at us with a disapproving frown, then looked at the computer screen and said, "I'm afraid we don't seem to have any more rooms available." She had traded in the singsong voice for a solemn tone, but maintained the smile.

"I just heard you on the phone," I said, confused. "You said you had rooms available, and you seemed prepared to give me one a second ago."

"I'm sorry, sir, I-I made a mistake. I just booked our last rooms for a family of four. You do know that this is our busiest time of the year—"

"Well, can you check again? You just told whoever was on the phone that you had rooms. How did they all disappear?"

"Sir, lower your voice. You will upset other guests. I can give you recommendations for lodgings, but your best bet is the Holiday Inn Express—"

"I'd like to speak with your manager or supervisor now."

"Chris, let's get out," Bubbles said, urging me away from the front desk. "I wouldn't want to stay here after this. We're not welcome here."

I followed her, too tired and upset to argue further. When I described to Bubbles how the lady's mood changed from day to night for no reason, she laughed, shaking her head.

"Chris, don't you get it? It was after she saw me that the rooms mysteriously disappeared. It has happened to me countless times. A sales agent in a store will change mood and tone from being super-kind and cheerful to being cold and rude. Welcome to my world. Your crime is being with a Black girl."

She was quick to pick up on the smallest negative attitudes, and I would only figure it out later, much to her amusement. In the beginning, I thought she was overdramatic and sensitive, but as time progressed, even I could identify the hostile behavior and subtle comments, especially during our house-hunting experience.

When I moved to Georgia, I splurged on my dream car, a 2003 Audi TT. My dream home was next in line. My realtor, a balding white man in his mid-to-late fifties, couldn't conceal his shock after I pulled up in my sports car with Bubbles sitting in the passenger seat. He didn't acknowledge her presence, not even with a greeting after she smiled and said, "Hi." He completely disregarded her the entire time he showed us the house. When Bubbles commented that the kitchen was outdated and asked about upgrades, he ignored her and addressed me instead. I could sense Bubbles' displeasure.

"Look here, Norman," I told him. "My fiancée will be living with me. It's our house we're buying, so please pay attention to any questions she asks."

The color drained from his Botoxed face. "Very well, I was simply talking to you as my client, the buyer—"

"I understand, but she just asked you if the seller is willing to make some upgrades to the kitchen, and you ignored her."

Speechless, he nervously flipped the pages on his clipboard and said, "I will talk to the seller's agent about upgrades."

I never called him again, and we resorted to attending open houses every weekend. I dismissed the first realtor's attitude as a one-off encounter until I met Britney, a thin, platinum blonde in her early twenties. She was showing a house in an upscale gated community in McDonough. When I spoke to her on the phone, she told me I had an adorable British accent and couldn't wait to meet me. She was standing outside the house in a short, above-the-knee, body-con dress, a black jacket and thigh-high leather boots.

"Wow, she's all dressed up for work," Bubbles remarked sarcastically.

She walked over to me as I stepped out of the car and said, "Hi, I'm Britney."

"A pleasure to meet you," I said.

"Oh my gosh, I just love your accent. I've always wanted to go to London," she replied excitedly. "I love your sports car. It fits perfectly in this community."

When Bubbles stepped out of the car, Britney stopped to stare like she was an unwelcome guest at an exclusive party. Bubbles smiled and said, "Hi."

"Hi," Britney replied with a quick nod, then turned to me. "Chris, you will love this house. It's got a brand-new kitchen and a grand master bedroom with a fireplace. Come on in."

We walked into the foyer, where a glamourous crystal chandelier hung from the high ceiling. A spiral staircase led to the upper level, and a shiny black grand piano was positioned awkwardly at the entrance. "It's gorgeous, ain't it?" Britney beamed.

She led us to the spacious great room with large windows, and the flood of sunlight highlighted the immaculate white couches and thick, luxurious white rug.

"Chris, this is one of our latest listings. My parents own the real estate company, and I tell you, I have seen plenty of houses, and this is a gem. We mainly sell in Buckhead and specialize in luxury homes. This house would sell for millions in Buckhead. It was a bit out of the way for me. Like, why do you want to live in the south of Atlanta anyway?"

Britney went on, in this annoying, creaky tone, "Chris, I can show you around Buckhead if you like. That's where I live. You might change your mind about living out here. So much more to do there. I can take you to some really cool places."

She was openly flirtatious, curling a strand of blonde hair around one finger, and now distracted from the task of selling us the house.

"So, how many bedrooms are there?" Bubbles asked. "And is

the master bedroom upstairs or on the main level?"

"Five," she replied dismissively, then she continued to focus on me. "Chris, come with me. You have got to see the basement, a true man cave that you can customize to your taste—"

"Britney, my girlfriend here is the one you should be talking to. Her opinion matters."

I pulled a stunned Bubbles close and wrapped my arm around her waist. Britney's eyes widened, then with a scowl she said, "Oh, I didn't realize... er... you were together like that."

"She asked about the master bedroom?"

"Five bedrooms, master on the main," Britney said firmly.

"That's too many," Bubbles said. "We don't need five bedrooms. Besides, this house is made of stucco, and I prefer brick."

"Then I guess we're done here," I said, much to Britney's dismay.

*****

In 2005, after I returned to Atlanta from London, I had lunch with my workmate, Jamal.

"Hey, Chris, you know there's another dude from England that works here?" he said. "I'll get you two together, and you can have tea with biscuits. That's what y'all call cookies, right?" He pretended to sip from a cup with an extended pinky, and we laughed.

That was how I met Liam. Because we were Brits, everyone at work expected us to become best buddies.

"The thing is, Liam and I would never be mates if we were back home," I said to Bubbles during one of our late-night phone conversations. She was still in London working, and I was alone in my apartment, counting down the end to her summer break.

"This bloke is a forty-something-year-old ex-con from Manchester. He has tattoos up to his neck and cusses like a sailor, and to be honest, he makes some very racist statements. I don't think he even realizes how repulsive it is."

"Does he know you're dating a Black African girl?"

"Not yet. I'm waiting for the big reveal when you come back. I can't wait to see the look on his face."

"What was he in prison for?"

"He said he first got into trouble as a teen for petty crime like pickpocketing. Then in his early twenties, he got involved with a local gang and started dealing drugs. He was at a nightclub when a rival gang attacked his crew, and there was a fatal stabbing. He was charged as an accomplice, served six years, and got out on good behavior."

"How did he end up in Georgia?"

"After he got out, he worked as a cabbie for his uncle's taxi company. His wife was touring England with some friends, and guess who gave them a taxi ride? He says it was love at first sight. By the time she returned to the States, they had hooked up. The rest is history."

Bubbles chuckled. "Summer holidays, taxi rides, and plane rides—you and Liam have lots to share."

A week later, on a Friday evening, I met Liam at O'Charley's restaurant and bar. He had been drinking at the bar for an hour or more and was visibly drunk. We didn't have much in common, and even though we worked for the same company, our roles couldn't be more different. I was at the management level and spent most of my days in board meetings across the country. He operated machinery in the factory. Our worlds seldom collided.

"I fuckin' miss smoking indoors," he moaned. "I have to step outside for a fag break, and even out there, I feel like I have to hide."

"Go on and have one, I'll place your order," I said, half wishing I could order my food to-go. I struggled to make meaningful conversation with Liam.

"I'll go later. So, you live around here? You got a house?"

"No, I'm still in an apartment. I'll start shopping for a house soon. I don't quite like the apartments, too noisy on the weekends."

"You can say that again, and I know what you mean." Then he whispered, "Too many of them people, you know, them darkies. Before we bought our house, we lived in an apartment in Jonesboro. They played that rap music all night, they laugh loudly like monkeys, and they have too many babies crying everywhere. I couldn't stand it, so we left and moved to McDonough. It's a lot more civil, you know?"

I agreed that the late-night music and the ever-crying baby from the apartment across from mine drove me nuts, but I wasn't comfortable with Liam's racial undertones.

He continued, now almost ranting, but still in a low voice.

"My wife was born and raised in Georgia, and she doesn't want to leave, but even she will tell you that over the years, those darkies have increased in number, and cities like Atlanta are unlivable now. You make a little money, you move out to the suburbs. Crime rates are high because of them. They don't wanna work, just feed off the system, deal drugs, and all."

I wanted to remind him of his past, but was too cowardly. I managed to say, "I don't think it's fair to judge them all based on the behavior of a few—"

"They're all the same, believe me, I work with them in the factory. There are only two of us white boys, and the rest are Black or fuckin' Mexican. I'm their boss in there. When I tell you they're bloody lazy, I mean it."

"I work with some Black people too. In fact, Jamal, head of logistics, is the one that told me about you. He's a decent fella, knows his job—"

"Yeah, well, there'll be one or two good ones, but a darkie is a darkie to me. Bloody uncivilized monkeys... except for one, just one, that hot bird, Beyoncé, the singer. Yeah, I'd like to get some of that pussy, good brown pussy—"

I rose from my chair abruptly, repulsed and ashamed to have let him keep talking, listening to such vile language, and most importantly, making him comfortable enough to say such things.

I cracked my knuckles, fighting the strong urge to throw a punch and make him shut up.

"I have to go," I said. "I just remembered I need to collect my shirts from the dry cleaner before they start to charge me for storage." A cowardly excuse and an elaborate lie. I motioned for the waiter and asked him to put my food in a to-go bag. There was no way I could sit through dinner.

In the days that followed, I received several phone calls from Liam, but I ignored him. I finally decided to talk to him and invited him to my apartment for a drink, *only* because I had a surprise waiting for him. He was happy to come and offered to buy beer and the wine I preferred. When he walked into the living room of my one-bedroom apartment and saw the pictures on the walls, he was gobsmacked. He stepped closer to scrutinize each photo, and with a dazed look he quietly walked to the couch, sat without a word, and failed to make eye contact.

After I returned from England, I'd printed all the photos that Bubbles and I had taken and enlarged them. My stay in the apartment was temporary, and I was tired of staring at the bare walls, so I sellotaped the pictures to the wall, like wallpaper. Everywhere you looked, you would see a picture of us, on the London Eye, standing outside Buckingham palace, kissing at the beach in Bristol, and even more photos of Bubbles alone, eating, laughing, and sleeping. I enjoyed looking at them, reminiscing, and anticipating more memories we would make.

"Who's the bird in the pictures?" he finally found his voice.

"That's Maita, my girlfriend," I replied with a smile. "She's from Zimbabwe. I reckon she'll fit right in with everyone here in Atlanta, don't you think?"

"Mate, I was drunk, and I know I said some stupid things. I take it all back. It was pub banter, you know—"

"I'm afraid I don't share your views, and I don't see how we can even pretend to be friends when you can't stand them, and when my girlfriend is Black."

"I shouldn't have said it. Look, mate, you can enjoy the wine. I think I'll head home." He rose to his feet. "You can keep the beer too. Maybe we can do this another time."

I didn't hear from him for days, then received a call from Carol, his wife, whom I hadn't met. She told me that Liam felt terrible and was extremely unhappy, so much she had to call on his behalf to apologize for disrespecting my girlfriend and me. Months later, I met Liam at work, and we got to talking like nothing ever happened. Then Carol called me again and invited Bubbles and me to their house for English tea.

"I'm certainly not going," Bubbles said. "Liam will poison me, no way."

"Please come with me. I want us all to get along. Let's just pop in, have a cuppa, chit-chat for bit and that's it. To be fair, Carol has tried to reach out, and I know Liam is behind it too. Maybe he was too drunk, and I don't—"

"You're making excuses for him. I will go with you, *for you.* But I won't drink or eat anything unless it's wrapped, canned, or bottled." She laughed, and I couldn't tell if she was serious.

After spending the afternoon with Liam and Carol in their house, located in a wooded area and isolated from other homes, Bubbles spoke up on our drive home.

"If you had never told me all the racist things Liam said, I'd believe I just met the friendliest and most non-racist couple ever. Carol was gushing about my beautiful hair, my stylish clothes, and how good my English was. Liam was the delightfully curious one, asking about growing up in Africa and my experience working in London. The endless flattery, how smart I am, a physical therapist enrolled in graduate school at Emory University. What a lovely couple we are." She shook her head. "Now I can't tell if they're Oscar-deserving actors, or they have magically converted to the good side."

I shared Liam's racist comments with Bubbles because I wanted to reassure her that I disagreed with him completely. The truth was that I would have to defend my relationship with Bubbles over and over again. However, it wasn't the challenges brought on by other people's perceptions that were the hardest for me. It was differences between *us* and our expectations—or rather, her expectations.

Bubbles complained when I asked her to go halves at a restaurant. When I offered a ride to Kroger supermarket, she seemed disappointed that I didn't pay for *her* groceries, as if driving her there wasn't good enough. During a recent argument, she accused me of being controlling and self-centered when I made her choose between studying on a Friday night, and spending that time with me.

"I can't sit here and fiddle my thumbs while you study. It's Friday for goodness's sakes."

"So you don't care that I could flunk my test on Monday? As long as I keep you company. Watch something on TV—"

"I don't want to watch telly on a Friday night, I want to be with you."

"Do I have to remind you that I'm a student?".

"I know, but surely you can take a break from your books."

"I have tests and assignments due next week," she said. "Can't you wait till next weekend?"

"Oh, come on, it can't be that big of a deal. So you can put off seeing me, but you can go to your book club meetings on Wednesdays? I'm not a priority—"

"Stop being so childish, Chris. The book club meeting is here on campus, and it's only an hour long. I do need some time to socialize with my classmates too—"

"My point exactly, you choose them over me, your boyfriend."

"Don't you go for a drink with your workmates? Do you hear me complaining?"

And the argument would go on and on, and we would sulk for a day or two, then make up.

Lately, we both seemed to get on each other's nerves quite easily, and a small issue would get blown out of proportion. I was annoyed when she talked endlessly on the phone with her girlfriend Lindy—it bordered on being rude, but Maita accused me of being petty, and wanting her all to myself.

I was determined to fix things, hence my New Year's

resolutions. I was tired of all the fighting. I just wanted to be in love again.

Chapter 17

Ade

Drafting an email to Maita proved to be more difficult than I thought. With no idea of what to say or how to say it, I stared blankly at the computer screen, searching my brain for the best first line. At this juncture, I felt an emptiness in my current relationship, and lately thoughts of Maita had been haunting me. Regret taunted me—memories of our time together, and the possibilities of what could have been occupied my mind constantly.

"It feels like a light has turned on in my head, and I can't switch it off," I'd confided to Gbenga a week ago, when we had beers at the local pub. He was on one of his rare visits from Birmingham, taking a break from his studies. I couldn't share what I was experiencing with Bola, because she would consider the situation from a female perspective, which always involved too much emotion. Although Gbenga was younger, he was more pragmatic.

"So, what do you think is bringing this on?" he asked. "You and Noma seem to be doing well."

"Don't be fooled by the outward appearance, as Mum always says. We aren't getting along. I think we tolerate each other." I took a sip of my beer, noting the confused expression on my younger brother's face. "I know it sounds crazy to be thinking about Bubbles, but Noma can never replace her, and I'm just discovering that now."

"Do you mean that you got with Noma to *replace* Bubbles?

Like a rebound? That's messed up, bro." He looked disappointed. Had I set a bad example? The confused older brother who couldn't manage his love life? But I had to vent to someone. Gbenga wouldn't judge me, and I didn't expect him to provide any solutions either. He was there to lend an ear, and that was all I needed.

"I don't know if it's wise to act on my feelings and contact her," I said. "And I'm afraid she may not be interested or willing to talk. We parted in a not-so-good way. My fault, by the way. I'm to blame this time."

"Then you have to make it right by Bubbles if you hurt her feelings. I'd call her and talk it over. Maybe after chatting, you'll get some closure and may have second thoughts about her. That might also help you to focus on Noma. Fix that too." My soon-to-be doctor brother sounded wiser than his twenty-five years.

Gbenga's smooth chocolate-brown skin, bushy eyebrows, slanted brown eyes, and a dimple on his left cheek made him a carbon copy of our mother. His well-maintained dreadlocked hair gave him an edge that the ladies loved. My mother's criticism of his hair fell on deaf ears. "You'll soon have to cut those dreadlocks if you want anyone to take you seriously as a doctor," she would warn. "It's bad enough you have an accent and a strange name. Add to that your hair, and no one will hire you."

Like my father, Gbenga was a good listener who studied situations, drew conclusions, and demanded quick and practical solutions, no beating about the bush. Combined with his sharp analytical skills, he would make a good physician.

"It's been over a year since Bubbles and I last saw each other or communicated via phone or email," I said. "So much time and distance between us now. I wish I had responded more kindly when she begged me to take her back." I stroked my beer mug, as if this would soothe away the feelings of self-reproach.

I thought of that rainy day in the summer of 2005, outside the Covent Garden Tube station. I couldn't erase the memory of Bubbles crying and pleading for a second chance. I remembered tears gushing down her face as we stood soaked in the rain, and she poured her heart out, vulnerable in a way I'd never experienced nor expected. I reminisced about how I held her in my arms, and without warning caressed her plump lips with mine. She'd immediately responded to my spontaneous affection, and we kissed passionately like the lovers we used to be.

"She came to London on a quest to get us back together, imagine that?" I said, shaking my head. "I was too stupid, maybe proud, or both, and I told her to move on and forget about me. Yet the moment she broke down and cried, I was drawn to her in a way that I couldn't explain."

"Sounds like a scene from a movie, a chick-flick," Gbenga said. He chuckled, then sipped his beer.

"After that, she never called or emailed me. Just like that, she disappeared again, this time for good," I said, expecting a sympathetic response.

But he said, "Are you surprised? She must have felt humiliated and too embarrassed to face you again."

"I'm pretty sure she has moved on, probably with the guy she mentioned on that day, someone she met that summer. The ball was in my court, and had I agreed to take her back, the new guy wouldn't have stood a chance. Instead, I told her off and left her crying."

Gbenga replied, "So, by getting in touch with her now, you expect her to dump her new dude for you? What's the point in all this?"

Always a straight shooter and realist, he was simply reiterating questions I had asked myself. Feeling the need to explain why I was so conflicted, I ordered a second round of beers, knowing it would take a while, that we may go beyond the two rounds.

"I don't know what I hope to achieve. I know that I miss Bubbles, and I'm not happy right now. When I walked away from her at that Tube station, I was satisfied with my decision. I didn't want to jeopardize my relationship with Noma, which was good then, comfortable and without drama. But with time, things began to change."

I felt like I was on a shrink's couch where I could let it all out. Gbenga continued giving me a disapproving look, leaving me with no choice but to pour out details of my relationship with Noma.

"There is tremendous pressure from her family for us to marry. She talks about it all the time, how her family isn't happy with our living together in sin…"

"But you know even Mum and Dad aren't thrilled about that," he said, as if taking Noma's side.

"It's frowned upon by most African cultures—I understand that— but no one complained when I bought the house and invited her to move in with me." My voice rose a bit. "Why is it a problem now? Then there's talk of paying *lobola*."

Lobola is the Ndebele word for the dowry paid by the prospective groom for his future bride.

I said, "They want a big traditional ceremony that we must do before we get legally married, have a white wedding and all. I'm not ready to make that commitment with Noma. Back then I was so ready for it with Bubbles, but she wasn't—"

"Do you love Noma?" Gbenga blurted, stopping my rambling with the one question that even I couldn't ask myself.

Pausing to consider this carefully, I gulped my beer and said, "I'm not sure. I think I'm coasting and don't want to rock the boat by adding marriage to the equation. The tension has been mounting. Noma is constantly moody and snaps quite easily. I'm also guilty of giving her similar treatment. When she's away at work on a night shift, I relish that time alone."

"You don't love her, but you're afraid to be alone. That's what I gather. You're looking for a way out and using Bubbles as an excuse."

"I thought you were going to specialize in neurology, not psychiatry," I said, feeling like an open book and embarrassed now to have my brother dissect my messy relationships. "About two weeks ago, Noma was gone for an entire week to stay with Thando in Luton. She never explained why, and I wasn't sure if she was protesting or something."

Thando is Noma's older sister.

"What do you mean protesting, like she needed a break from you?"

"Not really a break. I suspect Noma wanted me to suffer for a week without her cooking, cleaning, and—you know, sex whenever you want—the benefits of having a live-in girlfriend. Then perhaps I'd realize that I couldn't live without her, give in and get married."

He laughed for the first time since we began this serious conversation. "So, it's that good, huh? Sex whenever you want, and a personal cook. Should I be looking for a live-in girlfriend too?"

Ignoring his remark, I said, "She didn't even call me, but she later sent a text: *I will be in Luton this week. See you when I get back.* I never called to ask why. Frankly, I needed the space and time alone. That week was such a breath of fresh air. I didn't miss her at all. During that week, a light switch was turned on, or rather one light went on, and another went *off.*"

Returning to his serious demeanor, he said, "Your aha moment. If leaving you alone to fend for yourself for a week was intended to be some sort of punishment, it backfired badly."

He was starting to see things my way.

"I looked in the mirror and almost couldn't recognize myself," I said. "I had become content with mediocrity. I was happy just to have someone who loved me, kept me warm at night, and took care of my needs. I couldn't remember the last time I laughed out loud, or went out drinking with friends."

"I can attest to that. You've chilled a lot. Not a bad thing." Gbenga glanced at his watch, most likely getting bored by my rants, but I had so much to get off my chest.

"I couldn't recall having a big argument or even raising my voice, debating over issues on the news or silly celebrity gossip. No morning quickies before we run for the bus, and no more spur-of-the-moment weekends in Europe. Simple, good old fun."

"You're bored—I have made my diagnosis," Gbenga said.

"Boredom is putting it lightly. You know I haven't had a drink at this pub in months because Noma doesn't like the atmosphere. We stick to a monotonous routine of work, home, movie night, Bible study, and her family events—"

"Bible study? Now that's no fun. But aren't we supposed to be on the lookout for such good church-going girls? Don't they make the best wives?"

"It gets worse. I'll tell you what I can't stand: Noma's family parties and gatherings. I don't care if I never go to another *braai* or *goch goch*—what they call a barbecue. It's always the same, a house party with the same crowd talking in Ndebele or Shona, these Zimbabwean languages…"

"Have you tried to learn the language? You should be fluent by now, given that this is your second girlfriend from Zimbabwe." Again he laughed, and I joined in, shaking my head.

"The men stand around the grill, tending to the meat and drinking beer outside, and the women usually sit in the living area or kitchen, gossiping and sizing each other up. I always end up sitting away from everyone and drinking alone."

"The anti-social Nigerian boyfriend. Not a good look, bro."

"I've tried to make friends and to socialize with the guys, but I always sense some hostility. They call me *Chiremba*, which means doctor in Shona. But when my back is turned, they refer to me as *muNaija*, slang for Nigerian."

"I've been called *Naija boy* several times. Is it a derogatory word?"

"I'm not sure. Noma later explained that Zimbabwean men dislike their Nigerian counterparts because they complain that Nigerians take all their women. Nigerian men have a reputation for being wealthy and flashy big spenders. These men with money woo the Zimbabwean ladies. Meanwhile, most Zimbabwean men still work menial jobs, or are in nursing school, which makes them unattractive—"

"And they stand no chance against a *Naija* dude, let alone a doctor like yourself," Gbenga said, nodding. "I've heard about our reputation, and even the Kenyan dudes aren't thrilled with us."

"That explains their passive and sometimes hostile attitude toward me. What bothers me is that when Noma is with her crew—a gang of four girls—she's different. At these events, she doesn't give me any attention. In fact, most of the time, she ignores me. She leaves me to navigate my way around the kitchen and fix my plate and drink. Thando usually makes an effort to entertain me. We make small talk, but it always ends with Thando asking me when I will marry Noma, and I have to find ways to avoid answering."

"Phew, man, that's a lot to take in. Not only is she giving you grief at home, her friends and family are too. It's too much already."

"The source of all the negative attitude toward me is Noma's mother, Stella. She's a widow, you know, who raised three girls alone. She's protective of her children, but also very controlling. Stella made it clear to me that she doesn't trust Nigerian men, and believes that most are liars and thieves."

"Well, can you blame her, given all those *Nigerian Prince* scams out there? A few bad apples spoil the barrel."

"Painting us all with one brush is unfair," I said. "Noma's mother once threatened me to my face and said I better not have a wife in Nigeria, or she would sort me out herself. She half laughed when she said this, but I could sense genuine mistrust."

Stella had migrated to the United Kingdom years after her husband passed on. Unlike her daughters, she was uneducated and could only find low-paying work such as nursing assistance, janitorial, or housekeeping jobs. Her daughters paid for Stella's living expenses, including the rent, which I had no problem with, but I was uncomfortable with how she demanded it of them.

Stella dictated how Noma spent *her* money, including sending cash to aunts and uncles in Zimbabwe. Noma could afford all this because she didn't pay any bills in the house that we shared—she lived rent-free.

"I'm responsible for the mortgage, utility bills, and household expenses," I said.

"And she pays nothing?" Gbenga said with a surprised look.

"She occasionally buys groceries, and that's all. I finance Noma's upkeep, including getting her hair done and shopping sprees for clothes and other feminine spoils. When we travel, I foot the bill. Despite my generosity, her mom doesn't like me, and I know it. She tolerates me, and until I marry her daughter, she will continue to give me a cold embrace."

Gbenga shook his head. "Ade, you are way too kind. I make my girlfriend pay for dinner sometimes. Until she is my wife, I'm not going a hundred percent. Even then, she'd better have a job and help with the bills."

"You have become too Western. Back home, we take care of our women one hundred percent. I have no problem with paying—"

"How has that worked out for you, huh? Can't you see that she's taking advantage of your kindness?"

I wasn't surprised by his reaction. Because since he'd left Lagos for the UK at nineteen, Gbenga had never dated an African girl and didn't know why African men had to provide for our women. In most African cultures, the ability to provide abundantly for a woman brings so much pride to a man, and it's often a measure of success.

With a dedicated runner and soccer player's physique, Gbenga was a female magnet who attracted women of all races. He seemed to have a preference for non-Black and usually exotic-looking girls. His last girlfriend was English and of Brazilian descent, who looked like a model from *Sports Illustrated*. I never understood why he had an exclusive affinity for other races, and he explained it away by saying, "I like what I like, and race has nothing to do with it."

According to Bola, our mother often complained that neither of her sons would marry a Yoruba girl who would understand and value our customs and traditions.

Bola would tell us, "Mum has no problem with you guys

dating non-Nigerians. The thing is, a girl from any part of Africa can easily adapt to our culture, unlike the European and Asian girls that Gbenga dates." Always the messenger, Bola would relay whatever my mother wanted us to know but couldn't tell us herself. "I guess Mum just wants a relatable daughter-in-law who can cook her favorites, *Moin Moin, Amala, Pounded Yam,* and *Ewedu.*"

Gbenga would reply, defending his choices, "Well, Mum won't be living with me and my 'non-Nigerian' wife, so she shouldn't worry about the food my wife can or cannot cook. I'm cool with eating European or Asian food."

"You know what my friends say about you, Gbenga?" Bola once said, referring to her high school and hometown girlfriends from Lagos. "They say you're just another good-looking, well-educated brother who finds success and abandons his Black sisters for all other races. Don't shoot the messenger."

It wasn't the first time Gbenga had heard this. "Your friends are bitter, and it's not my fault they're unattractive. Come on, name one of your girls that's good-looking. None. I do like my Black sisters, Gabrielle Union was a longtime crush—"

"Oh, stop. We all remember your obsession with Gabrielle Union and Kelly Rowland, nice try. They are highly unattainable Black women, mere fantasies, but in reality, you choose the Chelseas and Fergies."

And they would argue for hours, leaving Bola upset and Gbenga gleaming in victory.

Rechecking the time, Gbenga said, "It's getting late, bro, let's head home. I have an early start tomorrow."

"Have I bored you with my problems?" I smiled. "Come on, let's have one last round."

He agreed, then as if to conclude our discussion, he put on a serious face and said, "You have a deep void inside and something gnawing at you. You need mental and social stimulation. You're happy to cruise along, playing it safe with Noma, but you're afraid to start afresh. Answer me this, can you go on for another ten or twenty years like this?"

"I can't go another day like this," I said. Talking to my brother was all the therapy I needed. Just like that, I knew what I had to do.

In the days that followed, I thought about Bubbles more and more, and yearned to hear her voice again. I missed her phone calls and emails that used to boost my ego.

It wasn't only Bubbles that I missed. It was her friends too. Unlike Noma's, her friends were a fun bunch, and her family was warm and friendly toward me—that *crazy gang*: Rosie, a nurse who indulged in expensive shopping sprees. Josephine was comical and sarcastic with a similar personality to Bubbles, and Grace, the serious one and the voice of reason. This group of girls loved to have a good time. They enjoyed exploring various entertainments and would venture into central London to try new clubs and restaurants, or watch plays. It was Bubbles who introduced me to the West End theater scene. *Chicago* was the first show we watched, and after that I developed a new interest in the theater. On the other hand, Noma was so bored by the theater that she slept through *Les Misérables* and never wanted to return.

It was a year and six months ago when I last saw Bubbles, beautiful as ever in her signature skinny jeans and hair flowing to her shoulders in thick, wavy black curls. When she cried, I knew I had broken Bubbles' heart the same way she broke mine once upon a time. Even then, I wanted to hug her and never let go. Sometimes when I closed my eyes, I could feel her soft lips on mine, and taste salty tears mixed with rain.

My heart was with Bubbles. After much consideration, and with Gbenga's words echoing in my mind, I decided to send her an email and test the waters.

On a cold Friday in January, twelve days after Christmas, I was home alone, and Noma was working late. I sat in bed drinking lemon tea, my laptop resting on my lap. I logged into my email and typed:

Hi, Stranger,

It's been a while since we talked, and I wanted to check in on you to find out how you're doing. I hope you are well.

Take care,
Ade

I read it over. The message didn't give away too much, and it read like an old friend reaching out. I considered if the message might be too vague. Since I had no time for cat-and-mouse games, perhaps it would be better to get to the point and tell her I was sorry and wanted her back, then ask her if she was still single?

In the end, I opted for the simple, friendly email, just to gauge her response.

I clicked *send* and watched it disappear. I placed the laptop on the nightstand, left it open, and prepared to sleep, confident that I had made the right decision.

I smiled at the thought of hearing her voice again. We were destined to be together, but had wasted so much time chasing other relationships. This time had to be it. Relieved after sending the email, I closed my eyes and prayed for a positive response. She was indeed the love of my life, and I would do whatever it took to get her back... unless she was happily married to someone else.

Chapter 18

Atlanta, GA
January 2007

Chris

January in Georgia was cold, with temperatures as low as forty degrees Fahrenheit. After a long, blazing hot summer with temperatures in the high eighties and mid-nineties, I appreciated the chilly weather. It was twelve days after Christmas, and I was finally taking down my outdoor Christmas lights. My second Christmas in this house, and the first one celebrated with indoor and outdoor decorations. Last year, after closing on the house a week before Christmas, I'd been too excited about buying my dream home, and decorating was the last thing on my mind. All I'd managed was a four-foot, pre-lit Christmas tree which I erected in the empty living room.

Not caring about the tree's size or the empty rooms, Bubbles and I were thrilled to finally settle into this four-bedroomed house after months of house-hunting. That Christmas, Bubbles had been on a two-week break from university and had stayed with me. With my furniture still in storage, we slept on an air mattress and used a futon and two giant beanbags for seating. That was all we needed. Like an extended slumber party filled with food, wine, sex, and lots of laughter, the first days in this house were a blur of euphoria.

This year I had the whole exterior of the house lit and had placed an inflatable Santa and reindeer on the front lawn. A twelve-foot Christmas tree stood tall in the living room, blending in with the Christmas-themed interior wall decor and lights hanging throughout the house.

As I climbed up the ladder to access the lights on the roof, my phone rang. It was Bubbles. Smiling, I said, "Hey, babe, are you coming back today?"

"Yes, I'm making my way home now. Simone is driving me there."

"That's great. I was getting a bit worried that you weren't going to be here for my work dinner tomorrow tonight."

"I'll be there within the hour." And she cut the phone. What a relief, I thought. After I'd talked so much about her at work, everyone expected Maita to show up for the fundraising dinner.

I hoped she had gotten over the most recent row we'd had three days ago, when she'd stormed out and taken a taxi to her friend's house in Marietta. It was costly to hire a cab from Stockbridge to Marietta, close to fifty miles away—and she'd gone despite the fact she couldn't afford it. Bubbles had opted for an early graduation in December, a small ceremony for the master's students because she didn't want to wait till May for the university-wide graduation day. Yes, she'd graduated, but was unemployed.

"It's a waste of money, especially in your situation," I tried to reason with her, after I heard her call the taxi company. She ignored me as she packed a backpack.

"Stay home, and let's talk it over," I pleaded. Yet she walked past me in defiance and went outside to wait—in the cold. She tended to overreact, and continuously threatened to leave me whenever we had the slightest disagreement.

I couldn't remember the subject matter of the argument. Of late, Bubbles often accused me of being selfish and controlling. Replaying the scene in my head caused me to hyperventilate, and my chest tightened, impairing my balance and causing my foot to slip off the rung on the ladder, but I managed to catch myself. I couldn't understand the effect she had on me, and why even the thought of her leaving so tore me apart.

Having lost concentration for the task of taking down the Christmas lights, I decided to take a break before I lost my footing again and tumbled to the ground. I longed for a shot of tequila, or any alcohol, to ease my mind from worrying about Bubbles, so I gathered my tools and went indoors.

Recently, our arguments had been getting louder, nastier, and more frequent. It was very troubling, to say the least, how we would have a go at each other like bitter rivals, shouting over each other and saying very hurtful things. Controlling my temper was difficult, and I always felt the urge to punch the wall or to smash something just to get the anger out.

Reliving some of our big fights provoked the very anger that I desperately wanted to bury. A recent example: two weeks ago, when I threw Bubbles out of the house at three a.m. on a cold and rainy morning, the police had to get involved.

I headed to my bar to mix a cocktail. The house was warm and toasty with the heat blasting at seventy-eight degrees, just the way Bubbles liked it—hot and tropical—so she could walk around the house in her tiny shorts and a tank top in the middle of January.

I poured myself a glass of vodka on the rocks—something different from my usual red wine—and headed to the study, my favorite place to drink and relax. It was Bubbles' idea to convert one of the four bedrooms into a study. "After all, we don't need a fourth bedroom yet," she'd said. "It will be a while before we fill up these bedrooms." I was glad she was thinking about the future and the possibility of having a family.

She wanted a place to study too, with enough room to place a large bookshelf for her many books. The desk was littered with papers, notebooks and cans of Red Bull, indicating that Bubbles hadn't cleaned the room since her last exam. Bubbles practically lived in this room every weekend when she left the apartment at the Emory University campus to spend time with me. After shutting herself in here, I wouldn't see her for hours as she studied and napped.

Surprisingly, her laptop was on the desk. Strange, as Bubbles took it everywhere. I suppose when she walked off in a fit of rage, the laptop was the last thing on her mind.

I settled into a chair behind the desk and took a gulp of my vodka. Thoughts of past arguments faded with each sip. Looking around the study, I spotted her pink UGG house slippers, the favorite comforter that probably needed a wash, and a pillow, bundled on the floor in the corner of the room next to the bookshelf. This area was her *resting corner*, as she called it, and it was where she took a break from studying, played her music, and relaxed. She often fell asleep in that corner, and sometimes I snuggled beside her. It had been three days since she'd gone to Simone's, and I missed her badly.

I stared at the laptop, which had seen better days. The screen had a thin crack from the upper-left corner to the lower right. With regret, I remembered how that crack had happened. During one of many heated altercations, I'd flung it off this very desk in anger, along with the books and all the papers. It'd crashed to the floor, cracking the screen. Fortunately, the carpet had buffered the damage.

"I'm sorry," I'd said, profusely.

"How am I going to complete my assignments with a damaged computer?" she yelled. "You know I can't afford to replace it." She picked it up and inspected the damage.

"I can replace it with a brand-new laptop," I offered.

"Don't bother. I think it's still working okay, just a cracked screen."

Bubbles explained that she wanted to keep the laptop as a reminder of the monster that I could be—and she meant it. To this day, I hated to look at that screen because it indeed reminded me of how I could lose control, something I was ashamed of; a score for Bubbles, the queen of passive aggression, playing her usual mind games.

I clicked the Start button and realized that the laptop was still on. I had never pried around her stuff—not my thing—but I was suddenly curious. She had no password, and I began to click around. There was nothing there, just a bunch of grad school-related documents. To be honest with myself, with only a high school education, an apprenticeship, and years of work experience, I was a little intimidated by her master's program.

Not only was she at Georgia's most prestigious university, but she was also an A+ student.

As I scrolled through the web browser, I noticed that a Gmail account was open. She had a good number of unread email messages. I must draw the line, I thought, and not invade her privacy by opening her inbox.

And yet, I found myself clicking it open and scrolling through.

It seemed like she had been looking for all kinds of jobs, because there were many email messages from Monster.com. At that moment a new email came in. Almost on reflex, I opened it.

Hi, Stranger,

It's been a while since we talked, and I wanted to check in on you to find out how you are doing. I hope you are well.

Take care,
Ade

That name Ade rang a bell. He was her ex-boyfriend, the one before me. She never spoke much about him, except that they'd broken up before she left London for Atlanta, way back in 2004.

What did he want? Perhaps he was just an old boyfriend reaching out. But why now? She never discussed past boyfriends, especially her last relationship; therefore, he couldn't have been that significant. She once mentioned he was a doctor from Nigeria or Ghana, or some other African country, but not Zimbabwe.

I sat upright and spun around as I considered my reaction to the email. Functioning on autopilot, and with the vodka in my veins clouding my judgment, I replied:

Hey Ade,
I am fine. How are you doing? It has been a long time, for sure.

I paused to think and whispered, "What would Bubbles write?" She would probably keep it short and to the point.

Thanks for checking in.
Take care,

Then I stopped to think again. Should I sign off as Bubbles or Maita? Most likely Bubbles, if they truly had a close relationship. Well, did they? How long did it last anyway?

I decided to use her nickname and immediately clicked the Send button. That should be enough for him not to email again. There was no room for a response unless he followed up on my *How are you doing?* I didn't want an ex-boyfriend getting too friendly. I felt justified.

Reading her emails didn't feel right. I certainly wouldn't want anyone reading mine, so I knew what I'd done was wrong. Responding to someone else's email was even worse. It had to be the alcohol that made me do that, because in my right mind, I would never invade anyone's privacy this way.

What had I done? I had opened the door to another big fight. I had to delete the email from Ade *and* my email to him so that Bubbles would never find out. I immediately did so, then rested on the chair, my hands behind my head, and closed my eyes. I wanted to nap.

How could I be threatened by an email from an ex-boyfriend who was far away somewhere?

I drifted off in my thoughts. I must have dozed off for a few minutes, as I woke with a start to a loud *ping* from the laptop. It was Ade.

A quick reply. What time was it in England, anyway? Assuming he still lived there.

Now I had no choice but to open it and make sure I ended this communication with him. I clicked it open and read:

Bubbles!

I am so happy that you replied, and I'm glad you're well. I was unsure if you would want to have anything to do with me after our last date in London two summers ago. I'm doing fine, just plodding on with work. How is Atlanta? Have you graduated yet? What is your next move? I doubt you will be returning to cold and gray England. I would like to catch up. Has your number changed? I thought of calling you once, but wasn't sure if that would be a welcome move. Plus, I don't know if that would offend your man if you have one. ☺ Please call me if you get a chance.

My new number is +44 7700 900915. I need to talk to you.

Ade

I stared at the screen for a while, not sure what to make of the email. It was apparent Ade wanted to open the lines of communication. What had happened that summer in 2005—the same summer I met Bubbles in London? She'd never mentioned seeing Ade or talking to him. But after all, we were just getting to know each other, and there was no obligation to talk about her past then—although it seemed something significant enough for Ade to mention. *I need to talk to you.* What was that about? He aroused my curiosity. I was suspicious and jealous.

I needed to nip this in the bud. I didn't trust him. I wished I had more vodka in my empty glass. I also now *definitely* didn't want Bubbles to get back in touch with an ex-boyfriend.

I'll tell him she's married, I thought, that he must bugger off and stop sending emails.

I began to type but stopped in my tracks, because the thought occurred to me that, indeed, I wanted to know what happened that summer between Ade and Bubbles. What was Bubbles holding from me if she never, *ever* mentioned it at all? She was open about her past with most things, but why keep this from me?

I thought, I can't exactly ask Bubbles directly now, can I? I was already typing a response:

Ade,
That was a quick reply. I assume you were sitting at your computer. I'm in a very serious relationship, and wouldn't want my man reading these messages. As you can imagine, he will not be pleased with me chatting online with an ex. Whatever you need to talk to me about, please text me on my new mobile. I have changed my number too. It is (404) 555 0187 TEXT ONLY, and please don't call or email me again.

After sending that email, I had an eerie feeling that I had started something dangerous.

I had just made Bubbles appear interested in whatever he had to say, and I implied that she was prepared to sneak behind her current partner's back and text him. I was second-guessing my misleading email, not confident about my actions. At least by directing him to text instead of emailing, I thought, I can make sure Bubbles never finds out, and I can control the way this plays out. To be extra careful, I blocked Ade's email address from her inbox.

Satisfied that by blocking his email and deleting the email messages he sent, Bubbles would never know they existed, and relieved by my handling of the situation, I decided I needed another drink. After pouring more vodka on the rocks, I returned to relax and fell asleep in Bubbles' resting corner.

The loud shrieking "Jingle Bells" ringtone from my vibrating phone woke me up. The room was dark, only illuminated by the ringing mobile phone. Trying to get my bearings and scrambling to get up, I grabbed the phone from the desk. It was Bubbles.

"Hey, I'm outside. I've been ringing the doorbell for a while now."

"Sorry, I didn't hear it. I passed out on the floor." I hurried out of the study and through the dark hallway to the front door.

"You passed out on the floor? Are you okay?"

"Yeah, I'm fine. Just had a little too much to drink."

I opened the door and hugged her tightly. Glad to see her

back home, because for a moment there, I thought she had gone for good. Bubbles seemed surprised at my sudden show of affection. "I'm glad you're back," I whispered.

She gently pushed me away. "I'm getting cold standing out here."

"Let me run you a bath and get you warmed up," I said, turning the lights on and leading her into the living room.

She didn't seem impressed by my enthusiastic welcome. "Chris, we need to talk, and I mean, we need to iron some things out before we get all lovey-dovey."

I knew this was coming, but I was hoping we could get comfortable and create a loving atmosphere before we talked about what happened three nights ago.

"We can't keep sweeping all these issues under the rug. We need to confront your anger issues—"

"My anger issues?"

"Yes, every time we get into it, you either break something or fling something across the room, and you start to talk of *your house* and *your stuff*. How can I ever feel like I belong in this house if you bring that up all the time? I get it; I haven't contributed anything financially because I'm unemployed and broke. But if you invite me to live with you, you can't keep saying stuff like that. I don't plan to stay this way forever. I just graduated, and I need time to sort out my immigration stuff so I can get a job and work legally."

I felt myself come down from the high and buzz I was feeling just moments ago. Careful not to let this explode into another argument, I pleaded, "Can we talk later, please? I want to enjoy this moment. I missed you."

Shrugging, she took a seat on the couch. It was apparent that she was unsettled. Bubbles was back home, but she wasn't the same. This time things had shifted, and if I didn't get my act together, I would lose her.

Then I remembered the email from Ade and realized that this was the worst possible time for Bubbles to even think about him, let alone email or call him. With emotions running high and our relationship constantly on the rocks, Ade could easily persuade her to get back with him. Overcome with anger—not at her, but at an ex-boyfriend who dared to try and start something—I took a deep breath and as calmly as I could said, "Can I run your bath, darling? Then we can talk. I want you to get warm and comfortable, please."

She rose and slouched to our bedroom. Not the confident Bubbles I knew. Something had changed. She seemed unsure of herself. I had to get things right. I needed to fix this and get my Bubbles back.

Chapter 19

Atlanta, GA
January 2007

Maita

Returning home to Chris seemed premature; I needed to be away from him longer to process what happened, and everything leading up to the big fight we'd had two weeks ago, before the row we had three days ago. I was beginning to lose count of the arguments. Now he was walking on eggshells, bending over backward to please me, and the bubble bath he was preparing was an attempt at appeasement.

"I'll light some candles too," Chris called out from our bathroom. "Soak yourself and take your time. Relax. By the time you're through with your bath, dinner will be ready."

It *was* a little charming when he did this sort of thing, going overboard. It reminded me of that day in London when I received the box of red wine. I had to admit, his ability to turn on the charm had been consistent.

"Thanks," I replied, hardly loud enough for him to hear, and I didn't care. Try as I might, I couldn't bring myself to smile. There was no joy in my heart, and I couldn't fake it.

He transformed the bathroom into a spa-like experience, with dimmed lighting, candles glowing, and the inviting aroma of sweet lavender diffusing through the mist from the tub.

"Indulge yourself," he said, pulling me close and kissing my neck. I tensed, forced a smile and clung to the towel covering my naked body. My body language screamed, *Don't you dare try to get fresh with me right now, and don't even think of taking this towel off. I'm not in the mood.*

He got the message and walked out without a word. I

unwrapped the towel, climbed into the tub, and slowly lowered myself into the warm water.

Chris popped back in. "Oops, I forgot the most important ingredient to this whole production: your music. What will it be?" He plugged the portable radio into the wall and connected it to my iPhone.

"Anything I want, right? Even if it's R&B, which you can't stand?" I asked, heavy with sarcasm. I couldn't help myself. After all, it was my music choice that had initiated the violent argument two weeks ago.

He turned red in the face, his muscles tensing as he tried to process my words without blowing up.

Realizing that I had opened up a fresh wound, which was uncalled for, and considering he was doing everything to make up for the way he'd treated me, I quickly added, "Please play the 'Babyface' playlist. Thanks."

Quietly, he scrolled down the playlist, and again left the bathroom without a word. He didn't even turn to look at me. With my eyes closed, I took a deep breath, relaxed, and submerged to the bottom of the bathtub. My mind drifted to the events that had led to this unhappy place in our relationship.

*****

After a series of small arguments and misunderstandings, things had truly fallen apart about two weeks ago. I was in a festive mood, because it was three days before Christmas. After graduating in December, I was excited to begin the next chapter of my life. I had made it through a rigorous curriculum and managed to sweat my way through my master's program, all the while working part-time on campus, paying my tuition and living expenses out of pocket. It had been an incredible challenge to which only an international student, with no financial backup or family ties in America, could relate. And yet I survived it, passing with a 3.9 GPA.

To add icing to the cake, my boyfriend invited me to move in with him to a house that I helped choose. It was from here that I would comfortably look for work, given that I had been granted an extra year in the United States through the Optional Practical Training program.

I had encountered many hurdles trying to secure a summer internship in the United States. Getting a public health job proved to be even more complicated, because most companies didn't provide sponsorship for an H-1B visa that would permit me to work legally. After several application rejections, I began exploring my physical therapist options. I realized there was a massive demand for physical therapists nationwide, and many companies offered sponsorship for a work permit and I could eventually qualify for a green card. So that was the route I decided to take. First, I would have to go through the credentialing process, then take the National Physical Therapy Examination. If I passed this challenging exam, I could choose in which state I wanted to live and work. As usual, I had a master plan for my next move, with a clear pathway to achieve my goal.

"You can stay with me, I want us to live together," Chris said after he saw me researching apartment rentals. "Bubbs, you shouldn't have to worry about paying rent now. You can't even find a decent job."

I agreed, not only because it was an opportunity to study comfortably without worrying about paying for housing, but because I believed I was in love. Chris was thrilled, even hinting at making this a longtime commitment as Mr. and Mrs.

So that Friday, two weeks ago, was a day to celebrate past achievements—and a bright, exciting future.

We ordered our favorite Chinese—General Tso's chicken and fried rice—and Chris began mixing a cocktail at the bar. We were having a good time chatting, laughing, and dancing to music. I loved moments like these when we enjoyed each other's company. They came naturally, like we were made for each other.

After a while, as Chris continued to mix his cocktails, I

switched to a glass of red wine.

All hell broke loose, though, when I changed the music to a song by Beyoncé, "Irreplaceable," which was my favorite song of the moment. Wineglass in hand, I got up to dance. With a disgusted look, Chris said, "Oh, come on, turn that off and play something better. You know I can't stand that music."

Ignoring him, I continued to dance and sing along, making dramatic gestures incited by the lyrics. "To the left, to the left," I sang.

"Turn off that *stupid* song," he snapped.

I paused the song. "Well, I really like it. Can I just dance to it?"

"No, you know I don't like that kind of music," he repeated.

"What kind? R&B? So I can't listen to the music I like?"

"Play something we both enjoy, like U2 or Coldplay. Not that shit."

"My music is *not* shit, and this happens to be a great song."

"You like U2 and Coldplay too, don't you?" he asked, sitting up from his slouched position on the couch. He placed his cocktail glass on the coffee table.

"I do, but I also like other kinds of music. I don't like Oasis, but I let you play their music on full blast in the car. Hell, I even went to an Oasis concert with you. It's called compromise." I was getting angry.

"So, you only came to the concert to please me?"

"No, I wanted to enjoy the time with you, because it's your favorite band. I had fun; I can be versatile. You should try that sometimes. You can't call my music shit because it's Black music." And with that, I pressed play and started to dance again.

"How dare you pull the race card on me in my house because I don't like your music."

I yelled back, "You never let me play any R&B and hip-hop songs, and you're only glad when I dance and sing along to pop and rock. You're lucky I happen to like a variety of music. Otherwise, we would never listen to *your* music either."

"Cut that music off. It's my house, and I won't tolerate songs, or anything that I don't appreciate."

Turning up the volume and shouting back in rage, I replied, "It's just a song, for goodness's sake. Let me have a moment to enjoy it, and it will be over." With that, I accidentally spilled some wine onto the carpet.

Chris jumped up from his seat and pointed at the floor. "First, you play that awful music, and now you're spoiling my carpet."

I stopped the music and ran to get a saltshaker from the kitchen. I'd read somewhere that pouring salt over the red wine would minimize the carpet stain.

"Stop it. That won't work. If you had just listened to me in the first place—"

I threw the radio remote at him. "Here, take *your* remote so you can choose the songs you like. After all, it's *your* house. You know what, Chris? I'm tired of your selfish tantrums. You only want to do things that please you. You invited me to move in with you for *your* pleasure, and to keep you company, but only on *your* terms." I fumed. "Why must I always be reminded that this is your house? I can never feel at home here."

He replied, "You're being dramatic. Tell me when I made you feel unwelcome."

I started to laugh in genuine disbelief. Chris had no idea how self-centered or unsupportive he could be.

"What's so funny?"

"That you still don't care about my feelings. I don't have to be here."

"Where are you going to go? You're unemployed and have no money."

"So, you think you're doing me a favor? I may be broke now, but I won't be this way forever. I can't stay here and have you treat me this way. I'm leaving now."

"Where will you go at two a.m. on a Saturday?"

"I still have the keys to my room on campus."

He snorted. "Good luck getting to Atlanta from Stockbridge at this hour. Have you forgotten that you don't have a car?"

He had a maddening smirk on his face. And he was right, it had started to rain earlier and getting a taxi on a rainy Saturday after midnight would be difficult.

"Do you *like* the fact that I'm at your mercy?" It dawned on me that I'd set myself up for a lousy situation of dependency. "I don't need you. I'm going back to my place now."

"You have nothing except some bags and boxes of books. What has all that time at that expensive university done except leave you penniless? You *do* need me," he shouted. "Sure, get your things and leave now. Let's see how far you can go."

I started to walk toward the bedroom, taking in what he'd just said. He perceived me as desperate and in need of his assistance. Since the day I met Chris, he'd never valued my academic achievements and ambitions, and seemed to enjoy having some control over me. We'd had this conversation many times before—for instance, when he insisted we go halves on dinner, and Chris couldn't understand why he had to pay for the both of us. He was never sensitive to my situation as a student and somehow expected me to be at his level financially.

I stopped at the bedroom doorway and said, "You know what? I'm not leaving, not tonight, anyway. You convinced me to leave my comfortable apartment on campus and move here because it was best for *us*. You can't turn around and tell me to leave when it suits you."

He replied, "You said you were leaving first, didn't you?"

"Well, I've changed my mind. I'm staying tonight. I'm going to bed now, but I'm not sure I want to stay here with you anymore. Good night."

I decided that if I were to leave that night, it would be on my terms. I must have struck a nerve, because Chris took long and quick strides toward me, grabbed my arm and hissed, "I want you out of my house now."

I looked him in the eyes. "Leave me alone, Chris. I'm too tired for this drama. I'm going to bed."

He tightened his grip. "Not in my bedroom. Get out."

I tried to release his fingers, but he squeezed harder. I felt his nails digging into my flesh.

"Let me go, please, you're hurting me."

He started to push me in the direction of the front door. I tried to resist, but he was much stronger.

"Get *away* from me, Chris," I shouted.

"I want you to leave now. How dare you pull the race card on me, in my house, then call me controlling and selfish? If you feel so uncomfortable here, then go now."

We began to shove at each other. I tried to pull away, but Chris wouldn't let go of his firm and painful grip. "You're hurting me," I groaned.

He released my arm and pushed me to the floor. I landed on my side with a *thud* and lay there, defeated, as he stood over me with a triumphant grin. Slowly getting up, my hip throbbing from the impact, I said, "You hurt me."

Once on my feet, I limped past him to get into the bedroom. He turned around and came after me.

"Please, let me go to bed," I said, wishing I had shut the bedroom door to keep him out. But I knew I didn't have the strength to keep him from pushing the door open, and it had no lock.

"Leave my bed alone," Chris snarled. "Do not touch my stuff. I'm mean and selfish, after all."

I sat on the bed, considering my options, just hoping he would let me to sleep. Surely he wasn't serious about throwing me out at this hour, in the cold rain. "Let's talk tomorrow morning," I said in a low, defeated voice. Tomorrow would be another day to organize and make a plan.

I was opening the bed covers when Chris lunged at me in a fury. "Get out of my house, *bitch*," he screamed. Again he grabbed me by my arm. He tried to haul me away from the bed, but I stubbornly held on to the bedpost with my hand. As he pulled harder, I held on tighter and refused to give in, and the bed began to move each time he pulled me.

"Stop it, Chris. Let me go!" I cried.

"Bitch, I said get out. You don't need me, right?"

I was shocked at the monster he had become, and disgusted by his foul language. His eyes were narrow and dark, and his face flushed in red. Possessed by a furious demon. I had never seen him look or speak that way.

"Let's calm down and have a civilized conversation," I said, but we had reached the point of no return. I was afraid, overcome with intense fear, a feeling I had never had in my life—fear of being harmed. So, I let go of the bedpost, hoping that it would appease him.

It didn't. Instead, he grabbed me with both hands and pushed me into the living room.

"Get your stuff and find your own way out of here. You think you're so smart? Well, let's see just how far you can go."

I decided to stop fighting, afraid of what he could do to me, and just too tired to resist. It was December, and almost three a.m., but I wasn't scared of the cold or the dark—just terrified of this person I couldn't recognize.

He let me go and disappeared into the bedroom. I began to look around the living area and couches for my phone, still trying to process what had just happened. He reappeared with my handbag and vanity bag in hand and walked to the front door. I watched in shock and horror as he opened the door and threw my handbag into the dark, wet, and cold morning. "Go on. Get your shit out of my house." He proceeded to throw my vanity bag and boots outside.

I was speechless. Chris wanted a fight, but I wasn't going to give him that satisfaction. Mumbling to himself, he grabbed my coat from the coat rack and tossed it outside too. I limped to the door and without looking back, I stumbled out, shaking in fear and disbelief.

With trembling hands I gathered my belongings, put on my boots and now-damp coat, and flung my vanity bag and handbag onto my shoulder as he stood at the doorway watching me. Thanking God for my phone, I thought about calling for a taxi or one of my friends. I wasn't sure who to call at this witching hour. Besides, most of my friends had left campus and returned to their homes.

On either side, vacant lots surrounded Chris's house, and across the road was a house under construction. There were no streetlights, and no traffic, just our Christmas lights and darkness. I slowly limped down the driveway toward the road, guided by the cobbles. My arms throbbed from his tight grip, and my legs felt like lead with each step into the dark. My mind was racing. Thoughts of serial killers and rapists flashed through my head, and still I tried to think of who I could call—the cops, maybe—to ask for a ride to the Emory campus.

I didn't look back and figured he must be pleased and satisfied to see me in this pitiful state. I scrolled through my phone contacts, praying to get some cell phone reception. I often had trouble getting a good signal in this area. Who could I call?

Just then, I saw the headlights of a car driving toward me. My heart began pounding. What should I do? Walk back to the house and beg Chris to let me in? Stop the car and ask for a ride to the nearest police station, and risk being taken by a serial killer?

I decided to step back and call my friend, Simone, who lived in Marietta. How embarrassing this call would be. What would I say? I watched in fear as the car drove past me. It slowed down, made a U-turn, and slowly drove back toward me. I thought I might go into cardiac arrest and realized that I'd been crying the whole time. The drizzle was doing an excellent job of washing the tears away, but I could taste the salt as the car pulled over and stopped.

I froze in fear. I had dialed 911 and was ready to press the call button when the driver rolled down the window and said in a slow, Southern drawl, "Ma'am, are you okay? Do you need help getting somewhere?"

For the first time since I had walked out of Chris's house, I looked back, not sure what I expected—maybe a witness—in case I disappeared. Chris wasn't standing at the door, but I saw him looking out through the window.

"Ma'am," he repeated. "Do you need help?"

I wiped tears off my face and stammered, "Yes, I need to get away from here. I need to get to Atlanta."

"Well, you need to get out of the rain. We can drive you to Atlanta or call the police to come and take you where you need to go, whichever option you prefer. Do you know the address of where you need to go?"

"Yes, I live on campus at Emory University."

He paused, then said, "That's a long way from here. We can take you to the local police, and they will take care of you." That's when I noticed there were two men; the one in the passenger seat sat quietly. I glanced back at the house and saw that Chris was now standing at the door.

"I-I think I'll w-wait here and call the police. Thank you very much for your k-kind offer," I said, not sure if I was stuttering because of the cold, pain, fear, or all three.

He turned his engine off. "Ma'am, you'll catch a bad cold in this rain. Please wait in the car. I'll call the police now." I hesitated, then thought of how warm it must be in that car. I agreed to wait with them in the car, which was just as warm as I imagined. I heaved a sigh of relief as I heard this stranger speak to the police on speaker. "The police are on their way. We'll wait here with you. Please, don't be afraid. It's very dangerous for a young lady to be out at this hour alone."

"Thank you so much," I replied timidly. I wanted to ask why they were out at three in the morning, but he spoke first.

"If you don't mind my asking, what happened to you?" He asked this as he turned on the light in the car. He was a heavyset man, probably in his fifties, with round cheeks and droopy eyes, the sort of person I would imagine to be a farmer or local pastor. His friend wore an Atlanta Falcons cap, and he looked younger, maybe in his thirties, with a thin mustache and a slim face.

"I just had a big fight with my boyfriend," I said truthfully. "He kicked me out of his house."

Both men sat up, shook their heads. "I don't care what the

fight was about, but no man should ever treat a woman that bad as to leave her out in the rain at three in the morning." His Southern drawl was charming, even comforting. "Did he hurt you, ma'am? My name is Pete Franklin, by the way, and this is my brother, Jeb. We live two blocks from here, and we're driving home from a game night with friends in McDonough."

"My name is Maita. I appreciate your kindness."

His silent brother spoke for the first time. "That's a strange name, and you have an accent. Where are you from?"

Here we go again, I thought. Every day since I had ventured into foreign countries, questions regarding my name's meaning, or how to pronounce it, had become the story of my life. "I'm from Zimbabwe."

"That's in Africa, right?" Jeb said. "Southern Africa?"

"Yes," I replied.

"You're a long way from home. How long have you been here?"

"I came here in 2004, as a graduate student at Emory University."

"That's an outstanding university," said Pete. "You must be a smart lady to come this far. I hope you've had a good experience in this country."

The irony of that statement at that very moment made me laugh. "Yes, until now, I guess." And they both laughed along.

"Well, ma'am, I hope we can show you that there are good people in this country." These two angels managed to make me forget that, not too long ago, I was trembling in the cold rain and afraid for my life. "Did he hurt you?"

Before I could answer, there was a loud knock on my window. It was so unexpected that it startled me, and I jumped in my seat. It was Chris, knocking and motioning for me to open the window.

"Is that your boyfriend?" asked Jeb, clearly surprised that my boyfriend was a white man and not a Black man.

"Yes, that's him."

"Do you want to talk to him?"

"No," I said firmly.

By this time, Chris had walked over to the driver's window, knocking desperately. Pete lowered his window. "Sir, she doesn't want to talk to you right now," he said, like a principal lecturing a wayward student.

"Maita, please let me talk to you."

I shook my head and looked away from him. His presence upset me. My eyes welled with tears.

"Sir, calm down," Pete said. "You can talk to her when the police get here."

Chris's eyes widened at the mention of the police. Before he could reply, blue flashing lights illuminated the street. The police car drove up quietly. I never felt so happy to see a police car in my life. Chris just stood outside, paralyzed by the events unfolding before him.

We all got out of the car as the officer approached us. He looked puzzled by this awkward group of people, and there I was in the middle of all the drama.

"Good morning, Officer. This young lady had an altercation with her boyfriend here," Pete said, pointing to me first, then Chris. "We found her out here in the rain after he threw her out."

Chris's face was now pale white, a clear contrast from a few moments ago when seething rage had turned it fiery red. He tried to say something, but the young officer held his hand out to silence him. "Young lady, are you okay? Did he hurt you?"

I had dodged that question before, maybe because I didn't want to admit that I felt violated by Chris's pulling, shoving, tugging, and name-calling. Did that constitute physical harm and domestic violence? Would they arrest him?

"Ma'am, did he harm you at all?"

I looked at Chris, who now seemed powerless, helpless and shaken.

"No, he didn't hurt me, but we shouted at each other angrily, and he threw me out. These gentlemen have been so kind to me. I don't know what I would have done if not for them."

The officer reached out a hand to Pete. "Thank you, sir, for helping. I'll take it from here." They shook hands, and both Pete and Jeb nodded at me.

"Thank you, and God bless you," I said, and meant it.

They waved, and as he entered the car Jeb said, "Take care, and all the best with everything."

They drove off, leaving the three of us standing in the blue lights.

"Ma'am, do you have everything you need?" the officer asked. "Before we leave, I would like you to know that you can press charges if he assaulted you, and I can take him in now." He spoke as if Chris wasn't standing there. "Do you have any bruises or signs of physical harm?"

The sheepish look on Chris's face was all the revenge I needed. "No, he didn't harm me, and I won't press charges."

"Okay then, where do you want me to take you?"

"I live on the Emory University campus, at North Druid Hills."

He paused. "I'm afraid that's out of my jurisdiction, so I can't take you all the way. However, I can drive you to the police station in Atlanta, and they can get you home."

The rain had stopped. Slowly nodding, I said, "That will be fine. Can I go and get a few things real quick?" I asked, rummaging through my handbag. "I can't find the keys to my apartment. I think I left them inside. Or they may have fallen out when Chris threw out my handbag."

The officer gave Chris a quick look of disgust. "Sure, do you feel safe going back into that house with him?"

Again, he spoke like Chris was nowhere in sight. I almost laughed at the confused look on Chris's face. He probably didn't think that what had happened between us was considered domestic violence, and clearly he was at my mercy. I was sure I had bruises on my arms, and could have him arrested.

An arrest—and involvement with the courts for domestic violence charges—could negatively impact Chris's job and visa status, putting an end to his American dream. Chris knew this, and that explained why, for someone with a hair-trigger temper, he remained composed. I was upset, but I couldn't jeopardize his career: the humiliation he was experiencing was enough.

"I'll be okay," I said. "I don't think he'll do anything to me."

The officer seemed determined to make Chris uncomfortable. "I'll escort you in, just in case."

I looked everywhere for my keys but couldn't find them, even after searching thoroughly under the couches and between the cushions, in the kitchen, and the bedroom. Chris was watching quietly, too afraid to speak. Frustrated and anxious, I imagined how disorganized I must have appeared as the policeman looked on helplessly.

"Any way I can help you?" asked the officer, most likely getting a little impatient.

"Maybe they fell outside, but it's too dark out there."

"I can use my flashlight. Let's go and have a look." So we went outside to look some more, but returned to the house with no luck. "Is there anywhere else I can take you?"

I took a deep breath and tried to decide whether it was even appropriate to show up at anyone's house now. Maybe a hotel would do, but I couldn't afford it.

Chris finally gathered the guts to say something. "You can sleep here, and tomorrow morning, or rather later this morning, you can decide where you want to go."

The officer turned to look at me. It was apparent I was considering this offer. After all, I was exhausted and frustrated from the early morning events, and now stranded with nowhere to go. "You don't have to stay here if you feel uncomfortable. Do you have a friend to call on?"

"Yes, I do have a few friends, but they all live far, and it's late."

"Maita, you can take whichever bedroom you like. I won't disturb you. I promise." He hardly ever called me by my real name. It was always Bubbles for him. He truly was shaken.

"I think I'll stay here for the night. I'm so sorry if I took up your time, sir."

"It's not a problem at all. I just want you to be safe. You don't have to stay here. I don't want anything to happen to you."

"Thank you for your concern. I'll be fine, I'm sure."

"Well, okay, you just call us back if you feel threatened. I will patrol around this area some more so I'll be close by if you need me."

I was so grateful for the police service. I'd never had to call 911, and this officer did an exceptional job in making me feel like I had support somewhere. The officer warned Chris that he was close by, and if anything happened, he would be back. I felt safe, and also enjoyed watching Chris's display of shock and fear.

As soon as the officer left, Chris turned to me and said, "I am so sorry. I know you probably don't want to hear from me right now."

"I don't," I replied. "I just want to sleep, thank you."

"Okay, you can have our room. I'll sleep here on the couch."

I nodded and mumbled, "Sounds good. Good night." I took my phone and handbag and walked away to the bedroom, relieved that all the mayhem and drama was over. My body was aching, and I wanted to sleep and forget about this crazy early-morning chaos that all started because of a song and dance.

Chris's reaction when I attempted to leave him later that day left me even more terrified. It was hours after our big fight, in the late afternoon, when he fell to the ground clutching his chest, gasping for air, having what looked like cardiac arrest and crying, "Don't leave me!" I remember how I panicked and fell to my knees beside him to check if he was okay. And when I said I was calling 911, he cried, "No, don't, just stay here with me," and he gradually simmered down and stopped crying. Before that panic attack, I had packed my bags to go to Simone's till I had a clear plan. But instead I unpacked and stayed. I couldn't leave him alone, not like that.

*****

That was how we had come to this point in our relationship, where Chris was treading carefully around me, and trying hard to impress me. And I was seriously considering my options. I deserved better than this toxic relationship. I had to figure out my next move. As much as I would have liked to walk away and prove a point to Chris that I was independent, I didn't have the courage because I *did* care for him, and I wanted *us* to work. I believed I was in love, but our misunderstandings were fracturing our bond, and this fight was a big blow.

I soaked in the warm tub, humming along to Babyface's smooth voice, and I concluded that I was staying—for now. Maybe we just needed time to work through this rough patch. But how much more insult could our relationship withstand?

Chapter 20

London, UK
January 2007

Ade

My relationship with Noma had deteriorated beyond repair. Her unpredictable mood swings made it unbearable to be around her, as if she suffered perpetually from premenstrual stress. Easily irritated by anything I said, she seemed to have a permanent frown on her face. Our sex life was virtually nonexistent, and we hardly cuddled or showed affection toward each other. Kissing her had become a distant memory.

We hadn't been intimate in over a month now, and I had begun to have erotic dreams like a teenage boy. I dreamed I was having raunchy sex with an unknown female, and at that moment, the steamy sexual encounters with this anonymous woman felt so real. I could feel her soft, full lips on mine, the weight of her petite body on me. And as she would ride me, thrusting her pelvis back and forth, I held her hip with one hand, the other grabbing her voluptuous breast.

Often I woke up with an erection, and sometimes to my embarrassment found I'd actually ejaculated.

Gradually, the recurring dreams became a nurtured fantasy. I started to imagine what could have happened between me and Bubbles, if I hadn't made an emotional decision driven by bitterness and vengeance. Could Bubbles be the faceless woman in my dreams?

Meanwhile, Noma lay beside me in deep slumber, wholly ignorant of my sex dreams. My attempts to touch or kiss her were often met with a hostile shrug. With each rejection, my sexual desire for her waned, and now despite my desperation for intimacy, I didn't seek satisfaction from Noma, not anymore. She never made time for us to discuss this problem, and when I tried to talk to her about it, she blamed fatigue from working long shifts, headaches, or premenstrual bloating and discomfort.

As time went on, I soon learned why Noma was increasingly cold and moody toward me. Her best friend Monica began texting and calling me, warning me about Noma and her family. The first time I received a text message from Monica, she said that Noma had given her my mobile number in case of emergencies. Right then, she couldn't reach Noma and was worried about her. I reassured her Noma was fine, and at home sleeping. That was the first of many texts:

Do you know any good Nigerian restaurants in North London?

I replied:

Try Abi's African cuisine, in Seven Sisters.

Noma's birthday is coming up. Let me know if you need ideas for a gift.

My reply:

I already got something thanks.

I'm at work on a night shift, Noma said you are on-call. Needed to chat with someone and it's 2 am. So I thought of you. Are you busy?

I replied:

Busy. Can't talk.

I told Noma about Monica's text messages, and that I was uncomfortable with her texting so much. She brushed off my concern, and said Monica meant nothing by it. Monica was like a sister to her, just being overly friendly. Then Monica's texts became too personal for comfort:

Are things okay between you and Noma?

Why do you ask?

Just curious. She complains a lot about stuff.

What do you mean?

Can't text. Need to call. But she can't know I talked to you.

Call me in 30 mins. I'm at work.

That was how Monica informed me that Noma's mother and sister had instructed Noma to give me the cold treatment, since I hadn't made any indication that I would be proposing. According to Monica, Noma complained that I avoided the topic of marriage, and never discussed having children or anything that implied a long-term commitment. Worst of all, I hadn't introduced Noma to my parents.

My parents owned several successful businesses in Nigeria, and they would visit England three to four times a year. Each time they stayed in England, they lived in their three-bedroom house in Surrey. I would see them often, but not once had I taken Noma with me.

"Why can't I meet your parents? Am I not good enough for them?" Noma would ask.

"Not now," I'd say, "but soon."

I couldn't explain why I was hesitant. Perhaps because I once introduced my parents to a girl, and they'd liked her a lot. They fell for Bubbles' charm, and they began to talk of her as their daughter. She checked all their boxes and they were excited that, finally, I would settle down. My parents would take us out to dinner, and sometimes my mother prepared traditional Yoruba meals for us, often insisting that Bubbles watch and learn like an apprentice. Mum even had a Yoruba traditional outfit made for Bubbles, an Ìró and Bùbá, and matching Gèlè. It was at least two sizes too big, and she joked about how Bubbles would soon grow into it, a heavy hint that didn't go unnoticed.

Mum and Dad were heartbroken when I broke the news to them that Bubbles had left me. "What did you do to her?" my father asked. "Such a nice young lady. Why don't you go to America and bring her back? She can study here in England. Why must she be so far away?"

They assumed that she'd left to study abroad, not realizing that we had broken up and she had left me for good. "We're not together anymore, and she's not coming back," I told them. But I couldn't provide a concrete reason why our relationship ended. "And just so you know, she walked out on *me*."

They were deeply disappointed, but my mother was affected the most. I later found out that she was more concerned about the impact the breakup had on me, because I couldn't mask my pain, not even from my family.

In the days and weeks that followed Bubbles' departure, Bola tried to cheer me up with movie and dinner dates. She was at my apartment every weekend, cooking my favorites like *jollof* rice, and *gaari* with *egusi* soup. She stuffed me with junk food and wine as we indulged in Nigerian movies and boring soap operas. Needless to say, Bola was glad when I met Noma. I had a girlfriend to take my miseries away. Bola liked Noma, but sometimes it seemed like she was trying too hard to create a bond between them, perhaps to ensure that this time my relationship would last, because she didn't want me to be lonely again.

"Mum is always asking about Noma, about when you will introduce her. She wants to know how serious you are."

"What have you told her?" I asked, a little annoyed that they were discussing my relationship.

"Nothing, just that she's a nice girl. She wonders if you have an obsession for Zimbabwean girls," she replied with a chuckle. "Your ex was—"

"Look, I will introduce her when I'm ready," I snapped. The reference to Bubbles constantly stirred up anger that I couldn't explain. I had been angry for a long time, and it had evolved into bitterness and resentment.

Now, I had come full circle and wanted Bubbles back in my life. And this time, I was willing to go to great lengths to do it. Despite all that had transpired in 2005, I never stopped loving her. I'd tried to, but I had failed.

After one of my sexy dreams, there was a time when my frustration intensified, and I sat up in bed and repeatedly banged my head against the headboard. However, it quickly turned into excitement when I remembered how quickly Bubbles had replied to my email, and that she had also given me her new mobile number. I understood why she didn't want to communicate via email, especially if she lived with her boyfriend. Besides, a cell phone was more private and intimate.

I decided to comply and reach out with a text. After calculating our time difference—England was five hours ahead of Atlanta—I had to figure out the best time of day to do so, a time that would not arouse suspicion from her boyfriend. I grinned at the thought, like a teenage boy waiting to call his girlfriend when her parents were out of the house. I must admit, sneaking to contact my ex-girlfriend behind Noma's back was arousing. The idea that we could have a secret relationship, and the fact that we were once lovers, had me fantasizing about a romantic rendezvous with Bubbles.

Assuming that she had graduated and was probably working, I decided to text her between nine and five p.m., when she would most likely be away from her boyfriend.

It was a cold, frosty Wednesday evening. I had completed my ward rounds and was in the doctors' office wrapping up the day.

The office was a tiny room on the second floor at the end of the hall that housed administrative offices. I sat at one of the five computer stations where doctors completed medical notes, reviewed patient records, or researched on the internet. Doctors took breaks here, away from the busy wards and background noise of humming and beeping machines, family members concerned about their loved ones, and other clinicians needing one thing or the other. I had waited all day to send a text and decided this was a good time.

With a slight tremor in my hand, I scrolled through my contacts to Bubbles, ashamed at how nervous I was. I had the number saved under her nickname, a name that Noma didn't know. I initiated the text conversation with a short message:

Hi, it's Ade here. How are you?

Expecting another quick response, I was disappointed when she hadn't replied after waiting five minutes. She must be occupied with work, I figured. I'd try later this evening. My workday had ended earlier than usual. I didn't usually leave the hospital before four thirty, so I decided to stop by the gym on my way home. I had resumed regular exercise, because after shedding all the weight two years ago, my belly was starting to bulge again, and the pounds were piling up.

My weight had always been an issue with Bubbles, who made it clear from our early days of dating that she preferred a leaner, athletic guy, and I was the opposite. At five-foot-ten with broad shoulders, a wide middle and a strong neck, I towered over her petite five-foot-three frame. And back then, when I stood next to her, she looked much younger than her twenty-three years, and I was just twenty-nine years old. She was obsessed with maintaining a slim figure and had what I called the *skinny girl complex.*

With time, my heavyset body didn't matter to her. She accepted me as I was. I knew this, because Bubbles was very blunt, saying what she meant and meaning it. She told me that I wasn't her type, but in her own words added, "I think judging a man by his looks is so high school. At this stage in my life, I need more than a Brad Pitt lookalike, the same way you probably need to stop fantasizing about Naomi Campbell."

We had both laughed. "So, I guess I do have a chance with you after all?"

"Yeah, of course." She chuckled. "Or else I wouldn't be entertaining you at all." Those were the conversations we had during the *getting to know you* phase of our relationship. She was brutally honest, but in the most charming way. She qualified her statement by saying, "I'm not going to date a dude with no career and no plan. I need financial security."

"You mean, no broke dudes?"

"Aha! You got it. It's a plus to have a man who can take care of his woman."

That evening I left the gym and threw my gym bag in the boot of my car. Before driving, I checked my phone for messages and was happy to see a text message from Bubbles:

I'm good. How are you?

I turned the engine on to start the heater, then began a series of text messages:

> *I'm fine, just left the gym. Still trying to be slim and trim. What are you up to?*

Nothing, just chilling at home.

> *So, where is home? You just graduated, right?*

I moved in with my boyfriend.

> *Big step. I guess that means you're serious with this guy. Reminds me of when you moved in with me. I miss those days.*

After a pause that lasted about three minutes, I began to wonder if I had pushed too hard to get details. But try as I may, I couldn't resist bringing up the past. I felt entitled, because she was mine first, and therefore I still had a right to talk about our history. I longed to hear her voice, and if I could, I would call and tell Bubbles to leave this man and come back to me. But in reality, I had been given that chance and I turned it down. Now I was on the outside and had to wait on Bubbles to let me back in.

Just as I began to put the car into reverse, my phone vibrated.

And who do you live with?

She had deliberately ignored my last message. *Why is she asking? Like she doesn't know I moved in with Noma?* I had told her on that day at the Covent Garden Tube station.

> *Still with Noma, but not sure how long that will last.*

Why?

> *Good question. I think I may have rushed the whole relationship. I must have been on the rebound. So, just a word of advice: be sure about this dude before you move in. Don't commit too fast unless you're sure.*

Another long pause followed. I assumed she was texting a reply, so I waited patiently. After close to five minutes without a response, I decided to call it quits. I had a strong urge to call and talk to her right then, but I couldn't bring myself to do it. After all, she had asked me not to do that. I had to respect that.

Ten whole minutes passed, and she hadn't responded to my last message. Had I upset her in any way? I punched the steering wheel, unintentionally blowing the car horn and startling a young lady walking nearby. I was too old for this foolish, childish game of secret texts. It was unnerving, having to hold my breath waiting for a text back.

"Call and talk to her," I said out loud. "And tell her exactly how you feel." We could cut through the niceties and get to the point.

I was determined to make a voice call, ready to make a direct international call, when a text message finally came in:

> *I'm sorry things aren't working out for you and your girlfriend. I'm happy with my boyfriend, and I don't think we should continue chatting. Thank you for reaching out. Please don't contact me again. Goodbye.*

I felt like I had been sucker-punched. The message and its tone hit me hard, and the impact was as damaging as Bubbles intended it to be. Oddly, that didn't read like something Bubbles would say. I had heard that when a person experienced hurt or pain, they were left scarred, and this could change them for the worst. Perhaps she had become that way—cold and uncaring in her words. I should have known better. I'd been in that exact situation not too long ago. I'd gone from being a very caring and loving boyfriend to being guarded and bitter, vowing never to fall so hard for anyone again. Now the tables had turned.

The Bubbles I knew would have made her point clear, but in a more pleasant way. This "texting Bubbles" bluntly told me off, wanted me to know that she was happy, and that I must leave her alone. I was too tired and downcast to think this through. This wasn't the end; I just knew it. I would make one more attempt—not today, but soon.

Chapter 21

Atlanta, GA
January 2007

Chris

I sat in my office, staring at my computer screen, unable to concentrate. I'd been on the phone with my sister Nicki, and was in a good mood, but now I was upset. After calling Nicki several times and leaving messages, she had finally returned my calls.

I said, "Lovely to hear from you, I thought you'd never call back."

"I can never figure out the time difference. Thought I'd chance a call before leaving work. I'm calling from my work landline. Don't worry, it's not a direct international call."

"I don't want you to get fired for running up a huge phone bill."

"I'm using a phone card, says I've four minutes remaining. How can that be? It's supposed to have five minutes of talk time."

"Those stupid cards are a scam, a waste of money. They charge you a connection fee. You want me to call you on your mobile?"

"Dropped it in the loo earlier today. Gotta get a new one."

It was typical clumsiness by Nicki, but I said, "That's terrible. How're you doing?"

"Good. Annoyed about my phone."

I imagined her sitting behind a desk and wondered how her office workmates put up with her gothic looks, including the studded boots and multiple piercings. She had kept that job steady for years. With little ambition and a simple lifestyle, Nicki was content with hanging with her gang of friends and shacking up with her boyfriend of ten years.

"How are Mom and Dad doing?" I asked.

"Good. Don't see them much. Two jobs keep me busy."

Nicki worked as a receptionist by day, and a bartender by night.

"Got your voice mails. You said you have something to tell me, what is it? Hurry because this phone card will run out of credit soon."

I felt rushed, but I had to tell her my plan. Her opinion mattered to me. We grew up as best friends. Nicki was a tomboy who preferred to play with the boys in our neighborhood. We drifted apart after graduating from high school when I enrolled in an apprenticeship program, and she opted to work odd jobs. She befriended the goth crew and transformed her appearance. In contrast, I became more formal in my relationships as I developed a professional career. As a result, we matured into very different adults.

We hardly discussed our personal lives, and I resented how Nicki continued to take care of her no-good boyfriend who was unemployed, smoked weed, drank excessively, and slept all day. He was a right-wing fanatic, hated Jews and Blacks, was an actual racist, and also gothic like Nicki. I had never asked Nicki what she thought about his bigoted views; we just never got into such deep conversations. That's why I had waited months before telling her about Maita, not sure of how she'd react. I was pleasantly surprised when Nicki said she was happy for me and couldn't wait to meet Maita.

"I've told you about Maita, my girlfriend—"

"Yah, how're you two doing?"

"Great." Not entirely true. But we were working on it.

"We've been together about a year and a half. I think I'm ready for Mum and Dad to meet her. I want to marry her. What d'you think?"

"What do you mean, what do I think? Wow, you are serious,

aren't you?"

"You think they have an issue with her being Black?"

I exhaled deeply after saying this. I hadn't realized how much I wanted their approval, and blessing. A beeping sound interrupted the silence.

"That beeping is a warning that I have less than a minute of credit left. Mum doesn't have a problem. Dad, well, you know him. He never says much. I don't think he cares. Bring her over. I'd love to meet her."

"Thanks Nicki, it means a lot to me."

"I hope she says yes. I gotta run and catch my bus. Bye. Love you."

The line cut off. I had her blessing, and that was good enough.

It was after that uplifting phone call when I received a text from Ade, followed by an exchange of messages that left me irate. He thought he'd been chatting with Bubbles and was ready to lure her into cheating on me. To add insult to injury, he was planting seeds of doubt in her mind, encouraging Bubbles to second-guess moving in with me. He had no idea how poisonous those text messages could be, given how vulnerable our relationship was right now.

After returning home a few days ago, Bubbles wasn't as cheerful and optimistic as she used to be. No morning and good night kiss, certainly no cuddling, and we hadn't had sex at all. She was just never in the mood.

She spent her days at home alone, and I'd call to check on her.

"Hey, babe, what are you up to? Had enough of *48 Hours* on telly?" I'd ask cheerfully.

"I haven't watched TV all day. Too busy doing some research online."

"All day? What are you looking for?" I tried to appear interested in her daily activities.

"Just looking up public health-related jobs and licensing requirements for physical therapy," she replied in a very solemn voice, and said nothing more.

Lately, I felt like Bubbles had shut me out of her life, with no plan to let me back in. I deserved it, because my actions the morning we had the big row were inexcusable. I was ashamed, and disgusted at myself. I had *never* laid a hand on a woman, but I had come close to it with Mabel, my ex-girlfriend. I couldn't blame it on the alcohol, not entirely. I still couldn't get over that the police got involved, and I could have been arrested for domestic abuse or assault. The thought terrified me. And yet, after everything I said and did, Bubbles didn't file charges against me; instead, she protected me. Even in that moment she cared about me. I promised myself I would do better, and even considered anger management therapy.

I had begged for forgiveness, and Bubbles assured me that we were fine and it was all in the past now, and yet she was holding a grudge. I had done the cliché thing and surprised her with flowers, which she'd accepted with a faint smile and a blunt, "Thanks."

I then decided to cheer her up with a weekend getaway to Las Vegas, something we wanted to do months ago but had to cancel after a quarrel about who was paying. Another one of our arguments where she called me selfish and uncaring. I had suggested we go away to Las Vegas because neither one of us had been there. We picked out some shows to watch and decided to stay at Caesar's Palace. I remember how, when I asked her if she was ready to make a payment, she looked at me in disbelief.

"What do you mean?" she said. "I have to pay for my ticket? I thought you were paying. After all, you brought up the trip to Vegas. You know I'm scraping the barrel for money."

"So, you think that I will just pay for you?" I asked, genuinely surprised that she'd even think that.

"Yes, since you're my boyfriend, I expect you to pay for me, especially after you *invited* me and you know my financial situation."

This concept was new to me. How could I be expected to

finance her holiday? I had always gone halves with my girlfriends, and it was never an issue. I replied, "That's bollocks. I am not a bloody sugar daddy who pays for your holidays. If you can pay for tuition to be at that expensive university, then you should be able to pay for your hotel and airfare."

She shook her head frantically, rolling her eyes. "You don't get it, do you? I have never asked you to take me on expensive shopping sprees or asked for a dime from you. You could never be a sugar daddy even if you tried. Cancel the damn trip, or go by yourself."

There was no Vegas vacation after that.

In hindsight, I acknowledged that maybe I had been a little insensitive to her financial situation as a struggling student. Today, I decided to make the flight and hotel reservations and pay for both of us. I was confident that it would cheer her up. We both needed the break, and the weather in Las Vegas wasn't too bad this time of year. The Caribbean islands would have been a better option, but Bubbles couldn't travel outside the United States yet. I didn't completely understand her visa extension or its limitations, and I'd never bothered to ask her to explain it all to me.

I was pretty pleased with myself for this idea to—hopefully— get us back on track, but then her ex-boyfriend began to text. He threw me off, left me in a bad mood. His last text message was infuriating. "He needs to back off," I said, after reading it a third time. Afraid to give my identity away if I responded in anger, I deleted all the texts and put away my phone.

Glad to have my own office instead of a cubicle surrounded by nosy workmates, I closed my door, sat back, and pondered. I had to decide if I wanted to continue communicating with Ade, or tell him to stop texting and end it all.

I completed the Las Vegas hotel and flight reservations. I even considered first-class tickets, an uncharacteristic move, and a desperate attempt to impress Bubbles, but settled for Economy. Then I decided to send Ade a message:

*I'm sorry things aren't working out for you
and your girlfriend. I'm happy with my
boyfriend, and I don't think we should
continue chatting. Thank you for reaching
out. Please don't contact me again. Goodbye.*

There was no way he could come back after this message that made it clear I wanted him to go away. And sure enough, he didn't respond to my very dismissive message. I felt relief like I had crushed a stubborn bug and—no pun intended—he would stop bugging me. Next, I planned to make dinner reservations, and there I would surprise Bubbles with a weekend in Las Vegas.

I expected Bubbles to be excited about a date night, something we hadn't done in a long while, but her response was the opposite.

"I don't feel like going out to eat," she said, lying on the bed and typing away on her beloved laptop. "Can we order pizza or Chinese takeaway instead?" She dampened my spirit further when I told her about the trip to Vegas, and she replied, "That's very nice of you, but I really can't afford to be going on vacation when I'm unemployed."

I immediately replied, "You don't have to worry about paying. I've taken care of it, and all expenses are on me."

She slowly sat up, with a confused look on her face. "What gives? You're paying for me?" And for the first time in days, she laughed out loud and said something in what must have been her Shona language. "*Mashura!*" she cackled. Bubbles often did that, expressing herself in Shona when she was emotional about something.

"What's so funny?" I asked.

"Well, not too long ago, you told me it wasn't your responsibility to pay for our trip to the Las Vegas you talk of now. So, what's changed? Are you feeling like a sugar daddy now?" There was spite in her voice.

Bubbles and her lethal tongue. She had a way of saying the most hurtful things—the queen of sarcasm, with a comeback for every scenario. I knew she was still mad at me, but I never expected sweet Bubbles to hold on to the anger for so long. How was I to respond to that? Maybe I ought to tell her that I was desperately trying to win her favor. I had stuffed up, and I was trying to clean up my mess.

Instead, I stood at the bedside, speechless. Struggling to contain my rising anger, I could feel my face flushing hot, and it took every ounce of strength in me to resist saying that she was a mean bitch—that she must get over the past or piss off. Rather, I turned away and walked out of the bedroom into the living room. I sat on the couch, angry and disappointed. She could at least be grateful that I had booked a vacation for both of us, I thought, shaking my head. "Unbelievable," I whispered to myself.

"What's unbelievable?"

I jumped in my seat. I hadn't seen Bubbles creep up on me. Afraid of what I might say and do, I decided not to respond.

To my surprise, she sat beside me and said, "Look, I'm sorry. I shouldn't have said that. I need to stop referencing the past." She took a deep breath. "I would love to go to Vegas, and you know that, but I'm so unsure about my future right now. I don't see how I could even enjoy myself."

And just like that, she was the Bubbles I had fallen in love with. All this time, I had convinced myself that she was sad and down because of me, but it was an uncertain future that worried her. She had one year to get a job, or she would have to leave the country and return to Zimbabwe or England. She was unemployed and broke. I could only imagine how stressful that must have been, especially after investing in a master's. I had been too concerned with how she felt about me, and never stopped to consider her situation and what she was going through.

I reached out and drew her close, and kissed her. She didn't resist. I was overwhelmed with passion and just wanted to hold her and never let her go.

"Bubbles, I will take care of you, I promise." She tried to say something, and I kissed her again. "Let me *be* your sugar daddy. I love you so much. You don't have to go through this alone."

Overcome by a lustful force, I ripped her shirt open. The buttons snapped off and fell to the floor. We undressed each other frantically, and for the first time in a long time, we made love on the couch.

With every kiss I surrendered myself, dissolving all the tension of recent weeks. At that moment, I knew that I would do anything for her. It was the best sex we'd had in months, and it felt good to know that we had both laid our feelings bare, and we could start over with a clean slate.

Afterward, we both lay on the couch in a tight embrace—naked, sweaty, and silent. In my mind, we had properly closed the last chapter of the recurrent arguments, and this was a new beginning. I knew now what I had to do to be a good partner. I was prepared to be that caring and supportive boyfriend, and soon—maybe—elevate our relationship to the next level. I was positive Maita was the one.

Chapter 22

Atlanta, GA
January 2007

Maita

Relationships can be complicated and stressful, and ours was no different with highs and lows, but we seemed to be lingering in the low phase. Although we got along fine, Chris's selfish and controlling tendencies often popped up, leaving me with no sense of security, unsure whether to continue with him.

We were together as partners, but it didn't feel like a partnership. I felt alone and afraid to get out into the world and start over. Our cultural differences were at play. I expected that, as the man, he would take care of his woman and provide for me, but this was a foreign concept to Chris, accustomed to being in a fifty-fifty relationship and an every-man-for-himself mentality. He had failed to show concern for my needs as his recently graduated and unemployed girlfriend.

The day that he surprised me with the all-paid trip to Vegas, I had been on the phone for over an hour with my childhood friend, Lindy—short for Lindiwe. For a change, she wasn't the one complaining about her boyfriend cheating or partying too hard; it was my turn to be the disgruntled girlfriend.

Lindy and I had a long history. We grew up in the same neighborhood in Bulawayo, and our mothers were good friends. Her parents received scholarships to study abroad in the early seventies. They met at university in Memphis and had Lindy and her twin brother, Dumisani, in 1979. A year later, in 1980, after a bloody guerrilla war, Rhodesia achieved independence from Britain, and it became Zimbabwe. Like many others in the diaspora, Lindy's parents returned home to a new Zimbabwe, with hopes of partaking in the development of a new democracy. Their advanced degrees and international experience enabled them to climb the professional ladder as high-ranking civil servants, affording them a comfortable, middle-class lifestyle.

Lindy always knew she would return to America. She was the envy of all the kids at school and in our neighborhood. Her mother convinced Lindy to study for her undergraduate degree at the University of Zimbabwe, because she said American universities were too expensive. Their family had been out of the American system for too long, and they couldn't help her financially. "Besides, at the UZ, you're given grants to study," her mother said, when Lindy insisted on taking the SATs. "In America, you get into debt after you graduate. Stay here and go to America for your master's degree."

Unfortunately, by the time we got to university in 1998, the UZ was a sinking ship, a far cry from the highly respected institute it once was. There were endless student riots and protests that became politicized and more violent. Eventually, the university was shut down for a few months, leaving many students in crisis. While some of us had no choice but to stay and stick it out, Lindy whipped out her blue American passport and left for Phoenix midway through her Economics degree. Her parents' friends in Phoenix took her in, and arranged for her to go to a community college.

Due to financial problems, Lindy never completed her Economics degree and only managed to get an Associate's in Business. She got a job as a customer service representative at Bank of America, vowed to complete her bachelor's, then advance to an MBA. Eventually, after several promotions leading to a branch manager position, Lindy gave up on going back to college and decided to focus on her career. I sometimes sensed regret when she talked about leaving the UZ, especially since those of us who stayed made it out with degrees and promising careers.

As preteens, we were inseparable, and experienced the woes of puberty and teenage life together. With my sister, Mercy, we formed a singing group that we called *Triple Trouble*, and together, we followed our dream to leave Bulawayo for university in Harare.

Now, distance and various circumstances had separated us as adults, but we always kept in touch, and we reunited when I moved to America.

As usual, we dissected my relationship with Chris. I gave her a detailed account of everything that had occurred since the big argument. We both agreed that Chris wasn't fond of Lindy and concluded that he was jealous of our close friendship. He couldn't stand our endless talking on the phone, especially when we switched from speaking English to Ndebele, and he was irked by our hysterical laughing or heated arguments.

Like a sulking toddler, Chris would complain, "I'm trying to watch telly here and can't hear a word with you cackling like a hyena." Sometimes he whined, "I bet it's Lindy calling again. Didn't you get all your gossip in just thirty minutes ago?" Or he'd yell, "Bloody hell, can you go and chat in the bathroom or somewhere else? I'm trying to sleep here."

There were times when I would cut my phone call short, lower my voice, or go to another room out of courtesy. Other times though, I stubbornly ignored his comments, convinced that he was trying to control me and alienate me from my friend. Chris wanted me all to himself.

"You know, Lindy," I said, "I don't know if this is what I want for myself going forward. I need a more supportive man. I can't deal with being made to feel like I must be grateful to be in *his* house."

She replied, "I don't know how you have survived this long. That would never work for me. I tell you, I don't remember the last time I paid a bill in this house. With the way Gift takes care of everything, even buying me a car and all, I can't imagine a man who expects me to go halves." Then she chuckled and said, "I guess that's what you get when you date these white boys."

She always annoyed me when she made a comparison between Chris and her boyfriend, Gift. I wanted to reply, *At least Chris treats me with respect and doesn't cheat on me with every skirt that walks by. Sometimes being a kept woman comes at a price.* But I didn't voice my thoughts and said, "I'm not asking him to buy me a car or anything fancy. He isn't a baller, like your Gift. It would be nice to have some reassurance that he could help me through this time when I'm looking for a job. Instead, he constantly reminds me it's *his* house, *his* car, and *his* this and that, and I must literally dance to his tune."

"Have you forgiven him for kicking you out of his house, and the whole fiasco with the police? Why else would you return to him? Has he not changed for the better after you almost left him?"

The question about *why* I went back to Chris after the big fight made me very uneasy. Deep down, I was still bothered by that incident, because it had revealed a side to Chris that terrified me. I wanted to avoid it, yet Lindy was one of the few people with whom I could comfortably unpack my feelings without fear of judgement.

"I'm not sure if I will stay with him," I said.

"What?" she asked, her voice booming so loud that I had to hold the phone away from my ear.

"There you go again," she continued. "Always so quick to walk away. You're seriously going to leave a man who loves you like crazy? And go where? You give up on relationships too easily."

I was taken aback, and a little confused, because she always agreed that what Chris had done was wrong, that he wasn't caring and supportive enough. She had even insinuated that I could do better.

"It may be better for me to leave now, and make a fresh start before I get too invested," I said.

"Just because he yelled at you and you had one big row? Do you know how many arguments I've had with Gift? Plenty, but I stick with it and work on the relationship, and now we're happy going on three years."

Again, I wanted to remind her that our situations were different. I really couldn't understand how she was still with a man who had physically abused her several times, even landing her in the ER. A man who had repeatedly cheated on her. They were happy for now, till the next fight, and then he would shower Lindy with gifts, including shopping sprees and the never-ending promise of marriage.

She stuck with Gift through all that, and loved him with all her being. She couldn't live without him, and sadly he seemed to take advantage of her obsessive love for him.

"Don't forget how you regretted leaving your ex-boyfriend in London, the Nigerian guy. What was his name? Ade? You went begging him to take you back, but he had moved on." And in a tone laced with malice, she added, "Soon you'll be asking Chris to take you back."

She seemed to get pleasure in my misery, and the mention of Ade, how he'd turned me down, added to the spitefulness. Lindy had a catty nature that occasionally reared its ugly head, and coupled with a rivalry, it sometimes caused us to drift apart, but we always made up.

"So, you suggest I stay in an unhappy situation because of the fear of regret and rejection?" I said. "Not all of us are strong enough to endure a bad relationship. I would rather get out of it now, suffer a major heartbreak, and get over it, than die a slow death from a toxic relationship."

I must have struck a nerve, because she was silent for a moment. It was intentional. After all, she had thrown the first punch.

She came back swinging. "Suffer a major heartbreak and get over it, you say. Are you even over that Ade guy, or were you *forced* to get over him after he refused to take you back?"

Offended that she would use that terrible experience to make a point, I said, "When was the last time you heard me mention Ade? He hurt my feelings, but I have since moved on and couldn't care less about him. You should try that sometime."

Even as I said this, it didn't ring true. The truth was that I thought about Ade sometimes, but less and less each passing day, week, and month, such that I had convinced myself that chapter of my life was over. But when confronted with the question of whether I was indeed over him, I doubted myself.

"Go ahead and walk away from another guy who loves you," she said. "Those of us who stay in the so-called toxic relationships aren't the strong ones. The strong ones are people like you who have the strength to walk away. I just don't know how you do it." She was subdued, almost whispering. Like she was thinking aloud and didn't expect anyone to hear her, or to respond.

I knew it had taken a lot for Lindy to admit that she couldn't leave Gift, despite the abuse and cheating. Such conversations reminded me why our friendship had lasted many years, survived the distance between us, and endured several hurtful verbal exchanges. We were honest with each other, didn't hold grudges, and cared for each other.

To lighten the mood and change the conversation, I said in Ndebele, "*Uyazi*, I should tell Chris to quit complaining about our daily phone calls, because you're actually on his side, even advocating for me to stay with him. If he only knew."

We both laughed.

"You're right, *Umtshele*. He owes me a drink. The next time I come to Atlanta, dinner and drinks will be on him, and I will not be paying for myself again."

Lindy was referencing when she came to visit me from Phoenix, and Chris took us out for a night of partying. Lindy was surprised when Chris refused to pay for her dinner and cocktails. Before that, when I told Chris that Lindy was planning to visit and she was excited to finally meet him, he replied, "That's great. Where will she be staying?"

"Here, with us," I answered. "She's only coming for the weekend."

"Why can't she check into a hotel?"

"Chris, why would she? We have a four-bedroom house to

ourselves, and she's coming to see *us*. Why can't she use one of the guest bedrooms?"

"I don't know her, and I've never met her, so why should she expect to come to my house? Most people would get a hotel room, then maybe next time *we* would invite her to our house. You don't tell someone, 'Mate, I'm coming to visit you, and oh, by the way, I'll be crashing over at your place.' Who does that?"

I was flabbergasted. "Where I'm from, it's a given that you open your home to friends and family who come to visit you. Even if it means offering your couch. I won't make my friend pay for a hotel room. She can stay in my room on campus, and I'll spend the weekend there with her."

Realizing that he had to choose between a weekend without me, or a weekend with a stranger, he'd opted for the latter.

Lindy continued to talk about how Chris had made her feel like a third wheel on the night he took us out. "I'm glad that I had my own money and was able to pay for my dinner. Imagine how embarrassing it would have been if I'd come out with you guys without a dime or credit card, like we used to do back in the day, going on a date without any money and relying on your date to take care of everything."

I replied, "*Manje*, things are different here in the States, and in the UK too. Men here will go halves with their girlfriends. Now add a friend to the equation. That's asking for too much. Honestly, when I look back, I see how ridiculous it was for a girl to expect her dude to pay for his girlfriend and her friends. It's insane, and shame on us for expecting that from our men." I was glad we were back on laughing terms.

Lindy said happily, "Do you recall how, back in college, when a guy would ask one of us out to the club, we'd all tag along and the poor guy had to pay admission for all three or four of us, including drinks and sometimes cab fare? How crazy was that?"

"And remember," I added, "when a dude offered to take you out for pizza or lunch, you'd always order an extra pizza to take away 'for the girls,' and he would agree, just to win you over—Speak of the devil, I have an incoming call from none other than

Chris. I have to get off the phone. I'd better pick up, or else he'll go off about how we talk on the phone for too long."

"No problem," she replied, still sounding jovial. "Just keep me posted on what you decide to do. Bye."

I answered Chris's incoming call.

"Hey, babe, get ready. I made a reservation for dinner." He sounded very cheerful—and yet somehow I went from being happy and cheery on the phone with Lindy, to a low mood with Chris. I told him that I didn't want to go to dinner, but wanted pizza or Chinese takeout instead. I couldn't explain why I continued to be angry at Chris, despite his efforts to show how sorry he felt.

Later that evening, when he told me about Vegas, my first instinct was to be sarcastic—to remind him of when he wouldn't pay for my hotel and airfare. I couldn't help myself.

Then, Lindy's painful words rang through my mind: "Soon, you will be asking Chris to take you back; go ahead and walk away from another guy who loves you." The words *regret* and *rejection* echoed over and over in my head. When I saw Chris's reaction to my sarcastic remarks about Vegas, I knew something had changed. He stood motionless, his face flushed red, the veins in his neck bulging like thick ropes, his eyes blinking to ward off tears, his lips sealed. He didn't retaliate in anger like he used to. He just turned and walked away. He looked like someone who had no fight left in him. I knew then that I had to stop holding a grudge and give Chris another chance.

I followed him to the lounge, feeling terrible for being ungrateful and unnecessarily mean when he was trying so hard to make me happy. In those few seconds, I made up my mind. So when he pulled me close and kissed me, my body was ready. I was ready for him. Maybe Lindy was right: I had to fight to make it work, even if it felt wrong.

Part V

Chapter 23

London, UK
February 2007

Noma

Something wasn't right, I could feel it. Ade had changed, for the worst. He didn't seem concerned about me at all. He had stopped asking where I was going and when I'd be back. He didn't keep up with my work schedule so we could plan our days off. He no longer called to check on me during the day like he used to. He simply didn't seem to care. Did he know what I'd been up to? I had been very careful— Well, I thought I had.

*****

Two years ago when I met Ade at work, he was a different man. I remembered how he looked sad and withdrawn, going about his work, reviewing a pile of medical notes at the nurses' station. I approached him, something I'd never dare to do normally, but his sadness caught my attention. Unlike the other doctors, he was friendly and approachable, even for the slightest questions regarding patients, and he was thorough and kind in his response. I asked him why he looked down and suggested he must not like working the ward rounds. He replied with a smile, "To be honest, I'm just starving."

"I can get you something from the snack bar, if you like," I offered.

"No, don't worry. I'll be heading out in a short while. The nurse manager paged me about some urgent reports I have to review. Thankfully I don't do ward rounds and the groundwork anymore."

I replied, "Well, I'm here till seven, and I'm already exhausted. Working these wards is no joke."

His pager rang, and he said, "I have to take this. I'm sure you'll be fine." And off he went.

There was something about him that left a lasting impression on me, and each day after our first encounter, I walked around the hospital hoping to see Ade again, but I didn't. I met him unexpectedly, however, on a Saturday afternoon when I was shopping around for a microwave, and he was inspecting some gas stoves.

Although he was dressed casually in jeans and a sweater, I instantly recognized his tall, muscular frame and gentle voice as he spoke to the customer service agent. Again I approached him.

"Hi," I said.

"Hi, there," he replied with searching eyes. I assumed he didn't remember me.

"So, what did you get to eat after that day at work?" I asked.

The twinkle in his eye showed that he remembered. "Ah, I think I downed a pint of beer with fish and chips at a local pub on my high street. I'm Ade," he said, extending a firm hand.

"And I'm Noma," I replied, cheerfully shaking his hand.

"Noma," he repeated. "Where is that from?"

"I'm from Zimbabwe. It's Nomagugu, but everyone calls me Noma." His face fell when I said this. Was it the mention of my name, or being from Zimbabwe that seemed to be a disappointment?

"What brings you here?" He tried to disguise that disappointed look with a weak smile.

"I need a top-quality, high-performance microwave. I'm tired of ordering cheap brands from the Argos catalog."

"So, you're prepared to spend a little extra; I like that. I'm here for the same reason. I just bought a new house and need a good stove and oven." He began scrutinizing a stainless-steel oven and ceramic hob combo.

My first instinct was to look at his ring finger to check if he was married, and to my relief, he wasn't wearing a ring, but I needed to be sure. I said, "Where is the missus to help you choose the best stove? Women have an instinct for such things."

He frowned and looked at me somewhat surprised, which made me feel embarrassed.

"Unfortunately, it's just me."

I was so sure Ade was about to brush me off for being so suggestive, but he added, "Hey, I need to get something to eat. I seem to be hungry every time I see you." He chuckled. "Will you join me for lunch?"

I smiled. "Yes, of course."

And so our romance began. We had several more lunch, dinner, and movie dates, which became a relationship and which led to me moving into Ade's three-bedroom house in North London. I later found out that he had been single for close to a year after he broke up with his girlfriend, who like me was from Zimbabwe. He didn't want to talk much about his ex, which made me conclude that the breakup had hurt. He referred to her once as Bubbles, which was an odd name. It was a nickname, and her real name was Maita. Whoever she was, she must have had quite an impact, because he tried hard to avoid any topics that involved this past relationship, and I sensed some resentment—or was it anger?—when I quizzed him about her.

All I knew was that she was in America somewhere at a university, and therefore she wasn't a threat to me, which was a relief. Ade had no pictures or any remnants of her. I had curiously searched and found no trace of her or any other girl, and I was satisfied that she was a thing of the past along with his other ex-girlfriends.

*****

I admit I had neglected him, and become too comfortable and satisfied in my own way— and gotten away with it for so long. This had to explain why he was cold and distant. I could lose Ade if I didn't act—now. I planned to reach out to Bola, and through her I could get Ade's attention. I knew this because he was close to his sister and Bola had a lot of influence on him. We could go back to being a trio, hanging out at home or going out to dinner or movies. I just couldn't afford to lose Ade—no *way*.

Chapter 24

London, UK
February 2007

Ade

After months of being unsatisfied with Noma and feeling trapped, my recent reconnection with Maita made me feel optimistic about the future, and I was constantly in good spirits. I was glad to have direct communication with her, even though in her last text she pretty much told me she was happy with her boyfriend, and I must never contact her again.

Dr. Patel, a work colleague, remarked once during a tea break in the doctors' lounge, "Your day must be going well."

"Why do you say that?" I asked.

"Well, you haven't stopped smiling since you walked in. Must be happy thoughts. Let me guess: it's a woman. It has to be."

I nodded. "Good guess, yes, I have to agree, there is a woman behind this smile."

"She must be doing something right. You've been smiling all day."

If he only knew that I was beaming with glee over text messages from an ex-girlfriend who was thousands of miles away and apparently in a happy relationship with her live-in boyfriend—he would think I was crazy. A far cry from what he assumed was the reason for my joy. I played along and replied, "I'm lucky to have her."

As I said this, I thought how stupid I had been to let Maita slip away after she'd come from Atlanta just for me.

Maita was now someone else's girlfriend. Why was I trying to break that apart? I asked myself this repeatedly. When did I

209

become the kind of guy that cheats on his girlfriend with an ex-lover, and has no qualms about breaking up her relationship? But what was I to do when I felt this strong attraction toward Maita? The right thing to do was to break up with Noma first, *then* pursue Maita. But I couldn't wait for the perfect time or scenario; I needed to connect with Maita now, for my sanity. I was dying inside.

I reasoned that she wasn't married yet, so technically, Maita was still single and therefore I was justified. The more countless hours I spent thinking of ways to get Maita back, the more I neglected my relationship with Noma, and it kept crumbling. We hardly had any meaningful conversations, and we didn't spend any time together. I didn't understand why we were still together. Neither one of us wanted to be the first to admit that the relationship had failed.

There were visible signs of hostility between us. The atmosphere was so tense that Bola felt uncomfortable when she visited, forcing her to cut the visits short, and she hadn't returned since. I didn't care that I was pushing Noma away, perhaps as some mechanism to force her into breaking up, but she wasn't about to make that move. Noma seemed determined to cling to this failing relationship. The only explanation for why she stayed was that I took care of her every need. It was purely logistical.

I believed that a man had to take care of his woman, to be the breadwinner who provided security for his household, with no expectations. But maybe, as Gbenga once suggested, I had been too generous. Noma drove a 2006 Mercedes ML350, for which I paid the deposit and made the monthly payments. Living rent-free, and with my credit card at her disposal, all the money she made from working as an agency nurse—sometimes over forty hours a week—was hers to do with whatever she wished.

We didn't discuss finances anymore. When we first moved in together, we shared everything, but now we had drifted so far apart, it seemed intrusive to ask about bank balances. It was no wonder that Noma was the envy of all her loudmouth girlfriends. As expected, there were internal wars among them, competition over who drove the most recent or fanciest car, who wore the best designer clothes, and of course, who attracted the most attention from men. And Noma was the one who had it all. That had to be the reason why she was still with me.

The rare times we were intimate were fairly routine, usually missionary position with no extras, just enough humps to get to the climax, and it was over. She hadn't had an orgasm in a long time because, unlike before, I now climaxed first. Previously, I made sure she came and was satisfied before I did. I had become selfish, and as long as I got mine, I didn't care much for anything else. Noma didn't complain.

Being stonehearted was out of character for me. Or could it be that I had no idea how ugly and mean I could be? I had evolved to be this way after Maita broke my heart into pieces, and as it slowly mended, it hardened and turned me into a harsh man. I wasn't too fond of this new tough-love Ade. I just wanted to be happily in love again. The only person who made me feel that way was Maita. That was why I wanted her back so desperately. The thought of having Maita in my arms again aroused me, warmed me up in ways that were hard to explain or understand.

I needed to deal with this once and for all. I had to meet with Maita and tell her how I felt. I could relocate to America if I had to, take the medical board exams, and work my way through a residency just to be with her again. Feeling rejuvenated, I convinced myself that the sooner I figured out the logistics of meeting up with Maita, the sooner I could win her back. I had to travel to America. The sooner, the better.

I planned to schedule some time off work and make the reservations pronto. I was filled with a sudden sense of urgency, as if I had to act immediately or risk losing her forever.

Later that week, on a Saturday evening, I was at home drinking cognac and listening to Sade's soulful music, when I decided that I would call—not text—and ask Maita to meet with me in New York City. Flights from London to New York were cheaper and shorter than to Atlanta. Plus, I wanted a neutral meeting place. The alcohol emboldened me, and I was coaxed by Sade's lyrics and the smooth taste of the cognac. Not caring about the time difference between London and Atlanta, or whether her boyfriend was with her or not, I was finally determined to make an international call to Maita. My mobile phone had the time in London at 6:32 p.m., which meant it was 1:32 p.m. in Atlanta.

I called her number, but she didn't answer. Not ready to give up, I called three more times. The third time she picked up and immediately cut the phone. Stubbornly, I called again. Now that Maita knew I was trying to reach her, she had to answer my call, and if she couldn't talk, she could text me back. But she did neither. After a three-minute wait, I decided to text her:

> *Hey, please pick up the phone. I need to talk to you.*

I waited for a reply, but none came. She was probably tied up with her boyfriend on a Saturday afternoon, like most happy couples—putting in stark relief the fact that I was drinking alone at home, while my girlfriend slept upstairs. Noma had been sleeping a lot lately, and I had begun to suspect it was her way of avoiding me. That didn't bother me because lately her mood swings had been so intense that I couldn't tolerate being around her anyway. I sent another text:

> *I need to see you. We need to talk. I know you're in a relationship and all, but I believe we still have a chance to be together, just like you wanted two summers ago. There is so much I need to say to you, but I have to see you so we can talk face-to-face. Please meet with me in New York. I will pay for your ticket to fly from Atlanta. Let's talk soon and make a plan. Or would you prefer to meet in Las Vegas? Remember how you wanted to go*

to Vegas? Let me know what you want, and I will make it happen.

I read the text message three times over and was pleased, so I pressed *Send* and watched the animated envelope on my phone disappear with a *swooping* sound. Even though she didn't answer my calls, I knew that she would read text messages. And if she were interested in giving us a chance, she would respond.

The response to my text message was the ultimate test, and if she ignored and never replied, then I would conclude that it was indeed over forever between us. I would have to permanently close this chapter of my life and let her go.

However, if she replied and said yes, we could meet in New York or Las Vegas, and I would know that we had a fighting chance, and that I would give it all I had.

Either way, I had also made up my mind that Noma had to go.

Chapter 25

Atlanta, GA
February 2007

Chris

"Hey, babe," I said. "I just got us tickets to watch your favorite play at the Cobb Theater. *My Fair Lady* is coming this summer."

We were having lunch at Naan, her favorite Thai restaurant in Midtown, after a day of window-shopping at the Lenox mall for a Valentine's Day wish list. It was my idea to have Bubbles look around Macy's, Dillard's, and Bloomingdale's to see if there was anything she liked from those stores, then choose what she wanted for a Valentine's Day treat. I deliberately suggested affordable department stores, because as a student who was forever scraping the barrel for cash, Bubbles had pretty expensive taste. If she had her way and the means, she would probably head straight to Neiman Marcus, but even I didn't shop at Neiman Marcus or the likes of Saks Fifth Avenue.

The idea for clothes shopping came about after noticing that Bubbles hadn't purchased new clothes and shoes since we started dating in 2005. She told me the last time she bought new clothes was that summer in London, when she was working and earning a decent paycheck. Even then, Bubbles had already budgeted for college expenses and couldn't splurge. Instead, she shopped around for summer deals. Since then, she'd made good with a limited but tasteful wardrobe, and spent a little extra on good-quality clothes that could be worn repeatedly and stretch out for years without looking outdated. And she did an excellent job of it. Bubbles had an eye for fashion, and her slender figure made everything look effortlessly classy.

"Buying my clothes in London gives me an edge," she would say. "I always get compliments from strangers and even my friends, because the styles are different from Atlanta fashion." Then she would add, "If they knew how old some of these clothes are, they'd laugh."

She always looked well put together, and no one would ever know she was perpetually broke and hadn't shopped for clothes in over a year. At work dinners or whatnot, I proudly showed Bubbles off to my friends and colleagues. Everyone said we made a beautiful couple, and I agreed.

I had never taken a girl shopping. Treating her to such a spree was all part of my new commitment to Bubbles that I would take care of her. It was awkward for me, totally out of my realm. I wasn't sure if I should set a fixed budget or give her my credit card to use without limitations— no way, I had to have a limit, but how would I do this without appearing stingy?

"Urrgh, I feel like a twat," I mumbled, after settling on letting her choose what she would like without limitations. And if she went beyond what I considered reasonable, I'd tell her.

I was expecting Bubbles to jump at the opportunity to be spoiled. I was disappointed to receive a very lukewarm response after she initially refused flat-out. "Chris, you really don't have to do this," she had said. "Please don't go out of your way to do stuff for me just because I said a few things in anger."

"Bubbles, let me do something for you. I want to do this, and it's not a big deal. Besides, you need to update your closet. It's so outdated, and soon you'll be wearing Hammer pants."

She laughed, and this made me happy. "All right, if you insist. So, let me get this straight. We window-shop so I know what's out there, then I let you know what I like, and you can *surprise* me with the item I choose as a Valentine's Day gift. How's that a surprise?"

"You're the one who said you don't know what the big stores in Atlanta have. You hardly ever go to the mall anyway and only ever see Macy's TV commercials with endless sales. You said you liked Bloomingdale's the one time you went there. So, I figured we could start there. We can always browse the other stores. Let's make it fun and then have lunch after."

I was getting a little excited about shopping for my girlfriend, then having lunch and cocktails afterward. It was a strange feeling, but I hadn't anticipated that it would make me feel proud and happy with myself too.

During lunch, after an exhausting morning at the mall, my work mobile phone rang. Somehow in a rush to get to the city early, I had taken my work phone instead of my personal phone. The only person who called me on my personal mobile phone was Bubbles, so whenever I was at home or out with her, I would forget that I even had a phone because it never rang. There were no close buddies in America to call me regularly, and my family and friends in the UK hardly ever checked up on me. The only phone that frequently rang, usually only on weekdays, was my work mobile. So, I was surprised when it vibrated in my pocket.

I couldn't believe my eyes when I looked at the caller ID. My expression gave me away, because Bubbles immediately asked, "Is everything okay?"

I faked a smile. "Yes. It's nothing, no big deal, it's someone from work." And I cut the call.

"On a Saturday?" she asked, chewing on her duck and rice. Before I could make up an answer, my phone rang again. "You can get it. If it's work calling, you have to."

I cut it again. "No, whatever it is, it can wait. Sometimes when we're behind schedule with a huge order, we go in on the weekend. Well, the guys that work in the molding factory have to go in, but management doesn't have to."

The phone began ringing a third time, and I could feel my anger stirring up. I was about to erupt, which could cause me to slam the phone on the table, or toss it to the ground in fury. The old me, that was. I struggled to stay composed.

She said, "The people at your job seem to need you badly. I think you should answer and find out what they want."

I cut it off once again and noticed that my hand was shaking as I did this—the rage was reaching its boiling point. I was fighting so hard not to smash the phone and wondered if Bubbles could see it in my face.

"You're right. I will step over to the loo. I'll be right back." I had to leave before I threw a wobbly right there. As I got up from the chair and walked toward the restrooms, the phone rang again. I answered it this time, then immediately cut it off. Fuming, I curled my hand in a tight fist. I thought I might explode.

The *nerve* of that Ade idiot. To bloody ring my mobile phone when I instructed him never to make a voice call. As a Bubbles impersonator, I didn't want my boyfriend to know we were chatting. He even chose to call back-to-back on a Saturday, obviously trying to get *me* caught so that he could swoop in and take over.

The men's restroom was empty, and I was glad. I locked myself in a stall, and without thinking I began to kick the door frantically. "Bloody bastard!" I shouted. "Taking the piss, you are."

I took a deep breath and stopped yelling when I heard footsteps enter the bathroom. I flushed the toilet, exhaled deeply, and unlocked the door. My face was red when I looked in the bathroom mirror. I splashed some cold water onto my face to calm down, asking myself why I had even started to text this fool—what I'd hoped to achieve. He wasn't a threat anymore, because Bubbles and I were, for the most part, back to our happy selves. I was already executing my plan to be a better partner, and I planned to propose to Bubbles on Valentine's Day.

Glad the restaurant had actual towels rolled up for single use, I took one and dried my face. Just then, a text message came in. I read it in complete disbelief. So, this ex-boyfriend had decided he would blatantly come between Bubbles and me, and convince her to leave me for him. If it weren't for the man who walked out of one of the bathroom stalls toward the sink and another gentleman entering the bathroom, I would have flung the cell phone into the mirror.

I was right to text Ade after all; I had to step in to ensure that he never got a chance to poison Bubbles' mind and lure her back. Relieved that my deceitful texting wasn't in vain, I whispered, "I knew he had something up his sleeve." I could only imagine if he had gotten through to her and said all these things during that rough patch we had. I would have lost her to him.

What had happened during the summer of 2005? I hadn't asked her. I couldn't. But I knew that whatever it was, it had a significant impact on this Ade man. Then I realized that I was still standing around in the restroom, talking to myself and probably looking dodgy and confused.

I decided to continue my lunch and not reply to his ridiculous text. He asked Bubbles if she wanted to go to Las Vegas, just as I planned to take her there. What a coincidence. I shook my head. He knew what Bubbles liked, and he would have had one up on me if I hadn't asked her first. What else would he offer? He was prepared to go all the way, including flying to New York just to talk. She must have meant a lot to him, just as she did to me, but she was mine now.

"Is everything okay at work?" she asked with a concerned look.

For a split second, I forgot my bluff about the calls from work. "Nothing that can't wait till Monday, so we're fine." I had lost my appetite, and struggled to keep a straight face. "You want dessert?"

"No way, I'm stuffed. I'll have another lychee martini."

I gestured to our waiter. I needed a potent drink myself. Unfortunately, as the driver, I had to opt for another of their fruity and sweet signature cocktails, just enough to taste some alcohol but not enough to get me in trouble if the police stopped me.

Anxious and inwardly enraged, I couldn't wait to get home and decide on my next move. I had two options: I could ignore Ade, change my phone number, and never contact him again.

Or I could call him back as the angry boyfriend and tell him to leave my girl alone.

Chapter 26

London, UK
February 2007

Ade

I was surprised at how quickly events unfolded via text-messaging since two days ago on Saturday when I'd called her several times, then sent the invite to meet me in New York.

I waited anxiously, eagerly checking for messages every so often, but time went by and she hadn't replied. I didn't attempt to call or text again. My conclusion was that Bubbles didn't want to see me, or have anything to do with me ever again. I was devastated and haunted by that all-too-familiar gnawing pain from three years ago. I had to be strong, to stop begging her for attention. After all, she *had* happily moved on. Was it so hard to believe that she could find love and happiness with someone else?

Finally, I received the long-awaited message on Monday. A loud ping alerted me as I sat on the couch, scrolling through TV channels, searching for something to watch. Noma had just made dinner and was calling me to come to get my food from the kitchen.

"Just a minute," I called back. I picked up the phone from the coffee table, and when I saw the text was from Bubbles, I made a fist, threw a punch into the air, and said out loud, "Yes!" I hadn't read the message, but the mere fact that she finally replied was good enough. She still cared about me.

"What is it? Why are you so excited?" Noma was standing at the doorway, holding two dinner plates.

"Nothing much," I replied, unable to hide my good mood.

"It must be something. Did you win the lottery? Here's your food."

She handed me a plate.

"Thanks, I need the toilet real quick." I set the plate down and rushed to the bathroom. With my heart dancing with joy, I read the message.

Let's meet in New York. I can only travel this weekend and I have to be back in Atlanta on Sunday. I can pay for my ticket and book my hotel. Let me know when you have made your reservation, then send me your details. Do not contact me after that. I will see you in New York.

That was all I wanted, just a moment alone with her, a chance to make right all the wrongs we both had done. She wanted a separate hotel—strictly business. It didn't stop me, however, from fantasizing about us together in a hotel room for an entire weekend, having wild sex, making up for the lost time. Separate hotels or not, I didn't care; I just wanted to see Maita face-to-face, even for just one day.

Part VI

Chapter 27

London, UK
February 2007

Ade

A single text, a single line, was all it took to bring my day to a crashing halt. It came from Monica.

Noma is cheating on you with a married man.

It stopped me in my tracks, on my way to a meeting with my medical team. I stared at my phone and read the message again. I excused myself from the meeting. They could go ahead without me. I had to call Monica immediately.

She picked up on the first ring.

"Monica, what is this about?"

"Exactly what the message says. Noma has been seeing this guy called Vusa—"

"Wait, what do you mean, like cheating with another man? Are you sure?"

"Of course I'm positive. I was her best friend and I've known since the beginning, but that bitch decided to talk shit about me to *my* man, so why should I keep her secrets?"

I headed for the hospital exit, out into the cold February air—I needed an open space to breathe and digest these explicit details. I had mindlessly walked to my car, the phone pressed to my ear, listening in disbelief as Noma's former best friend narrated how Noma was sleeping with another man.

I leaned against the car, armpits and palms sweating, even as my face was freezing in the cold. I gritted my teeth. I was speechless.

Monica told me how Noma had met this married father of two at Club Afrique, a South African nightclub they frequented. He was a nurse by day, and a DJ by night at the club.

"Noma is with you for your money, we all know that. Vusa is the one she loves," Monica said, rubbing more salt onto my wound. "My conscience has been eating at me. I wanted to let you know sooner but—"

"You have told me enough for now." I snapped back to reality and finally found my voice. "I need to get back to work. Thank you for letting me know. I'm going to have a word with Noma."

"I don't care if she knows that I told you. You deserve better than her. You are a good man—"

"Monica, I have to go. Please, let's discuss this another time." I didn't want to hear any more details about how they had quickies in the DJ booth—it was too upsetting. Noma had played me for a fool, and all her friends knew about it.

The timing of all this couldn't be more complicated: it had come on the eve of my departure to New York to meet Bubbles. I was indeed devastated and furious that Noma had cheated on me, but on the upside, I now had a solid reason to leave her. Was I a hypocrite to be upset? My pending meeting with Bubbles was deceitful, but I was planning to break up with Noma soon, I just needed the right timing.

I gathered myself and returned to work, distracted and absent-minded as I thought about my next move, and how to confront Noma.

*****

That evening, when Noma came home from work, I was packing my carry-on bag, trying to decide which shirts to take with me and if two pairs of jeans were adequate. I wanted to stick to my goal of traveling light. I planned to fly to New York the next day, Thursday, and return to London on Sunday in time for work on Monday morning. I was glad my request for personal time off work was approved on such short notice.

She walked into the bedroom, threw a handbag onto the bed and asked, "What's this? Are you going somewhere?"

"Yes, I'm flying to New York tomorrow night. I have to pack now, because I won't have time after I come back from work tomorrow."

She sat on the bed, and with a confused expression asked, "Why are you going there? You never mentioned it before."

"We haven't had a decent conversation in months, have we? I'm attending a cardiology conference, and I'll return on Sunday."

"Really?" she said with a scowl. "So, when were you going to tell me?"

I looked at her. Monica's scandalous revelations crossed my mind, repulsing me with Noma's mere presence. I wanted her to leave me alone to pack, to continue riding this wave of excitement that I had been on since getting the text from Bubbles, but I had to confront her.

"I'm telling you now, aren't I?" I snapped. "Instead, let's talk about how you have been cheating on me with a married man." I looked her in the eyes.

Her mouth gaped.

"Don't even try to deny it. Monica told me everything, and frankly, I'm disgusted."

She shook her head in protest. "It's not true, I… he was just a friend—"

"Save the lies for another day. That explains so much, and why you refuse to have sex with me so often. You were getting it from him, huh?"

"Ade, it was a long time ago—"

"I don't care," I shouted, finally releasing my anger and frustration. "I don't want to continue like this. I think we need to call it quits and go our separate ways."

Taken aback, she gasped. "What do you mean, go our separate ways?"

"Don't act surprised. The writing is on the wall. We hardly do anything together, and we've drifted so far apart, we're practically living separate lives in the same house."

"Ade, what do you mean—"

"Oh, come on. You know what I'm talking about." I got louder, finally reaching a tipping point.

"Why must I endure this, huh?" I said. "You won't let me touch you, and the atmosphere in here is always hostile. It's not like we're a married couple staying together for the kids or some complicated marital assets. So, why torture each other?"

I most certainly had nothing to gain from this unhealthy relationship, but she, on the other hand, was certainly benefiting from my generosity.

She stared at me blankly, surprised by this sudden outburst. She had never seen me react this way. I paused to collect myself; the silence in those few seconds was deafening.

"Noma, I've been thinking about this for a while now, but thought maybe things would change. But after what I learned today, that you have been sleeping with another man, there is no reason to drag this on."

"I'm sure we can talk about this. Monica has always been jealous of me, why else would she do this? I-I can explain everything."

For the first time, I saw desperation and heard it in her voice, and it was pathetic. I should have done this earlier, I thought. "It's been a long time coming, and we both know it—"

"Are *you* seeing someone?" she interrupted.

"Of course not," I said defensively. "And you have a nerve to ask that. I want out. I will give you time to find another place to stay, then you can leave."

"Ade, please don't do this to me." She broke into tears. "I'm sorry if I haven't been good to you. Please, don't leave me." Sobbing loudly with tears streaking down her face, Noma hunched her shoulders and wept. It struck me that I had never seen her cry in the two years we had been together. For a moment, I felt a pang of guilt. Once again, a woman was begging me to be with her, to choose *her*. And again, I would turn her down, just as I did Maita, albeit under very different circumstances.

This time, unlike that dreadful day with Maita crying outside the train station, I wasn't acting out of a vengeful and broken heart, and neither was it a show of pride. In this case, I was no longer in love and had been unwilling to face the facts. I had instead chosen to languish in a relationship that was long dead, hoping that things would get better, but they'd gotten worse. I felt nothing as she cried, and I continued packing my bag.

"Noma, let's not waste each other's time anymore."

"We can at least try to work things out. Don't go to this conference. Please stay and let's talk. I have something important I need to tell you."

"Look, I won't be canceling my plans now, and whatever you have to say can wait till I return on Sunday, but my mind is made up. You can't blame me after what you did."

Postponing the discussion to Sunday seemed to calm her down. Perhaps she thought there was hope of reconciling, a chance to change my mind when I returned.

Wiping tears away with the back of her wrist, she sat upright and asked, "What time will you arrive Sunday? I can pick you up at the airport."

Her manner had changed from a weeping, jilted girlfriend to a loving and caring partner. She was already making plans to worm her way back. Noma wouldn't go away without a fight.

Could this be an opportune moment to tell her that indeed I was in love with another woman, and there was no going back? Or was it best to wait until Sunday so she could tell me whatever she needed to say, and then I could tell her about Maita?

Not ready for a heated discussion, I chose the latter.

"Don't worry about picking me up. I'll get a taxi back. Listen…" I paused, zipped my bag and looked her in the eyes. "I have pretty much made up my mind, but I will hear you out on Sunday when I return. For now, I just want to be left alone."

She got up from the edge of the bed, evidently taken aback by my determination for a breakup. Nodding in defeat, Noma slowly walked out of the bedroom. I felt a huge relief, a heavy burden taken off my shoulders. I had been suffering under its weight for months.

Chapter 28

New York, NY
February 2007

Chris

I had to lie to Bubbles about an unexpected meeting at one of our manufacturing facilities in Dallas, Texas. It wasn't unusual for me to travel to Dallas once or twice a month for a day or two. Bubbles didn't like it when I had to work out of town. She didn't like being home alone, so we Skyped as frequently as possible—pretty much each time I returned to my hotel room, I called or Skyped her. However, this time, when I told her I would be gone from Friday to Saturday, she didn't seem to care at all. She was nonchalant and didn't question why I would have a meeting on a Friday, which was unusual. I figured she was preoccupied with not getting any leads on her job hunt.

We were in a good place now, no arguments like before, and we got along well. I did my best not to rock the boat, and I tried to be that supportive boyfriend she wanted. Despite all this, I could sense that something had shifted in our relationship. Bubbles wasn't the same, and she seemed to be trying just as hard to keep the peace. So, in the end, we had an almost too-perfect relationship, with just the right amount of pleasantries and affection to convince each other that we could make this work. It felt manufactured and unreal. I yearned for the raw and uncensored Bubbles, who said whatever was on her mind, criticized me when she wanted to, and kept me on my toes with her next move. So, I wasn't completely surprised that she didn't question my trip to Dallas.

Little did she know that I was in a private war with her

unsuspecting ex-boyfriend. I had rehearsed the upcoming meeting with Ade in New York several times in my head, how I would tell him in person to leave Bubbles alone. I couldn't wait to see the look on his face when he realized that it hadn't been Bubbles on the other end of the phone the entire time, that it was *me* instead.

I arrived in New York and went to my hotel to leave my backpack and change out of my work clothes.

Ade had already sent a text message with his hotel room details. Feeling pumped, I confidently stepped out of the yellow cab and walked up to the hotel, a three-story building tucked between two restaurants. As I approached his room on the second floor, I nervously clenched my fists, as if preparing for a fight.

I knocked on the door several times and got no reply. I had to look up my text messages to make sure I had the correct room. I banged louder on the door and almost called out his name when I heard some movement in the room. Then I knocked again, and he replied, "I'm coming."

As I waited, I paced back and forth. With each step, I began to doubt my actions. Was I that insecure? And did I not believe that Bubbles was in love with me? It wasn't too late to turn back. What was I doing at this hotel room on a Friday evening?

When the doorknob turned and the door slowly opened, I stopped pacing and stood at the door as confidently as I could, determined to meet this Ade and get this done with—once and for all.

Chapter 29

New York, NY
February 2007

Ade

The flight to New York was a smooth six hours. I slept through most of the journey with the help of a few shots of whiskey. I had been a bundle of nerves since the day I received Bubbles' text message. I was energetic, chirpy, and generally in high spirits—a far cry from the days, weeks, and months before.

The news about Noma's cheating weighed heavily on me, but the prospect of going to see the love of my life neutralized the feeling of betrayal. This was no ordinary trip, but a crucial one, because finally I would get to have a one-on-one chat with Bubbles, and I could plead my case in person instead of via secret text messages, like silly teenagers.

Just before the plane took off, I called Bola. She picked up my mood from the tone of my voice.

"You sound weird," she said. "What's going on? Are you on something?"

"Nah, I'm just glad to be taking a break from it all."

"What do you mean?"

"It's a lot to talk about over the phone. I'll fill you in as soon as I get back, because I may be returning with even more news."

"What are you talking about? What are you going to bring back after a stupid cardiology conference? Stop talking in riddles and spill the beans already."

"Okay, for starters, I told Noma it's over between us."

"What? Why? I thought you guys were doing fine. I'm confused."

"Now you see why you have to wait for my return. It's too much to tell over the phone. Anyway, I've got to go now."

She was silent, probably still digesting what I'd just told her, then replied in a subdued voice, "Okay, I guess I'll wait. Are you doing okay—?"

"Yes, yes, I'm fine. Don't worry about me. I'll call you on Sunday when I land."

"Fine, call me when you get to New York. Enjoy yourself. I love you."

I couldn't remember the last time Bola told me she loved me. She always gave me big bear hugs, but never actually said the words. I knew right then that she would worry about me till I returned, so I made a mental note to call Bola first thing when I touched down at Heathrow Airport on Sunday.

I arrived in New York on a frigid morning with temperatures in the low forties. Even on a cold day, the New York streets were crowded with people and cabs. It was my third time coming here, and I loved the vibe. That I was here to meet Bubbles made me truly happy, definitely the happiest I had been in a very long time. My sunshine had come on this cold February day.

I had made a reservation at a boutique hotel in downtown Manhattan, the sort that Bubbles would like—modern, but with the more intimate feel of a traditional bed and breakfast. I checked into my room on the second floor of the hotel. The room was tiny but elegant, facing a brick wall and an alley, not flattering at all. But I wasn't here for a view of the city, I was a man on a mission, and nothing else mattered.

Before I took a hot shower and ordered food, I sent Bubbles a message with my hotel name and room number. I told her I would take a nap and included my room phone number if she wanted to call me. Finally, we would ditch the messaging and start to talk.

Too tired to go out, and not ready to face the cold in search of a restaurant, I ordered a steak with fries from the limited hotel menu. I timed it all so that the food would be ready after my shower. After eating, I collapsed onto the bed and immediately fell asleep.

I woke up to a loud knock on the door. Disoriented and sluggish from a combination of fatigue and jet lag, coupled with the room's darkness, I sat up in the bed, confused. Then that loud and urgent knock again. This person must have been knocking a long time. I suddenly remembered where I was and why I was here. That could be Bubbles knocking.

I leaped out of bed and fumbled to turn on the light switch. A white fluorescent light lit up the room. "I'm coming!" I called, looking around for my clothes. I put on my pants and shirt in haste. I wasn't sure for how long I had been sleeping. I must look terrible, I thought. I needed to brush my teeth. This unkempt state wasn't exactly how I imagined our first meeting.

I had lost track of time. Winter days were short, and night came too early. My food tray was on the chest of drawers, with leftovers and a big steak knife on the plate. I felt the urge to tidy up the little mess I had made with the food tray and my luggage on the floor, but another loud and angry-sounding knock made me rush for the door instead. I took a deep breath and slowly opened the door. I was so nervous, and I hated myself for feeling that way.

"How can I help you?" I asked the stranger who stood before me. He must have the wrong room. I was disappointed it wasn't Bubbles, but slightly relieved that she wouldn't have to see me looking so clumsy.

"Are you Ade?" he asked in an English accent, completely unexpected.

"Yes, and who are you?" I replied, studying this white man who seemed very sure of something.

"I'm Maita's boyfriend."

Part VII

Chapter 30

London, UK
February 2007

Noma

It was Sunday, the alarm clock read 10:33 p.m., and here I waited, impatiently, for Ade to come home. His flight from New York should have arrived at 8:45 a.m. I contacted British Airways, and the customer service lady confirmed that the flight made it to Heathrow from JFK on time.

I had called Bola shortly after one o'clock. "Have you heard from Ade? He hasn't come home." Unlike me, she didn't seem worried and casually replied, "He may have extended his stay in New York. He's probably having a good time there."

"Have you tried to call him?" I asked, since they talked regularly on the phone.

"No, strangely his phone has been switched off since Friday. I figured he forgot his phone charger, and the battery is dead."

Surprised at her dismissive tone, I asked, "Do you have any information about the conference or his hotel? I can call him there." She didn't have his travel details. "Let me know if he contacts you. Bye."

I looked up cardiology conferences in New York via a Google search, but that came up with no results. There was a conference in Las Vegas scheduled for the last week of March, so it hadn't even happened yet. Even though he was mad at me, he still had to return home, and he had to go to work on Monday. So where was he?

I couldn't stop thinking about Ade, how he'd practically broken up with me. I'd cried all night at the thought of Ade leaving me. The next day, I called in sick to work and canceled a night shift. Ade had been nothing but good to me in the two years that we had been together. He was a gentleman who knew how to take care of his woman, and I knew that I was fortunate to have him. However, I was tired of being his girlfriend and wanted more than the live-in girlfriend status. I wanted a ring, a white gown, and all the benefits that came with being married.

That Sunday night I lay in our bed, staring at the ceiling, thinking about what went wrong in our relationship. Regrettably, I was responsible for pushing him away, and I was the one that cheated. Monica, the backstabber, used to say, "You don't love Ade, you love the idea of being with him because he fits the profile of a perfect boyfriend."

She was right. Ade made me feel safe and secure, and because of the way he provided for me, I was the envy of all my girlfriends, especially Monica. Unlike the men my friends dated, Ade didn't enjoy being out in the pubs and clubs every weekend, drinking and chasing girls. He didn't have a clique of guys he hung with, but was more of a loner who chose to stay home and watch movies. He preferred to go into the city for dinner, or watch a play on the West End, go biking with the local cycle crew, and occasionally take impromptu trips to European cities. All of this had been fun early in our relationship because they were new experiences, and I was willing to learn new things. But it certainly wasn't my cup of tea.

I couldn't stand musicals or West End plays with their endless singing, and to this day I found it all so dull. Dining at fancy restaurants was fun initially, but when my friends couldn't join us because they couldn't afford the pricey menus, it became taxing to sit with his friends and their boring wives, talking about work, books, and politics.

We went out dancing at some London clubs, including the African and Caribbean clubs that I preferred. That was always fun, and my girlfriends would join us. Ade took care of my single girlfriends, paid for their food and drinks, and made sure they were comfortable. He tried to strike up conversations with my friends' male companions, but it was clear that he was a fish out of water in the African clubs that I liked. However, as time progressed, Ade had complained that my girlfriends were too materialistic, behaved wildly in the clubs, and switched boyfriends so often it was worrying.

So, as time went on, we drifted. Ade went out with his group of snobbish, intellectual friends, and I went with my girlfriends to the African clubs and Zimbabwean barbecues that we enjoyed. There, I let loose, and shamefully I would flirt with guys, including ex-boyfriends. I was one of the best dressed, because I could afford expensive clothes and shoes, and I drove the latest Mercedes Benz, so naturally I got a lot of attention from both the guys and girls. That was my scene, and I would rather be there than sit through *Les Misérables,* or go to some jazz festival.

At Club Afrique, I met an old high school boyfriend, Vusumuzi, whom we called Vusa. At Milton High School in Bulawayo, where we grew up, he'd been a skinny, lanky nerd who couldn't come up with a decent chat-up line. Despite this though, we hit it off, and dated for two years. He was my first everything—date, kiss, and sex.

Now he had morphed into a handsome ladies' man who all the girls were crazy over. My relationship with Ade went south when I began having an affair with Vusa. Both of us were cheating on our partners when we made out in his car after a night at the club. I enjoyed being with Vusa, especially the spontaneous sex in his car or in the DJ booth, where I would often give him a blow job. It was risky, naughty, and fun every time. We talked daily on the phone, and we were careful to never call each other after hours, except when we were on night shifts. Sometimes we booked a room at a bed and breakfast for quick sex, before returning to our respective partners. I began to find Ade downright boring, and I didn't complain when he stopped touching me, or when we'd go weeks without sex.

That was the only time I ever cheated on Ade. Six months after we started our romance, as we became more reckless, word got around to Vusa's wife and her friends, and they came for me at a mutual friend's baby shower.

"There's that whore, messing with my husband," Vusa's wife called out in front of everyone. When I tried to make an exit, she lunged and pulled me by my weave.

"Leave me alone," I screamed. I don't remember much from that day, except for being dragged to the floor and viciously kicked as she called me names. "*Hure!* You're a bitch and a slut!"

There was no way I could return home to Ade bruised all over, with a black eye and swollen face. How would I explain all this to him? So, I went to my sister's house in Luton and stayed there for a week. I called in sick from work.

By then, my relationship with an unsuspecting Ade had eroded to irreparable levels, and he didn't call to look for me until the fifth day. No questions as to why and no concern at all. He obviously didn't miss me.

This Ade was the new, coldhearted Ade, different from the broken, kind, and gentle Ade I'd met a little over two years ago.

Unlike me, I doubt that Ade ever cheated. My only concern was that he didn't seem at all bothered by our dry spells, or lack of intimacy. When we went for days without talking outside of daily greetings and small talk, Ade continued like everything was fine. As a result, I began to wonder if maybe he *was* seeing someone else.

I suspected that since Vusa fulfilled my sexual needs, Ade was probably doing the same with someone else. A forensic search of every corner of the house, and prying through his phone, yielded nothing. And to top it off, I could account for all his time between home and work. He was either at home, work, the gym, or with Bola, and that left no window of opportunity to indulge in another relationship.

Then he dropped a bomb on me and confronted me about Vusa, and after he said we should go our separate ways, I realized how good I had it, and I didn't want to leave. I had something to share with him and hoped that this was what would bring us back together, that maybe he would finally marry me. I was eager for his return, and I'd laid out my presentation and speech. I planned to give a full confession about my dealings with Vusa, apologize and promise to be faithful. Tell him I loved him, and that I was willing to do whatever it took to fix things.

I planned to remind him of a night about three months ago when his sister and cousin came for dinner, and we were all in good spirits—drinking, eating, and laughing. A rare thing in our house, but we knew how to put our issues aside for a while when we had people over, and sometimes we showed each other bursts of emotion, usually over a bottle of bourbon or cognac. That night we had wild sex like two dogs in heat. We hadn't been intimate for weeks, and the raw sex that erupted had me screaming, and screaming for more. I'm certain I woke our guests—and the neighbors.

It had to be that night that he planted this tiny seed inside me, and I was glad it was on a night that we were in love, even if it was just for that night. After weeks of feeling extremely moody, lethargic, and nauseous, I found out that I was pregnant. I used the IUD birth control and so this came as a surprise. The doctor said it was possible, as no birth control had a one-hundred-percent guarantee.

I planned to take Ade to dinner and give him the good news on Valentine's Day, just three days away now. This news would surely bring us closer. We could revamp our relationship, get married, and build a solid family together... but he'd broken up with me before I could tell him. He had no idea that I was carrying his baby and was close to twelve weeks pregnant already. It was bittersweet, because it would take me getting pregnant to get Ade back, and hopefully force him to marry me.

We would be eternally bound to each other. He couldn't possibly leave me pregnant. That gentle, caring, and loving man I met two years ago would be back.

I smiled to myself as these thoughts raced through my mind, and when my phone rang, I sprung up from the bed, hoping it was Ade.

It was Bola. "Hey, has Ade called or anything?" she asked. "I'm getting worried because I called British Airways, and after much convincing, they disclosed that he wasn't on the flight." She sounded urgent and anxious, unlike the calm and collected Bola I'd spoken to earlier that day.

My heart was racing. "What are you saying? He's still in New York?"

"Most likely, and the puzzling thing is that I asked a cardiologist friend of his about the conference, and he said there was no conference in New York. He attends all the annual conferences worldwide, and New York wasn't on the calendar."

"Are you saying he lied? Why would he go to New York then? Who's in New York?" My emotions changed from worry to anger. I was angry that he'd lied to me.

"I don't know of anyone in New York. We do have an uncle in Florida, but why would he lie about going to see him, if that's where he went?" Then Bola paused and asked, "Did something happen between the two of you? He told me you broke up just before he left."

"What does that have to do with any of this? He's supposed to be at work tomorrow, right?" I was trying to make sense of it all. "He'll show up. Ade has never missed a day of work, not in the two years that I have known him."

"That's my brother, always an honest and upright guy. Gosh, I hope he's okay. Something doesn't feel right. If he doesn't show up by morning, I'm calling the police. Let's touch base tomorrow."

"Okay, and please, if you hear from him, call me. Good night."

I sat up at the edge of the bed, gazing at the wall. Ade had lied and gone to America after breaking up with me. He never had a connection to America, except that he once considered relocating to practice medicine there. But that was before I met him.

It suddenly occurred to me that he *did* have a connection to America—his ex-girlfriend. Was it a mere coincidence that he would break up with me just before leaving for an unexpected and random visit to America, on the pretense that he was going to a conference? The so-called upright and honest guy was lying. What else was he hiding? Was he getting back with this Bubbles? Why after so long? How could that be possible?

Well, I was the one carrying his baby, so he'd better hurry back. And forget about Bubbles.

Chapter 31

London, UK
February 2007

Bola

I hadn't slept all night. Something didn't feel right. My brother had promised that he would call me as soon as he landed from New York, but he hadn't made contact and had disappeared into thin air, which was very much unlike him. I planned to call my parents and ask if they had heard from him, but I didn't want to worry them. I knew my mum would panic over her beloved Ade.

On Monday morning, a cold and windy day, a calm Noma called and said, "Bola, I don't think there's anything to worry about. I think I know where Ade is."

"What do you mean?" I asked, starting my car engine and turning up the heat.

"I think he went to see his ex-girlfriend. That's why he lied about a conference in New York, and another reason why he broke up with me the night before he left."

It seemed far-fetched that Ade would be going to see Maita, yet Noma could be right, because Ade had been rather *too* excited about going to a conference, and when he told me about the breakup, he hadn't been that sad about it. On the contrary, he seemed happy.

"Are you sure?" I asked. "What makes you think that?"

"I'm sure. Don't bother calling the police and causing unnecessary alarm. Ade is a grown man, and he knows what he's doing. I'll wait for him to return. If he calls you, let me know."

"Okay, I'm sorry about the breakup and all. I'm sure you two will work things out somehow." I didn't know what else to say.

I sat in my car with the engine roaring, heat at full blast, thinking everything through. Ade *might* have gone to see Maita. She meant a lot to him, but she'd also broken his heart terribly when she left for America. The excitement in his voice when I last spoke to him, just before he'd boarded his flight, was undeniable—not that of a man who had just broken up with his live-in girlfriend of two years.

I exhaled deeply with relief. He was okay, after all. Yet something still nagged at me, and I decided to contact Maita and check if indeed Ade was with her.

How would I begin to find Maita's contact information? I could probably find her on Facebook, I thought, tapping the steering wheel with my fingers. I was sure I had her email from years ago, when we'd shared some party photos. That was assuming Maita hadn't changed her email address. Was I taking this too far?

I decided to wait a day or two, and if I didn't hear from Ade, I would try to contact Maita. Feeling reassured by the possibility of Ade being with his ex, I drove off to work, satisfied that there was no need to panic or call the police. My brother would be home soon. I had to be patient, but I couldn't help being worried that he hadn't tried to reach out. Any excuse for missing his flight was better than this silence.

After work that evening, I drove to Ade's house, agitated and overcome with worry since I still hadn't heard from him. He hadn't called into work either.

Noma was home, and she wasn't as calm as she'd sounded over the phone. She was pacing back and forth in the living room, worried.

"Have you called Gbenga?" she asked me. "Could Ade have gone to visit him in Birmingham?"

"Gbenga hasn't spoken to Ade in over a week. I called him on my way here. He is always so busy studying, and he never checks on us anyway. I think I need to call my parents now. I've been holding off thinking Ade would surely be back by now. If they haven't heard from him, then we should call the police."

It was 7:45 p.m. in Nigeria, and I knew my mother would be preparing to watch the eight o'clock news before retiring to bed, so it was a good time to call her.

"*Oluwa mi, ki lo se le si omo mi,*" she cried in Yoruba. "Where is my son? Are you telling me that he's missing? Have you called the police?"

I could hear my father mumbling in the background. Then he took the phone from her, and his voice boomed into my ear: "Bola, you must contact the police now. Call us back immediately after reporting him as missing. I'm going to make flight arrangements, and I will be there as soon as possible. This is not a small issue."

Talking to my parents heightened my sense of urgency. Noma now sat on the couch, biting her lower lip and fighting back tears. I called the local police station and reported Ade as missing. I provided his flight details and the little information I had about his trip to New York, and the police officer reassured me that they would immediately investigate.

My mind raced with ideas on what to do next. I had to track Ade's steps. I already had his flight details checked with British Airways, so I needed to follow any hotel reservations.

"Noma, did Ade take his laptop?" I asked. "He probably did. Does he still have a desktop computer?"

"It's in our bedroom, and we hardly use it," she replied in a whisper.

I rushed to the bedroom, fired up the desktop, and rapidly logged into his email—I knew his password.

I felt a sense of relief when I saw the email with his hotel reservations—one step closer. I scribbled the details on a piece of paper and continued scrolling through his inbox, looking for an email from Maita. I was about to give up on the search when I decided to search through his *sent mail,* and there I found an email he'd sent to Maita.

I began to cry tears of hope, because I wanted to believe that he was somewhere safe with Maita, that Noma was right—he had run off to his ex-girlfriend. I wanted it to be true.

"Are you okay?" Noma asked, standing behind me and reading the email. Ade was *checking in* on Maita.

"I knew it, the lying cheat," she said. "What a hypocrite. Ade is with his ex-girlfriend."

"Let's not jump to conclusions," I said, wiping away tears. "At least we have Maita's email address, and now I will email her to ask if she's seen Ade. I also have his hotel reservation. Let me send the email to Maita, then make some calls."

I emailed Maita and included my mobile number, urging her to call me back; it was an urgent matter. Then I called the hotel in New York—and it was that phone call that shocked me to the core.

When I mentioned who I was and why I was calling, the lady at reception said, "Please hold the line. You need to speak with my supervisor." I knew then that something was wrong. When the hotel supervisor came to the phone and told me he would connect me to the New York Police Department, I crumbled to the floor and screamed, "What has happened? Tell me *now*."

Noma knelt beside me. "What is it, Bola? Is Ade okay? What did they say?"

Something terrible must have happened to Ade. I put my phone on speaker as we waited for a connection to the NYPD.

Chapter 32

New York, NY
February 2007

Chris

"What? Where is she, and what are you doing here?"

Ade looked nothing like I had imagined. He was tall, muscular, and broad-shouldered. I had envisioned him to be of more diminutive stature, perhaps because Maita was petite. But standing next to this guy, she must have looked tiny.

Now intimidated by his presence, I failed to make eye contact and looked him up and down instead. He must have just woken up, because he looked disheveled.

"I'm here to talk to you. Can I come in?"

It had to be strange and unexpected to have me there instead of Maita, but I pushed on. "Please, may I come in?" I persisted, surprised at my steady and controlled voice. Ade, on the other hand, looked confused and worried.

"Is she all right? Where is she?" he asked, opening the door wider to let me in.

The room was small, and as the door slammed behind me, I felt a little awkward to be alone with a stranger in his hotel room. I decided to just get to the point. "I need you to stop communicating with my girlfriend. You've been trying to get her to leave me, and I don't appreciate it—"

"Wait, what are you talking about? How did you find out about our texts, and how did you know where to find me?" He spoke in a West African accent mixed with an English tone, but very different from Maita's, which sounded much softer.

"You've been texting *me* all this time, thinking it was Maita. I read the first email you sent, and I'm the one who's been sending all those text messages."

His eyes widened in disbelief. "What? I've been chatting with you all this time? You've been *playing* me? Maita doesn't know?"

"She never read any of your messages, and she wants nothing to do with you," I replied.

I could see Ade's chest rising and falling, his breath getting deeper and faster. "You can't be serious," he shouted. "How do you know that Maita doesn't want me, huh? If she never saw my messages, how can you be so sure? You're a sick man. Get out of my room now."

"What happened in the summer of 2005?" Whatever happened that summer was a question that had been nagging me, but I couldn't ask Bubbles directly.

His shoulders dropped, and he wiped beads of sweat off his forehead. "Why don't you ask her yourself? You came all this way to ask me that? Get out of here before I call the police."

I lashed out. "What were you hoping to get by flying all this way from England? You came to break us up, you jealous fuck."

"You need to leave now," he said, pointing to the door. He was sweating and breathing heavily. I could tell he was seething with anger.

"Maita doesn't give a shit about you. She's mine now, and I intend to marry her. You had your chance, and you lost out, so now bugger off and don't ever try to contact her again."

"You made me fly all this way to tell me that you want to marry Maita? You're a sick man. Why didn't you just tell me over the phone? Are you that insecure?"

Ade's words stung. "I made you come here because I wanted to see just how desperate you are, and to tell you to your face to fuck off. Maita never talks about you. You were insignificant—"

"In June 2005 she begged me to take her back. She cried in my arms and told me she loved me. She had flown from Atlanta for one reason: me. So, you can't tell me she doesn't love me. She told me she met some dude that summer, and he was after her, but she wanted me instead. Was it you?" Ade chuckled and shook his head slowly. "She settled for you because I wouldn't take her back. After telling her that I had moved on, she cried for me. So, there you have it; you were second best." He had a satisfied look on his face, as if he had won a competition, which infuriated me. "Think about it. You're a coward to pretend to be Maita and not give her the chance to either turn me down or leave you. You spoke for her, and I know if she had the chance, she would take me back. You can never have what we had."

I ran my fingers through my hair. "Listen to me, you fat fuck. You stay away from Maita, you hear me—"

"Or what? What will you do? You're the sick one, pretending to be someone and luring me here. What do you think Maita would say if she found out, huh?"

"Stay away from her, you hear me, and don't try to call, text, or email her again."

Ade took a step toward me. With an arrogant smirk, he whispered, "Or what? What will you do?"

I stepped back, aware that he was much bigger and taller than me. I backed up against the chest of drawers that held a TV and a tray of leftovers.

I spat back at him, "Be a man and stop begging like a bitch for her to take you back. Leave us alone. I'm going to marry her."

"She settled with you because you were her rebound," Ade hissed. "Now get out before I call the police. You lied and tricked your way here. Let's see what Maita has to say about *that*."

The mention of the police didn't frighten me. But the thought of Maita finding out that I had pretended to be her? She would never forgive me, and this could be the final straw. "You wouldn't dare tell her," I said, blood surging like a storm through my veins.

"So, how did you think this would end?" Ade asked. "That you would come here and tell me to leave her, and I'd just let her go? That I wouldn't tell her? I know how to get to her directly. Don't think you own her. I will tell her; she deserves to know you're a sick psycho."

When he said this, I reached for the steak knife on the food tray, and without thinking I lunged at him. He was taken off guard and reacted a second too late. Before he could block the knife, it landed deep in his neck. There was a moment when time stood still, and then it all happened in slow motion as he staggered backward toward the bed, then fell to the floor, clutching his neck. Blood gushed down his hands and chest.

I froze and felt a warm sensation spreading down my thigh. Looking down, I realized that my bladder had reacted to my shock. He was gurgling, and his eyes rolled to the back of his head. Still, I stood there paralyzed, not knowing what to do. Bloody hell! How would I explain any of this? Why was I there? Should I call for help or make a run for it?

Ade was writhing and moaning, his eyes bulging and glaring at me, pleading for help. In shock and trembling with fear, I turned to leave. Then it dawned on me that I had left traces of my fingerprints. Nauseous and feeling weak, I muttered, "Oh, shit."

Using a washcloth from the bathroom, I wiped down all the places I had come in contact with, which wasn't much more than the chest of drawers, and the doorknob. I had wet my pants, but no leaks, just an embarrassing wet patch. I used the washcloth to open the door and wiped the doorknob again.

Before I shut the door, I remembered his phone, which could link me directly to Ade, especially if he'd saved all the messages. I had to find that phone. How could I do this without leaving prints? I ran my fingers through my hair in panic.

Then I had an idea. I ripped out the plastic liners in the bathroom trash can, wrapped the plastic around my hands like makeshift gloves, and began searching the room for his phone.

Ade had tucked his phone under a pillow. He must have gone to sleep expecting a call from Maita. Wishful thinking. I put the phone in my pocket and quickly made my way out. After taking one last glance at his big, motionless body, I shut the door.

I looked around the hallway and didn't see a surveillance

camera—perhaps the one good thing about this small hotel. I was sure there were cameras in the elevator or other public areas of the hotel, so I kept my head low and didn't make eye contact with anyone. The lobby was busy with people checking in on a Friday evening. No one paid attention to me—just another white bloke walking out of a New York hotel. I slowly and steadily walked out and away. After watching so many crime shows, I knew that I had to distance myself from the hotel before I hailed a taxi. There should be no witness connecting me to the hotel. As calmly as I could, I walked into the cold night.

The horrendous scene played over and over in my head. My legs felt like lead, and my chest felt tight, a sharp pain piercing through it with each step. I had *killed* a man… killed for Maita. She had warned me about my explosive temper, and how when I got angry I often reached for the nearest object and threw it at the wall. Once I had thrown her handbag and smashed her glasses. I had to replace the lens and get the frame repaired. That was one of many examples, and today in a fit of rage, I'd used a steak knife to kill a man.

Walking with my head down and covered by the hoodie on my jacket, I began to cry. I was sure I had walked at least three blocks when I finally hailed a yellow cab and instructed the driver to take me to my hotel. My mind was playing tricks on me—what happened in that hotel room had to be a nightmare from which I could escape by merely waking up, but it wasn't.

In a dark and twisted way, though, I felt slight relief that Ade would never bother us again.

He was gone, and Maita was all mine.

Chapter 33

Atlanta, GA
February 2007

Maita

My flight to Phoenix had been delayed. I waited impatiently at the American Airlines gate, listening to Rod Stewart's raspy voice sing "My Heart Can't Tell You No" from my iPhone. The sweet melody served as a distraction from the constant worry about my uncertain future—and my bold decision to move to Arizona.

Chris had no idea that I had left him. After weeks of debating whether to stay or go, I'd finally made up my mind and waited for the best time to leave him for good. Things had never been the same since that altercation two months ago. Although we continued as if nothing had happened, the damage was profound and irreversible. I couldn't erase from my memory his dark eyes and violent outburst when he shoved me out of *his* house at three o'clock in the morning. That incident, compounded with all the other things he did or didn't do, had left me deeply shaken.

We both tried hard to make things work, maybe too hard, and it wasn't organic. Chris was going out of his way to please me, and I couldn't help but think it was fake, that he would soon default to his selfish ways. As usual, I had called Lindy to vent, and she accused me of being a complainer.

"You whined about how he didn't show concern, but now that he's trying, you think it's fake. What do you want?"

"I don't know," I replied. "But I know that I'm not happy, and I'm not feeling Chris like before. I can't pretend anymore."

"So, let me guess, you want to leave him and go, where?"

It dawned on me that, like Chris, she assumed that I couldn't survive in America alone. Offended by this, I cried into the phone, "I came to this country by myself and got this far by my sweat. Why should I suddenly be dependent on a man and stay in an unhappy relationship? For what?"

"I meant, where will you go since you don't have a job and you're broke? At least Chris is providing a place for you to stay rent-free, and without worries about bills. It can't be that bad that you can't hang in there till you get sorted."

I was speechless listening to Lindy's continuous rambling. That was the moment that I'd decided to leave Chris. I never subscribed to the idea of staying with a man for convenience. I wasn't going to be one of those long-suffering wives or girlfriends, like Lindy, who would endure an unhappy marriage or relationship because of their fear of being alone.

"I refuse to be reduced to the sort of woman who pretends to be in love just to get ahead, and it's not fair to Chris. I'll take my chances. I need to get a job, get my own place, and start from there."

"When will you tell him it's over?" Lindy seemed to be enjoying the idea that I'd be stranded and helpless.

Ignoring that, I said, "I've done some research, and I can get a job as a research associate in public health, or as a rehabilitation technician. That will be an easy job for me. I'm overqualified for it, but it will keep me going till I get credentialed, take the national physical therapy examinations, hopefully pass and get licensed. The next available date to take the exam is in April, so I have two months to prepare."

"Typical Bubbles, always with a grand plan. How far with your papers? Any luck with the immigration situation?"

I sighed. "I've consulted a lawyer, one of those free phone calls before you sign up and start paying through your nose. I need to change my status before my OPT expires. If I pass my physical therapy exam and get licensed, the lawyer can help me apply for a green card, or I could apply for a job, and the employer will sponsor my work permit—"

"Or, Chris could marry you, and you automatically get a spousal visa or something, right?"

"I don't want to get married for that reason, and I just told you that I'm not that girl."

"Of course, you'd only marry for love. Has Chris even offered to help you with your papers? I'd be surprised if he did. He doesn't seem interested in that part of your life."

Lindy's venomous tone was causing its desired effect, but I wasn't in the mood for a fight. After all, she was right. Chris had never showed the slightest interest or concern about my immigration woes. As long as we were happy, living in the moment, he didn't care about anything else. I ignored this too.

"I'm glad I don't have to deal with all that immigration drama," Lindy said.

"Yes, be grateful that your parents had you here before they returned to Zimbabwe."

Lindy was an American citizen, born in Memphis, and raised in Zimbabwe.

"I've started looking for work around Atlanta, and I have some good leads," I said.

Lindy surprised me by saying, "Why Atlanta? Apart from Chris, who else do you know there? Why don't you come to Phoenix instead?"

"Staying in Atlanta seems like the natural course, I guess."

"Come here and stay with us while you get yourself situated, or with my cousin, Noni. She just bought a house, and I know she wouldn't mind a housemate for a while."

That was how the idea to leave Chris evolved into me running off to Phoenix. I was afraid to break up with him in person.

When Chris told me he had to go to Dallas for work, I knew instantly that this was my chance to get away without any drama. It was odd that he would travel for work on a Friday, because his offices were usually closed on the weekend, and he would arrive there late in the afternoon or evening. Who wanted a meeting at the end of the day on a Friday? Maybe Dallas folk? I didn't care to ask; I was glad for an opportunity to escape. He would return to an empty house. I didn't want to leave him this way, but I saw no other option.

I couldn't admit to anyone, especially not Lindy, a victim of repeated domestic abuse, that I was afraid of Chris's reaction if I told him to his face that I was leaving. I had seen the darkness in his eyes many times before, and on the night of the big fight, they had looked evil. It wasn't his fake anxiety attacks that scared me—I was frightened of what he might do to me. I had a deep fear that Chris could easily snap and possibly harm me.

"I've planned my escape for this Saturday, when he's out of town." I told Lindy. "I arranged for my friend, Simone, to come by the house and collect all my boxed belongings. She's volunteered to store them in a garage for a while."

"That's quick. What's the rush? Saturday is four days away. Have you talked to Noni already? Does she know you'll be coming this weekend?"

"Yes, I did, and she's fine with me coming there at short notice. I have to act now while Chris is away on business. It's simpler this way."

"Sounds like you're running away. After everything you have shared, does he deserve this? Just tell him it's over, then leave. Don't burn your bridges."

"Who knew you cared that much for Chris? If he only knew how much you always support him. Look, I don't feel comfortable telling—"

"Are you afraid of what he might do to you? No need to explain. Just get your crazy self to Phoenix soon. Let me know if you need help paying for the ticket."

As soon as I got off the phone, with Lindy's help I purchased a one-way ticket to Phoenix. Noni had agreed to have me as a housemate for a few months while I settled in and found a job. There, I had it all worked out. Now, on to the next chapter.

I felt relief—no sorrow, no regret, no loss, and no love. In fact, I felt free. Ready to get my life in order, away from Chris breathing down my neck. He would probably try to find me, but I planned to change my number. And since he never befriended Lindy, he didn't have her contact. There was no way he could find me. I wrote him a cliché Dear John letter and left it on his kitchen counter.

Dear Chris,

I will start by apologizing for leaving this way, but I had no choice. I know that this will hurt and I am sorry. I decided to leave because we both can tell and feel that things haven't been the same for months. I'm not happy anymore. Please forgive me for leaving this way. I need to figure myself out and get my life in order—alone.

I did love you, and I will cherish all the memories, but I must leave. Please don't try to find me. I know our paths will cross one day. I wish you love and happiness.

I will always care about you,
Maita

I cried as I wrote the letter, because I could already imagine how painful reading this letter would be—another broken heart, courtesy of Maita. Maybe Lindy was right: I gave up too soon, and I was a heartbreaker. I had done something similar to Ade, and then later, I was the one begging him to take me back. Would I be back here asking Chris to take me back? Would he reject me and move on as Ade did?

I hardly thought about Ade anymore; I'd made a conscious decision not to. But now, after writing a break-up letter to Chris, Ade was on my mind. I imagined him happily married with kids and a perfect family. Did I ever cross his mind? For the first time in a very long time, I considered calling or texting him to find out how he was doing. Try as I may, I couldn't ignore the sinking feeling in the pit of my stomach— revived by thoughts of Ade. I still cared about him.

My reality was that I had just broken up with Chris, who loved me obsessively, declaring that I would rather be alone than unhappy. What if I never found happiness? I contemplated tearing up the letter, unpacking my bags, and pretending none of this ever happened. But I knew what I had to do, and staying was not it.

I was ready for a new start—no ex-boyfriend drama. Once again, as I sat at the American Airlines gate on that cold Saturday morning listening to my soothing music, I toyed with the idea of reaching out to Ade. As a newly single girl, I could. I hoped that he had changed his mind about me, that things never worked out with his girlfriend, and he was single too. Maybe getting back with Ade would be my happy ending.

"Forget it," I said out loud. "Have some pride and forget about him."

Chapter 34

Phoenix, Arizona
February 2007

Maita

It was Monday evening, my third day in Phoenix, when I got an email from Bola. I was still adjusting to my new environment, staying with Noni in her new townhouse. I planned to stay there no more than six months. By then, I would hopefully have a job and my own place. I had ten months left on my current visa, time was precious, and I had very little of it.

I spent countless hours on internet job sites, searching for public health jobs. I frequented blog sites run by Indian and Philippine immigrants who provided information about applying for a work permit with immigration lawyers, and how to study for the NPTE exams. As a result, I always had my laptop with me, doing research and occasionally checking my email.

I hadn't been in contact with Bola in years. Therefore, when her email popped up, I was stunned, and immediately opened it:

Hi Maita,
I hope you're well. I know this will come to you as a surprise. I realize that Ade has been in touch with you. He left London last week Thursday for New York, and we have not heard from him since. He didn't show up for work today. Have you seen or heard from him? Are you with him? We are worried. Please call me on my mobile as soon as you get this message.
My number is: +44 7700 900 639
Regards,
Bola

I sat up on the couch and turned off the TV that was now noise to my ears as I processed what I had just read. The most disturbing thing was that I hadn't contacted Ade since 2005, so why would Bola apparently think I would meet him in New York? What was this about?

I immediately called Bola. It was probably close to midnight in London. When she heard my voice, she began to cry and continued to sob without saying a word. Someone was in the background, asking Bola who she was talking to on the phone.

"Hello, Bola, what's going on? Are you okay?"

"Hi, Maita, Ade is … oh, I can't breathe… Ade's in a coma, he could die…"

I could hear her hyperventilating, and someone offering a glass of water.

Why was Ade in a coma? And what did I have to do with this? It hadn't sunk in yet that Bola had just informed me that Ade, *my* Ade, could die.

She returned, sounding more composed. "We were told by the NYPD that Ade was found stabbed in his hotel room in New York. They're investigating the case. I can't believe this…"

She continued to cry.

I was shocked, devastated, and speechless. I cut the phone in denial. Ade stabbed in New York? How could it be? I sat in silence. The world around me seemed to have stopped except my heart, now beating fast as it bled. After close to fifteen minutes of silence and paralysis, I called Bola again.

This time she wasn't crying, and made more sense. She told me how things had unfolded since Sunday, how Ade didn't return to England as planned. She had gone through all his emails from as far back as September last year, looking for clues, and had come across emails I'd exchanged with Ade in January. She found the email in which I gave Ade my cell phone number to communicate via text messages, and not email.

I was stunned. "Bola, what do you mean I sent Ade an email? I haven't had any communication with him since June or July of 2005."

"What are you saying?" she stammered.

"He moved on, and so did I."

"But in the email, you gave him your mobile number."

When she told me the phone number mentioned in the email, I immediately recognized it as Chris's work cell. It was all too much to take in. How did Chris get involved with Ade? What was going on? I was confused.

For the first time since I'd learned about Ade's condition, I shed tears.

"I know that phone number," I said. "But it's not mine. I'm not sure what's going on here, but someone else sent that email, not me. And I think I know who. Let me look through my email and figure this out. I can't believe this…"

Now I was sobbing uncontrollably.

"My parents are flying to New York from Nigeria tomorrow, and I will meet them there. We need you to come too. I'm sure the police will want to talk to you." She spoke in a low, hoarse voice from too much crying. Then she added, "Ade had broken up with his girlfriend just before he left for New York. He's going to be a father. His girlfriend, Noma, is pregnant, but Ade didn't know. She didn't get an opportunity to tell him before he left for New York. Oh, God, I can't take this, God help me…"

"Bola, I knew *nothing* about the email and the trip to New York. I can't think straight right now. Let me call you tomorrow, and yes, I will come to meet you in New York."

His girlfriend was expecting his baby—it hurt like hell. I was already an emotional wreck, and this somehow worsened everything. Why did he break up with her? And what was he doing in New York? I had lost Ade in more ways than one. This one was a different type of loss. A baby signified an unbreakable bond between Ade and his girlfriend, which meant I would *never* have any chance to reconcile with him.

Then again, if he didn't survive this, we would all lose him forever.

Chapter 35

Atlanta, GA
February 2007

Chris

I returned to Atlanta on Saturday, scared out of my mind and visibly shaking. After leaving Ade's hotel room in New York on Friday night, I had successfully returned to my own hotel without being stopped by the police. No one looked for me, and there were no police banging on my hotel door. The world around me had continued, and yet I had just killed a man. I was a murderer, a killer, and I would have to live with this for the rest of my life.

That night in my room, I headed straight for the minibar and guzzled every drop of alcohol. I paced up and down in the small space, trying to think of what to do next. For fuck's sake! How the hell did I end up here? My gut swam, my head spun. *End it*, a voice whispered to me, *you're done for, jump over the railing and end it. Now you've really done yourself in,* another said. Mad. I was going mad.

Even though I didn't stop to check, I was sure that Ade was dead. I considered calling the police to turn myself in; after all, it was a crime of passion. I didn't go to that hotel room with plans to murder Ade. However, I had deceitfully lured him into what now appeared to be a premeditated trap, confronted him, stabbed him, and ran off with his phone.

No one would believe me, and Maita would never, ever forgive me. I would lose her forever, and everything I had done to protect our relationship would be in vain. I had to return to Atlanta and pretend that none of this had happened.

Paranoia was what would eventually eat me up and consume me. In my haste and panic, I cleaned everything else, but left the murder weapon at the crime scene with my prints on it. Had I been too afraid to approach a dying man? How could I be so stupid!

"Fucking hell, I should have pulled out that knife," I mumbled repeatedly, slapping my forehead hard, over and over. "What have I done?" It was a matter of time before the police would find me.

But no one came.

I thought about my family in Oxford, how devastating it would be for my mother to have a killer for a son. I had finally told my parents about Maita, and even mentioned my intentions to marry her.

"I can't wait to meet her," Mom had said cheerfully, to my astonishment. "If she makes you happy, then I'm happy." Dad's response wasn't as terrible as I expected. "It's about time, and where is she from again, Zambia? Trust you to bring home a foreigner. I'm not sure I care anymore."

The next day, on my way to the airport, I was sure that strangers on the street were staring at me with accusing eyes. I was certain that every police car I heard or saw was coming for me. So absentminded and dazed as I navigated my way through the airport, I was clumsy with my luggage, and when a security officer asked my destination, I fumbled for a reply. I couldn't focus; my mind was wandering in fear and confusion.

As I sat at the United Airways gate, I saw a trio of police officers walking purposefully in my direction. I felt myself shrinking into my seat; my time was up. I was relieved when they walked past me to another target. Not me.

Not this time.

When I arrived home that Saturday evening, Maita wasn't there, and she wasn't answering my calls. Not ready to speak to her or anyone, I was partially glad to get her voicemail.

Then I found the letter she left on the kitchen counter. Words could not describe the pain... followed shortly by anger.

How could she do this to me? There had been no warning signs, and I believed we were doing fine. I was livid: I tore the letter to pieces and banged my fist on the kitchen counter. What I had just read was unbelievable, utter rubbish. I was in the middle of an awful dream. I had killed a man *because of her,* and then she decided to leave me. The nightmare that had begun on Friday night was still playing out.

I called her. Again I got her voice mail.

"Maita, call me back," I cried into the phone. "We need to talk. You can't just write a note and leave me. You need to call me today."

I drowned my sorrow and spent the rest of the evening drinking alone.

The next day, Sunday, was a blur. I only got out of bed to go to the bathroom, get a snack from the kitchen, and top off my glass with vodka or whiskey. Maita still hadn't returned my calls. I tried several times, sent an email, checked Facebook for any updates and found no leads. I wasn't sure where she was; I guessed in Marietta at Simone's place. When Simone and her other friends in Atlanta said they hadn't heard from Maita, I was certain she was with Lindy, but I didn't have Lindy's contact details, and therefore had no way to confirm it.

I lay in bed in a drunken stupor, distraught and unshaven. Eventually, Maita sent me a text message:

Hi Chris. I need some time alone to settle in. I'm so sorry for leaving you the way I did. You, of all people, should understand why. I will get in touch soon. Take care.

I had no strength to respond.

On Monday, I called in sick and didn't go to work. I couldn't pretend that everything was normal, and eight hours at work would be torture. Confronting Ade in New York had turned my world upside down, and I still feared a visit from the police. I even contemplated running away to London.

I finally received a call from Maita as I prepared to go to work on Tuesday morning. After shaving my face, I was studying the bags under my eyes when my phone played her ringtone. I immediately answered.

"Hello, Maita. Where in the heavens are you? I've been trying to get through to you."

"Hi, Chris," she said in a low, soft voice. "I need to talk to you."

"Are you okay?" I said. "Where are you? I need to see you."

"No, I'm not okay," she replied. I heard her sniff as if she were crying.

"Maita, are you okay?" I repeated.

"Can you come to Phoenix?"

"Yes, of course, just tell me where you are," I said. "I will get the next flight out."

After I wrote down her address in Phoenix, I called the office and told them I would be out for the rest of the week. I booked an evening flight to Phoenix, made a hotel reservation for the night, called Maita, and told her I would see her first thing the following morning.

I felt alive again, because *she* had called me and invited me to Phoenix. She missed me after all and maybe realized that she needed me and wanted to come back home. Then it struck me: the next day was February fourteenth. Valentine's Day. It was the day I had planned to propose—before the incident with Ade derailed my plans, and my life as I knew it had been changed forever.

Chapter 36

Maita

I pondered the connection between Ade and Chris, and it left me feeling guilty. If Chris had anything to do with Ade's attack, it was ultimately my fault because I was the only link between them. It was too much of a coincidence that Chris had gone to Dallas the same weekend that Ade was in New York. Furthermore, I had made a mental note that Chris traveling for a business meeting on a Friday evening always seemed odd. I was preoccupied with my plan to leave for Phoenix at the time, and I didn't question him.

The thought of Chris masquerading as me online, emailing Ade, was unsettling. If it were true, he had to have done it stealthily, because I never suspected anything. Bola later told me that she believed that Ade had broken up with his girlfriend, because he hoped to meet with me in New York to rekindle our relationship. This was shocking—what would have changed his mind about me? I was convinced that Ade resented me for breaking his heart. How did Bola come to this conclusion? Perhaps she'd deduced this from reading his email. She told me how happy he was the last time she'd talked to him when he was boarding his flight.

Within minutes of calling Lindy and telling her about Ade, she showed up at Noni's house with two cups of hot chocolate and a box of donuts. At five feet and seven inches tall, Lindy could pass for a model. Her latest short haircut accentuated sculptured cheekbones, and her beautiful, smooth ebony skin was a perfect canvas for any makeup and lipstick. At university, she was crowned as Miss UZ and automatically qualified to enter the Miss Zimbabwe beauty pageant, but she'd left for America before she could compete.

After placing the donuts on the kitchen counter, she gave me a tight hug, and I cried in her arms. "He's hanging on by a thread for his life. He could die."

"Hush, hush, *ungakhali.*" When we sat down on the couch, she gave me a donut and a Kleenex. Between sobs, I relayed everything Bola had told me.

"They believe that what saved his life was that the attacker left the knife in his neck, which minimized the bleeding. The knife cut his internal jugular vein. Thankfully it wasn't severed by the blade; it nicked his vagus nerve—"

"Hold up, Bubbs, you have to simplify this medical jargon."

"He's lucky that the knife missed his carotid artery, a critical blood vessel that is close to the jugular vein, and if it had cut that artery, he would have bled to death. He somehow managed to drag himself to the nightstand, pulled the hotel room telephone down, called the help desk, and said 'I'm dying.'"

I started to cry again, imagining how he must have felt, facing death alone.

"The lady at the front desk called 911, and the hotel staff ran up to his room. He was rushed to the hospital and straight to the operating room. He bled so much, they couldn't anticipate the outcome until he woke up."

Lindy moved to sit next to me and wrapped her arm around my shoulders. "Oh, Bubbs, I'm so sorry. I know he meant so much to you. He will make it."

"He came to New York to see me. He wanted to see *me*, Lindy. He still wanted me after all." I sobbed. "It may just be speculation, but it hurts to know that he wanted to see me, and maybe, just maybe, if he'd been able to get in touch with me, we could have been together, and none of this would have happened."

"It's not your fault, Bubbs. How could you have known? It's Chris's fault; I always knew there was something shady about him. You told me that he covered his apartment walls in Atlanta with your pictures after just one date in London. That's creepy." She took a sip of the hot chocolate, leaving a bright red lipstick stain on the Styrofoam cup.

"What hurts the most," I said, "is that despite his desire for us to reunite, in reality, there was probably no chance of ever rekindling our relationship, because his girlfriend is now expecting their baby, and he didn't know."

"He's having a baby?" she said, with an arched eyebrow and a frown. "Hmm, that's a sticky point. The poor guy didn't even know he was going to be a dad. If he loves you, I don't think that a baby would stop him from being with you. Lots of men have babies with one woman and still get married to another. Take Gift, for example. He has a child with another woman—"

Hearing this for the first time, I gasped, my eyes wide, and for a split second Ade was off my mind. "Wait, what? Gift has a child? When were you going to—?"

"Look, the point is, baby or not, I'm sure if he loves you, he'll make it work."

I decided to let the issue with Gift slide— for now anyway. We were dealing with a bigger crisis. If my suspicions were accurate, what would have prompted Chris to impersonate me via email? The degree of deceit it would take for Chris to pull this off indicated disturbing and sociopathic behavior, and this had me thinking of the dark look in his eyes when we had our big argument.

I hadn't told Bola about my suspicions. I only mentioned that I recognized the phone number that was in the email. I wanted to be sure before I drew any attention to Chris. I also considered reporting him to the police. They could easily look through Chris's phone records and determine if indeed he had been communicating with Ade, but I decided to do some digging first.

I voiced my suspicions to Lindy, who immediately concluded that Chris was the culprit who attacked Ade. "He's shown that he can be violent. Besides, the police can easily verify the information regarding his trip to Dallas, and they can check his work phone for clues. What are you waiting for? Report him already."

She made a good point.

"I want to talk to him face-to-face, because a part of me can't believe that he would go as far as trying to kill Ade. He deserves the opportunity to explain himself to me."

"Okay, then you had better meet him soon, or I'm calling the police."

I needed time to think through my course of action, and waited till Tuesday morning before I called Chris to invite him to Phoenix. I had to see him soon, before I traveled to New York on Thursday to meet Bola and her parents. Hopefully, before I met Ade's family, I could alleviate my fear that Chris was involved, and the guilt I felt would end.

That Wednesday morning on Valentine's Day, Noni had left for work, and I was talking to Lindy on the phone.

"Chris just called to let me know he's on his way," I told her. "I'm so nervous."

"I think this is a bad idea. You should just report him to the NYPD when you go to New York tomorrow. I booked the flight for you, don't worry about paying me back on this one. For everything else though, I'm keeping your tab open."

"Thanks Lindy, I couldn't do all this without you."

"I still think you should call the police now and tell them your suspicions."

"A part of me doesn't want to believe that I spent the past two years of my life with someone capable of such a horrendous act. Why didn't Ade just call me directly on my phone?" I began to cry. The pain I felt each time seemed to be worse than the day before, as the reality of his condition slowly sank in.

"He didn't call you, because your psycho boyfriend diverted all communication to *his* work phone. Is that not what that email said?" When she realized that I was crying, she said, "It's not your fault. Please don't cry. Listen, I have to go to a doctor's

274

appointment, and I will come by and see you as soon as I'm done."

My head was aching terribly, and after taking a Tylenol, I took a nap on the couch. The doorbell woke me a short time later. I got up slowly, still feeling a little tension in my head and around my eyes, which felt puffy and tender. The bell rang again, and I remembered that I was expecting Chris.

Overcome with fear, and having no idea how I would confront him, I contemplated ignoring him and calling the police, but just went and opened the door. His frail appearance was shocking. His sagging jeans and baggy sweater highlighted weight loss, and the bags under his eyes were pronounced. I must have surprised him with my red and puffy eyes too. We stared at each other for a few seconds in awkward silence as he stood at the door.

"Can I come in?"

"Sure, please come in." I could smell alcohol on his breath, which struck me as odd this early in the day.

I led him to the lounge and offered him a seat on the couch. He looked around uncomfortably, then broke the silence. "You don't look well. Are you okay?"

Fighting back tears, I shook my head, unable to find the right words to answer.

"I was deeply hurt when I read your letter," he said. "I don't understand why you left me like that. I thought we had made progress, and were in a good place. I even had big plans for today…"

Finally, I gathered the strength and courage to speak. "I'm not fine because I found out that someone stabbed my ex-boyfriend, Ade, and now he's fighting for his life."

His expression wasn't one of surprise or confusion at the mention of Ade's name. Strangely, he lit up and said, "Fighting for his life?"

I knew, right then, that I was sitting across from Ade's attacker.

I began to cry again. "I know about the email exchange you

had, impersonating me. Tell me how and why you got in touch with Ade, lied to him, and then hid it all from me."

"Maita, please, don't cry. I don't know what you're talking about, I never—"

"Don't lie to me," I snapped. "You went to meet him in New York, didn't you?"

He had his head in his hands, elbows resting on his knees, as he shook his head in denial. Or was it regret?

"Tell me where you were last Friday. Did you go to New York?"

He stood and slowly began to approach me, which prompted me to get up. He stopped and said in a steady voice, "Maita, you know I love you, and I would never do anything like that. Ade sent you an email, and I… happened to be there right when it came through. I felt threatened by him, I guess. So I told him off, pretending to be you so that he would leave you alone. I didn't mean anything by it, and that was all. What makes you think I was in New York? Why would I go there?"

"Did you ever contact Ade on your phone?"

"No—well, yes, I gave him my work cell phone number. Then I told him to stop trying to get in touch—"

"So, you *did* communicate with him. Why did you give him your work cell phone number unless you planned to keep in touch? You could have told me about his email and allowed me to make a choice, to decide for myself if I wanted to chat with him or not."

"Would you have considered him then?" Chris asked firmly.

I was furious. "It was a gross invasion of my privacy. I had the right to hear from Ade directly and make my own choice. But you chose for me, again with the controlling."

"I can't believe that you would admit to me, your boyfriend, that you wanted a chance to have a word with your ex-boyfriend. I was protecting our relationship—"

"Protecting it from what? From who?"

"Don't play dumb. You know he wanted to get back with you. Why else would he email you out of the blue?"

He had no idea how painful it was to hear from a second person, after Bola, that Ade was trying to get back with me. All along, I thought he didn't want to have anything to do with me.

"So, you were jealous of Ade, afraid that I might leave you for him. That's motive right there."

"Are you accusing me of something? Would you have run back to him? After you once begged him to take you back, and he refused?"

I was stunned that Chris seemed to know about what happened that summer in 2005. He must have spoken to Ade in depth; how else could he have known this? I was silent, processing the implications of this revelation. I looked around for my phone. It was on the coffee table between us. He noticed how I eyed my phone and must have guessed what I was thinking. He had given himself away. First, Chris lied about *never* talking to Ade, then admitted that it was just to tell him off, and now he'd disclosed information he could have only gotten through a detailed conversation. How far did this go?

I reached over for my phone, but Chris was closer and quicker, and swiped it off the coffee table.

"Give me my phone," I said, breathing heavily.

"I can't do that. Maita, I need you to listen to me. Let's go back to Atlanta—"

"No, I'm not going anywhere with you. Give me my phone."

"You want to call someone in the middle of this serious conversation? Let me guess, Lindy—"

"I'm going to call the police, and you will explain to them what you were doing calling Ade and pretending to be me. And then you can prove to the police that you didn't go to New York on Friday."

I attempted to take the phone out of his hand, but he grabbed my wrist, and a struggle ensued.

"Maita, listen to me, let's talk—"

"I don't want to talk. Give me my phone."

With great force, he pushed me, and I fell to the floor, screaming in pain. My phone fell out of his hand and landed a few inches from me. I immediately reached out to get it. Chris kicked it further away. I grabbed his ankle and began to pull him. He lost his balance and fell next to me, before we both scrambled for the phone.

That was when my phone began to ring.

Chris grabbed my legs and pulled me by my ankles. I tried to kick but failed. I was on my back, between his knees, and I looked into his dark eyes as he began to choke me.

"You selfish bitch. You don't appreciate that I was trying to protect us."

He tightened his hands around my neck and squeezed. I kicked and tried to wriggle from under him, at the same time clawing my fingers at his hands to loosen his grip and dislodge him, but all in vain. His hands were at my throat, and I felt light-headed. I was powerless.

"You don't know what I've gone through for you. You made me do it."

I knew then that this was how it would all end. I would die at Chris's hands, and unlike Ade, I wouldn't survive this attack. I had no more strength left in me, but I was determined to fight till my last breath. The more I resisted, the more he tightened his grip.

Then, just as my body was about to surrender, his hands relaxed, relieving the pressure on my throat. I sucked in precious air. My lungs came to life, and I was disoriented for a few seconds, coughing, inhaling deeply and rapidly. Then I saw Chris lying on the floor beside me—and Lindy standing over him with a table lamp in her hand.

She knelt beside me. "Bubbs, are you okay?"

I looked around and then at her, confused.

"I decided to cancel my appointment with the doctor. After talking to you, I figured you shouldn't be alone to deal with this Ade mess. And honestly, I wasn't comfortable with the idea of you meeting Chris alone."

I looked over at Chris, worried that he might get up to finish me off, and also concerned that he might be badly injured.

Thankfully there was no blood in sight.

"I called from outside the front door, just to check I wasn't going to interfere," Lindy said. "And when you didn't answer, I got worried. I called the police too. I knew something wasn't right…" She still held the table lamp.

"Thank you," I said, still in shock. I moved over to Chris and checked for a pulse. Relieved, I said, "You knocked him out good, but he's breathing."

We heard a police siren, and I exhaled.

"He did it," I said. "Chris attacked Ade."

Lindy sat beside me, wrapped an arm around my shoulder, and said, "Everything will be all right; the police are here."

I didn't have the strength to get up, not yet. I was grateful that Lindy had saved my life, but I felt a deep sadness and unimaginable pain because I had suffered so much loss in the space of five days. I had to pick up the pieces and find a way to live with endless *what-could-have-beens.*

Chapter 37

New York, NY
April 2007 – Present Day

Ade

Everyone keeps telling me how lucky I am to be alive. The doctor said it at least twice, and all the nurses repeat it too. My parents have been here to see me every single day, taking turns to come round the clock dutifully like shift work. Mum says it constantly: "You're lucky to be alive. The Lord favored you, my son."

They tell me that I've been in this New York hospital for two months and spent three weeks in the ICU, hooked up to machines that kept me going until my body was able to take over. The doctor eventually weaned me off the ventilator, and now I'm in a private room on the medical floor. The physiotherapist has already come to get me up to ambulate, and he said I'm making good progress. After achieving two goals, to sit up at the edge of the bed unsupported for fifteen minutes and to walk twenty feet with a walker, I felt accomplished. My joy was short-lived after I started to feel light-headed and extremely exhausted.

I remember the day I opened my eyes. It felt like I was waking up from a profound slumber, the sort you have after a night of binge-drinking cheap alcohol, along with the throbbing headache. My ears were the sharpest, and I could hear the beeping and buzzing of machines, in perfect harmony, a familiar sound after years of working in the ICU. My ocular muscles seemed to be the only ones awake, because I couldn't move anything apart from my eyes.

Then I heard her voice, and for a moment I thought I was dreaming. Or in heaven.

"Ade, oh, my God, he opened his eyes. Ade, can you hear me?"

I could hear her sweet voice, but she couldn't hear me shouting, "Bubbs, is that you? What are you doing here? Is this real?" The words were loud in my head but trapped there, because I couldn't move my lips, just my eyes.

I felt her soft hand hold mine, and she squeezed it. "Ade, it's me, Bubbs, I mean, Maita. Oh, *Nkosi Yami,* you're awake."

I opened my eyes again, and this time I could see more clearly. She hovered over me with that unmistakable beautiful smile. I could smell Chanel Chance. Then she repeated it, her favorite phrase, "Nkosi *Yami,"* which means "My Lord."

I was smiling, but on the inside, because I still couldn't move any part of my face.

Shortly after that, I heard a nurse telling Maita to wait outside so the medical team could do some tests. That was what I counted as day one to recovery. And I couldn't be happier to have experienced it with Bubbles.

Ten days later, I was alert and oriented to person, place, time, and situation. Like my parents, Bubbles came to see me every day, usually before lunchtime, and she would stay with me till evening, even taking naps on the hospital recliner in my room. Inevitably, she became reacquainted with my parents, and they included her in discussions about my progress. I was happy to have all three of them in one room.

Now that I was stronger, my parents updated me on all that had happened since the day I was stabbed. I was shocked when they told me that Noma was pregnant. It all made sense now, her mood swings and long naps, and of course Noma did say she had something to tell me before I left for New York. I didn't know how to react—I had mixed feelings. A part of me was excited to be a father, but the other part felt like it was with the wrong woman. Would I have to stay with Noma, for the baby's sake? What kind of father would I be? I didn't think my life could get more complicated, just when Bubbles had re-entered the scene.

Today Bubbles brought me lunch, her favorite chicken and pasta dish that I always liked, which she'd cooked at the place where she was staying. With dark bags under sunken eyes, she appeared drained and exhausted. I noticed prominent clavicles, a thin neck, and loose-fitting clothes. She was stressed.

"My physiotherapist says I'm making progress after being bed-bound for weeks," I said. "I should be able to go home sooner than predicted. He said for a doctor, I make a good patient. Apparently doctors are generally difficult patients. I sat up for a whopping fifteen minutes, and get this, I walked twenty feet today."

She smiled. "That's great news. I'd like to sit in on your next therapy session, and maybe I can take over as your therapist after you get discharged." She quickly added, "I'm just kidding. I mean, I could get some tips on what you need to do—"

"It's okay, Bubbs. I'd love to have you as my physio, anytime."

She smiled, and before she could say anything, I said, "Thank you so much for being here with me. I know what a sacrifice it's been for you. Commuting daily from Brooklyn. That's where you are staying, right?"

She nodded quietly.

I said, "Bola calls me every day, and she said to thank you. She'll be here next week. She took four weeks off work. We'll travel back to London together, and she will stay with me for a few days. My parents can't stop singing your praises."

"I'm glad to be at your service, and I couldn't be happier to help out. After all, it's my fault you got into—"

"Don't you dare blame yourself for what that psycho did." I raised my voice and winced from the healing surgical wound on my neck. "You didn't know what he was up to, and maybe I should have been more vigilant."

"How could you have avoided it? You shouldn't blame yourself either. More vigilant? How?"

"I should have called you directly from day one. I should never have been a coward and emailed or texted. I could have insisted on talking and not—"

"Stop it," she shouted, suddenly crying. "We didn't know, and it's no one's fault. Let's just be glad you're here. Please stop blaming yourself."

It was best to change the subject, but I wanted to talk about that Friday night, not just to anyone but to Maita. We hadn't discussed her ex-boyfriend, or the events leading up to this moment, with me in a hospital bed. I needed to offload and was tired of ignoring the elephant in the room. One thing this experience taught me was to stop holding back my feelings.

I shifted from my sitting position to the edge of the bed. I knew now I had the stamina for it.

"I've lost muscle mass, strength, and physical mobility," I said. "But I still have my faculties intact, and a surprisingly sharp memory. I remember everything from that night when that devil came by. What with the endless hours I spend lying in bed, I replay every scene over and over in my head. I can see his red face and dark eyes. Sometimes he visits me in my dreams, and most times I can't tell the difference between my dreams and reality."

She wiped away tears, and looked at me with tired eyes, sitting upright and listening attentively.

"You know, after I realized that he had stabbed me, the cardiologist in me immediately took over. Amazing how the brain works. I knew that if he pulled out that knife, I would surely bleed to death. I thought the knife had dug into my carotid." I stroked the dressing on my neck. "I was afraid he had come to kill me, and I played dead, so he wouldn't pull out that knife and finish me off. Secondly, I knew I had to keep still so that I wouldn't over-exert my heart; increasing my heart rate would be dangerous. When I heard the door shut, I had to decide: use the little strength left in me to get to the phone on the nightstand and risk dislodging the knife, or lie still and hope someone found me."

Bubbles rose from the chair at the bedside and sat beside me on the bed. She took my hand and placed it on her lap.

"Right after I called the front desk, I blacked out. And yes, I must have moved the knife because the doctor told me that I'd lost so much blood the paramedics didn't think I would make it to the hospital."

"I'm so sorry, Ade," she said. "I'm glad you made that call. It saved your life."

"What's the status of the investigation into your ex?"

"He was arrested for attempted murder. You know he tried to strangle me." She paused and took a deep breath. "I still can't believe he would do all that. They have a solid case against him, his fingerprints on the knife, the text messages, and flight records. It's an open and shut case. He will need a good lawyer."

"I'm ready to get back to my life. I've been given a chance to start over," I said, changing the topic deliberately.

She let go of my hand and said, "You have a … never mind."

"What is it? Say what you want to say. Remember, we can't keep holding back our feelings."

"You have a whole new life ahead of you, with a baby on the way," she said, speaking fast.

Before I could reply, the door flung open, and my mom and dad walked in. "Hello, hello!" Mum said cheerfully, carrying a basket of fruit. She placed it on the chest of drawers near the foot of the bed, adding to the clutter of flowers, get-well-soon cards, and books.

"Hello, my daughter," she greeted Bubbles, smiling broadly, arms stretching to offer a big and loving embrace.

Chapter 38

New York, NY
April 2007 – present day

Maita

Lindy came through for me again. When I told her I had to return to New York to check on Ade, she connected me with a friend who lived in Brooklyn. Her friend was generous enough to offer me a couch for as long as I needed to be in New York. With the embarrassment of a child who never left the coop, I turned to my mother for financial assistance, and when Mercy heard about the horrific incident that led me to New York, she generously chipped in and sent cash for my daily upkeep.

On the move again, I packed and left Phoenix for New York.

I made sure to take my NPTE study guide and physical therapy textbooks, to stay focused on studying for the physical therapy board exam. The physical and mental strain that resulted from the daily commute to the hospital, and the late nights studying, began to take their toll: drastic weight loss, falling asleep on the train and missing my stop several times, being irritable and withdrawn.

Thankfully, witnessing Ade's progress as he got better and stronger each day filled me with joy and kept me motivated. His parents stayed at an extended-stay hotel in New Jersey, a cheaper option than being in New York. Like me, they commuted daily to visit our convalescent.

I played his music, our favorite '90s old-school R&B, and his beloved "Purple Rain" by Prince on repeat. Sometimes I massaged his feet, and every day I read to him. When I read him his favorite book, *The Alchemist* by Paulo Coelho, I thought I saw him smiling, ever so slightly, or maybe that's what I wanted to see. Strangely, I felt that the author had directed some of the messages in that book at me. As if Paulo Coelho was speaking to me in code. I paused when I read about how no one can ever escape his or her heart; therefore, it's better to listen to what it has to say. What was my heart saying? Was Ade abiding by the wise words of his favorite author, when he flew from London to come here—and almost died?

I had become a constant fixture at his bedside, blending in with the walls and furniture, and now considered a "family member" by the medical team. I knew his nurses on a first-name basis, and even though I was on a tight and minimal budget, I bought the day and night staff donuts and trays of cookies. My gratitude was sincere, because I watched them fuss over Ade every day, and I couldn't thank them enough. I was glad to be the first person he saw when he woke up from his coma.

We hadn't had an opportunity to talk further about Noma's pregnancy since three days ago, when his parents interrupted us. In those past three days, we always had company, because his uncle from Miami was in town with his wife and kids.

Today, on a warm spring day, he was alone, sitting in the chair beside the bed. With a fresh haircut and new clothes, he looked less like a patient, as if he could simply get up and walk out. He had lost a significant amount of weight, which didn't look natural on him, but he was still the good-looking Ade I'd fallen in love with years ago.

After the usual pleasantries, I sat on his bed and got straight to the point. I didn't want his family interrupting us again.

"When you left London to come to meet me here, what were you hoping for?"

I wanted to hear it from him, not Bola or anyone else. It had to come from him.

"Okay, you mean business today," he said, smiling and turning the TV off with the remote. I hadn't noticed it was on, and that he was watching soccer.

"I wanted to see you and to ask you if you would... er... if you wanted us to… if we could get back together. I knew you had a boyfriend, but… I couldn't stop thinking about you. I had to try to get you back—"

"What about your pregnant girlfriend?"

He looked away at the window, then down at his hands. I could see he was grinding his teeth.

"I broke up with her before I left. She told me she had something important to tell me, but I didn't want to hear it." He shifted uncomfortably in his seat. "Mum told me about the baby as soon as I was able to comprehend stuff. Noma told Bola she was twelve weeks pregnant. My parents were also informed about it, but with so much going on, we haven't really discussed it in depth. Obviously they want to know my plans. As you can see, Mum is always in such high spirits because I'm getting better, and also because she's going to have her first grandchild."

He was looking at me now, searching for my reaction. I was hurting inside. As I had predicted, Ade having a baby meant we could never be together again. I stood no chance and had foolishly consumed Lindy's optimistic mantra about men leaving their baby mamas and marrying the women they love.

"Have you talked to her, your girlfriend?"

"You mean my ex-girlfriend? Yes, I have. I call to check on her and … the baby."

"You say she's your ex-girlfriend. Are you planning to leave her while she's pregnant?"

"When I left her, I didn't know she was pregnant. A baby can't miraculously change the way I feel about her, and how I feel about you. She's been begging to come and visit me. She wants us to work things out, but I've made up my mind. I'll be the best father I can be to my child, but I can't be with Noma."

"Why not? She's carrying your baby."

"She was cheating on me with a married man. I can't go back there. Even my parents will have to understand that—"

"Wait, what? Cheating? That's terrible."

Although I wanted details, I sensed that it wasn't the best time to probe. But I had to ask one thing.

"Are you sure it's your baby?"

He again looked out the window in silence, shaking his head. I knew I'd struck a nerve.

"That has crossed my mind. It infuriates me that I have to consider a DNA test. And if it isn't my child, my mother will surely break down."

The situation made me uneasy. I was glad that he was prepared to father his child, and still be with me, but that meant leaving the woman who was carrying his child. And now, I secretly wished that the DNA test would prove that the baby *wasn't* Ade's. It was bittersweet.

"Will she let you go without a fight?" I asked, already anticipating future drama.

He shook his head again. "She can try, but I have made up my mind. She cheated, I owe her nothing."

"And the plot thickens," I said wryly.

He attempted to get up from his chair. I quickly got off the bed and stood beside him, unsure if he was strong enough to stand up unassisted.

"Don't get up," I said, but he insisted.

"I can do this. I got off the bed myself. It's only three steps to the bed."

I helped him push up from the chair, guided him to the edge of the bed, and sat beside him.

"Bubbs, do you remember our last date, the summer of 2005?"

"How could I forget the summer of rejection?" I chuckled.

"Do you remember when you asked me if I'd move to America, if you asked me to?"

I was nodding, unsure where he was going with this, a little afraid that this could be the makings of a spring 2007 rejection.

"Well, I was foolish to say no, but you were bold enough to say that you would move back to England if you had something to move back for, and I knew what you meant by that." He took my hand and held it. "Does that still stand? Would you move back to England with me? Am I reason enough—"

"Yes, yes, of course, I'll gladly move back with you," I replied, stopping short of jumping excitedly on the bed.

"You would abandon the great American dream for cold, gray England?"

"Ade, I'm putting away my physio exam study guide. It's over for me here. I want to be with you. Just like I did that summer of 2005. I can get a public health job in the NHS, or return to work as a physiotherapist. I don't need to take any exam."

"We wasted so much time, and it's my fault for letting you go—" Ade said, beaming.

"No, I'm the one who let you down when I came to America. I turned down your proposal, and I hurt you first—"

"Bubbs, stop. Let's start over together. Nothing would make me happier." Then, without warning, he wrapped his arms around me, and we kissed for the first time in a very long time.

The door opened. His parents, uncle, aunt, and cousins walked in carrying trays of food.

"Hello, hello," his mum said, like she always did when she entered the room. "I cooked your favorite *Jollof,* plantain, and fish." She turned to me. "My daughter, come help me prepare this food."

A note from the author

I would like to thank everyone that helped me fulfill my dream to be a writer and author. A special thanks to my best friend, husband, and the father of our two children, Ngano. Thank you for your patience when I rumbled on and on about my characters, and typed late at night in my favorite writing spot—our bed (thank you for the foldable laptop table for the bed). You listened attentively when I whined about the challenges of writing and publishing, and you always encouraged me to continue and give it my best shot. You were editor-in-chief for my first drafts and your invaluable feedback made for a better manuscript. I am blessed to have you.

Thank you to Nyasha Mapuranga-Aboim, Zanele Siziba, and Reyna Jones who had the task of reading the very first draft, or rather very rough draft. Your feedback was honest and ever so encouraging, and I knew I was onto something. To Ndidi Ike and Catherine Nwosu your input was essential and it made my Nigerian characters authentic. I knew if Catherine could read it in two days it was a page-turner! To my sister Dadirai Zemura, you challenged me to add more tension to the plot, and I think it worked. A big shout-out to my team of cheerleaders: Brendah Kigwe, Madeline Chadehumbe, Lilian Pswarayi Takawira, Tasha Seecharan, Dr. Lisa Moody-Kier, Nyarai Kapisavanhu-Forestieri, Zukiswa Wanner, Bukekile Dube, and Chiedza Goronga. You have no idea how your words kept me going when I was clouded with self-doubt, and to think you hadn't read the manuscript, but you believed, thank you. My friends and family on Facebook and Instagram thank for your support.

To my editors at Polgarus Studio, Mike Robinson, Graeme

293

Hague, and Stephanie Parent, you turned my manuscript into a clean and tidy piece of work. Mike Robinson, you helped me to elevate my writing and storytelling abilities to the next level, and the story is better for it.

I am grateful for Anesu and Tanaka, our beautiful children, who were so invested in the entire writing process, they knew the characters and *some* of the story. My eight-year-old daughter Anesu challenged me to publish before she turned twenty-one—the three-year process was taking too long. Thank you for the laughs along the way, I can count on Tanaka to make fun of *"Mommy the wanna-be writer"*.

I cannot write this part without tearing up. I need more than a few lines to thank my dearest mother Pauline Zemura. My mother knew I loved reading books and as a young reader, she agreed to enroll me in three libraries! I had an endless supply of books. She cheered me on when I began to write books in high school. I was fortunate to have her locked-down with my family in Atlanta during the three-month COVID-19 lockdown of 2020. It was then that I made strides in my writing. Day and night I wrote and edited the manuscript over and over. And as she sat on the couch knitting, she always said, "don't give up, hard work always pays off". And when we binge-watched *Fauda* on Netflix, she said jokingly, "Soon, we will be watching an adaptation of your book on Netflix". Nothing is impossible, right? Thank you mama for believing in me. Keep watching over me from heaven. Rest in Peace.

About the Author

Alice Takawira was born and raised in Zimbabwe. After receiving a bachelor's degree in physiotherapy from the University of Zimbabwe, she relocated to London for work. In 2004, she moved to America to attend Emory University and graduated with a master's in public health. Alice currently lives in Atlanta with her husband and two kids. When she's not working as a geriatric physical therapist, she enjoys binge-watching foreign-language dramas, exploring new places, trying exotic foods, and learning new languages.

She is the proud creator of the Verenga Girls Book Club on Facebook, a place to connect with fellow book lovers. To learn more about Alice and her work, visit:

Website: www.alicetakawira.com
Instagram: www.instagram.com/alice.takawira.writes
Twitter: twitter.com/RudoTaks
Facebook: www.facebook.com/alicetakawirawrites
GoodReads: www.goodreads.com/user/show/114073414-alice-takawira
Book club: www.facebook.com/groups/2719502594794960/

Printed in Great Britain
by Amazon

82302813R00174